Resounding praise for Pulitzer Prize winner

EDNA BUCHANAN

and

THE ICE MAIDEN

"A supremely expert yarnspinner."
Los Angeles Times Book Review

"Buchanan has improved, novel to novel . . .
The Ice Maiden demonstrates
her mastery of mystery fiction."
St. Louis Post-Dispatch

"Edna Buchanan does it again . . .
She has given us a gripping adventure
starring her alter ego, Britt Montero.
The book careens from subplot to subplot without
ever seeming disorganized or implausible . . .
Highly recommended."
Raleigh News and Observer

"One of crime fiction's national treasures."
Newsday

"Edna Buchanan is outrageous and unrivaled."
Patricia Cornwell

"The Queen of Crime."

Los Angeles Daily News

"Powerful . . .
a real knockout, with unexpected revelations leading to a deadly conclusion and a tragically ironic aftermath . . . A highly entertaining tale that's really tough to put down . . . A terrific, compelling, page-turning mystery that's definitely one of the best in her series."

Lansing State Journal

"There's a grabber of a lead . . .
The ending has so many twists and turns, executed so well, that my reaction when I turned the last page was a simple, breathless, 'Wow.' And there is a bunch of good stuff in between."

New Orleans Times-Picayune

"Buchanan writes killer prose."

Austin American-Statesman

"She is familiar with the worlds of crime
and newspapers. And for the last several years she has been writing novels that effortlessly—or so it seems—capture the essence of both."

Chicago Sun-Times

"Buchanan's books are the best in the business."
Kirkus Reviews

"A compelling tale . . .
Every detail ultimately matters in the resolution of the mystery . . . Character and nuance are the author's strongest points . . . Her unveiling of her characters—layer by layer—raises this mystery novel above the conventional."
Pittsburgh Post-Gazette

"Vivid and real . . .
Deep in the heart of *The Ice Maiden* lies a gripping story about crime tearing apart families, victims, and criminals alike rebuilding their lives . . . [It] is strongest when Buchanan focuses on the police culture. The cops' camaraderie, determination, and personalities—and how this helps or hinders their work—fuel some of the best scenes."
South Florida Sun-Sentinel

"A first-rate storyteller."
Michael Connelly

"Get Britt and Buchanan on the trail of a story,
and the writing, as well as the action, simply sizzles with power, passion, and pizzazz."
Cleveland Plain Dealer

Also by Edna Buchanan

THE CORPSE HAD A FAMILIAR FACE
NOBODY LIVES FOREVER
NEVER LET THEM SEE YOU CRY
PULSE
CONTENTS UNDER PRESSURE
MIAMI, IT'S MURDER
SUITABLE FOR FRAMING
ACT OF BETRAYAL
MARGIN OF ERROR
GARDEN OF EVIL
YOU ONLY DIE TWICE

EDNA
BUCHANAN

THE ICE MAIDEN

AVON BOOKS
An Imprint of HarperCollins*Publishers*

This is a work of fiction. Names, characters, places, and incidents are products of the author's imagination or are used fictitiously and are not to be construed as real. Any resemblance to actual events, locales, organizations, or persons, living or dead, is entirely coincidental.

AVON BOOKS
An Imprint of HarperCollins*Publishers*
10 East 53rd Street
New York, New York 10022-5299

ISBN: 0-380-72834-6
www.avonmystery.com

First Avon Books paperback printing: December 2003
First William Morrow hardcover printing: November 2002

Printed in the U.S.A.

10 9 8 7 6 5 4 3 2 1

For Teresa Johnson,
who tamed the Dragon

Some say the world will end in fire,
Some say in ice.

—ROBERT FROST

THE ICE MAIDEN

1

The shoes startled me. They dangled in midair, at eye level. They were scuffed, meant for running, and they were occupied by a dead stranger who was stuck in the ceiling.

The cops were furious at the stranger.

The firefighters were irritated.

He had left them a problem: his corpse and how to extricate it. Homicide detectives, a fire department battalion chief with the personality of a pit bull, and an assistant Miami–Dade County medical examiner noisily debated how to tackle the job.

The dead man had missed a spectacular dawn. The rising sun had ignited a magnificent city of fire, its own face reflected in glass- and steel-walled skyscrapers. Their flaming towers pierced a radiant blue sky, their golden glow an empty promise to shell-shocked commuters still haunted by smoldering images of carnage and death.

The fire chief insisted that the corpse, tightly wedged in an air-conditioning grate, be pried free and lowered to the floor. Far more efficient, he claimed, than dragging dead weight up to the roof and then down a ladder. Three of his bravest, he pointed out, were still recovering from injuries suffered when they removed an eight-hundred-pound heart patient from his tiny apartment and down three flights of stairs. He wanted his men to tug the dead man's legs from below as others exerted pressure from above.

A sweaty homicide detective disagreed. The corpse was caught at the thighs. His hips were wider and his pockets stuffed with bulky items. He would have to leave the way he arrived, through the roof of this small shop, similar to so many others along Miami's downtown fringe.

"How did it happen?" I asked a young uniformed cop. "Was there exposed wiring?"

"It's absolutely shocking," he said, grinning at his little joke.

Hector Gomez, a small man in a well-pressed but shabby suit, did not smile. The proprietor of Gomez Jewelry and Watch Repair stood stricken amid plastic and cardboard displays of cheap watches and costume jewelry, his dark eyes soulfully regarding the skinny, dangling denim-clad legs.

"He was like this when I unlocked the store this morning. I think it's the same one as last time," he confided, misery on his face, voice barely audible. "I recognize the sneakers. It was raining that night. He left footprints when he climbed over the counter."

We studied the soles of the well-worn Nikes. There was a distinctive pattern visible in the tread.

"The seventh break-in in two months," he whispered. "With times so hard, nobody is buying now. How do I make a living? How do I feed my family?"

"Well," I said, "this one won't be back."

He wasn't cheered. When I told him I was a reporter, he was pathetically eager to explain.

"First I installed an alarm; then I thought burglar bars would stop them, but they come in like cockroaches through the roof, stealing everything, even the watches here for repair. My customers want their watches back. Some threatened to sue me. I begged the city, the police, for help. I even wrote to the mayor. Twice. Write that down," he said, actually wringing his hands. "They didn't answer. Nobody did. The cops don't come anymore. My place was burglarized so many times they stopped sending anybody. They take the report over the phone. If only they had listened, this never would have happened . . ."

"I'm listening now, pal," interrupted a burly curly-haired detective named Oscar Levitan. "You got my undivided attention. Okay?"

The detective also squinted at me, as though I too were a cockroach who had skittered in through the ceiling. "Britt Montero, ain't you supposed to be on the other side of that line?" A gangly, pimply-faced public-service aide had nearly finished stringing yellow crime-scene tape between light poles along the sidewalk outside.

"But . . ."

"Outside," Levitan repeated, his stare hard.

"Okay, okay." His attitude irritated me. This was no major murder mystery. Like everyone, burglars have bad days. Breaking and entering is risky business. They crash through skylights and are cut by broken glass, caught by bullets, or nibbled on by Dobermans. Some thieves are exterminated along with the termites inside tented buildings. One of a pair of burglars slipped while maneuvering a heavy safe down a dark and narrow stairwell; next morning he was found crushed beneath it at the bottom. Another thief executed a perfect swan dive from a third-floor ledge. He would have successfully eluded police if he hadn't missed the pool and kissed the pavement instead. Death is an occupational hazard for thieves—or poetic justice, depending on your point of view.

I left the shop reluctantly.

"Did anybody advise this guy of his rights?" Levitan bawled to the uniformed officers.

"You're charging him?" I asked, as the detective steered Gomez out into the harsh and unforgiving glare of the relentlessly climbing sun. "Why? The burglar was electrocuted as he broke in, right? Exposed wires or poor electrical work is only a code violation, not a crime."

"Homicide," the detective said, snapping metal cuffs around Gomez's wrists, "was still a crime, last I heard."

"Homicide? You think it was deliberate?"

Gomez's resignation, shoulders slumped as Levitan led him to a cage car, answered my question.

We spoke through the patrol car's half-open window

as detectives and a crime-scene photographer scaled a ladder to the roof. Huddled in the backseat, wrists cuffed behind him, Gomez trembled as though cold, despite the scorching early-morning heat.

"Never would I hurt anybody," he swore, eyes moist. "I only wanted to shock them, to make them leave my shop alone." His voice cracked. "It was . . . you know, *prevención*. Not to kill."

"A booby trap," I said sadly. "You built a booby trap."

He gave a weak shrug. "Nothing fancy. Only an electrical cord connected to the metal grate where they come in through the ceiling. I plug it in, that's all. I didn't think it would hurt them. Only household current, a hundred and ten—fifteen—volts. A deterrent."

He'd succeeded. This thief had been deterred—permanently.

Levitan waved me away from his suspect.

"You really aren't going to arrest him, are you?" I asked.

"Kidding me?" he demanded, his loosened tie hanging limply from his thick neck. "Only question in my mind is whether to book him for manslaughter or second degree. Look," he muttered under his breath, "I have to charge him." He said an assistant state attorney he'd consulted by phone had advised him to make the arrest.

"It's not fair," I said, aware I had abandoned my professional level of objectivity. "The man was a repeat victim, trying to earn a living and protect his property."

"Since when is burglary a capital offense? You can't use deadly force to protect property; it's against the law. You know that, Britt. What if some fireman went in there to fight a fire and got zapped, or a police officer chasing a suspect?"

I saw his point.

The corpse, wrestled unceremoniously down the ladder, was ready to be removed. Gomez was asked if he recognized him.

Levitan peeled back the sheet to expose the dead man's face. The watchmaker nodded solemnly.

"That's him," he said, his words nearly drowned out by angry shouts from a growing crowd. "Came into my shop once, tried to sell my own merchandise back to me. He just laughed when I threatened to call the police."

Nobody was laughing now. The dead man appeared to be in his late thirties. His pockets yielded pliers, a screwdriver, a small wrench, a crack pipe, a couple of joints, and seventy-five cents in small change. He was black. So was the neighborhood. Gomez was Hispanic. Was the quick decision to arrest based on race? I wondered. The already surly crowd became more unruly as the body was loaded into the medical examiner's van.

A few rocks and bottles flew. As we left, community-service officers were fanning out into the neighborhood in an attempt to avert further hostilities.

Both men were now in custody, en route to county institutions: Gomez to jail, the dead man to the morgue. Each would be photographed, fingerprinted, measured, and weighed. One difference: Nobody escapes from the morgue.

This story was more than a parable about life being unfair, I thought, as I drove to the big *Miami News* building at the edge of Biscayne Bay. The store owner's arrest would certainly generate controversy in this volatile and passionate city. In my business, the newspaper business, we thrive on controversy. Sudden death and good intentions gone bad are always good copy.

Bobby Tubbs, the assistant city editor in the day slot at the city desk, the heart of the newsroom, half listened as I explained.

"After being burgled to the brink of bankruptcy, the owner built a crude booby trap to zing the next thief with a little electrical jolt, a deterrent," I said.

"So why is the guy dead?" Tubbs's round face puckered into a skeptical scowl. "I've been zapped by household current a dozen times. The Christmas-tree lights knocked me on my ass again last year."

That could explain a lot. "Maybe a bum ticker?" I said. "Or drugs he had on board that were incompatible with electricity? I don't know."

"Find out," he snapped.

I knew who to ask, so I drove over to number 1 Bob Hope Road. I liked visiting the morgue. The dead always reveal something new, and I want to know all their secrets. What went wrong? What happened? What brought them there? There are always surprises.

This time was no different. The chief was performing an autopsy. The corpse's toe tag was bar-coded like all the others, a practice borrowed from supermarkets to prevent mix-ups, but this man's slim and hairy naked body would never be confused with any other. It was decorated with sparkling silver glitter, chicken feathers, and several large-caliber bullet holes, both exit and entrance. The glitter that adorned his skin was the sort used on greeting cards and children's school projects. Chicken feathers, lots of them, had been glued to it.

The chief looked up, his shiny pink face alight with a warm smile. "My secretary tells me you have questions about the electrocution."

"Yes, but first, what . . . ?" I watched, distracted, as a single chicken feather took to the air, fluttering in slow motion to the quarry-tile floor. The chief shut off his bone saw, silver flecks of glitter twinkling like grains of stardust from his immaculate scrub suit.

"Oh, this fellow?"

The shooting victim, he said, had been alarmed by an imminent confrontation with an irate husband. So he did what any sensible Miamian would do: He consulted with his clergyman, a Santería priest, who assured him that if he wore only glitter and chicken feathers he would remain invisible to his enemies.

I scribbled notes and then inquired about the dead burglar.

"Here he is." The chief gestured accommodatingly, as though introducing me to a new friend.

The corpse appeared normal enough for a man who'd lived hard and died the same way. His face had an innocent quality, almost childish in profile. But from his neck to his groin he was horribly disfigured, his skin shriveled and distorted, deformed by odd grapelike clusters.

"Ouch," I said. "Are those electrical burns?"

"Nope. Had nothing to do with his death." He studied them thoughtfully. "Interesting, aren't they? Probably a childhood incident. Those nodules are keloids, old scar tissue caused by severe burns. You can see the splash pattern."

"Think he was scalded by hot water?"

"Nope. Most likely battery acid, lye, or some other equally corrosive substance. That spatter configuration indicates that, unlike scalding water, even the smallest drop of whatever he was splashed with destroyed the tissue."

I shuddered. "So this guy had a bad start and his luck never got better. If it was only a hundred and ten volts, why was the shock fatal?"

The chief patted a gloved hand to his left chest. "The heart has its own electrical system. A foreign electrical shock can interfere with that system and shut it down. It's not so much the voltage but the path it takes through the body. To be fatal, the current has to pass through the heart during a certain part of its cycle. When most people receive electrical shocks, their hearts aren't involved. No problem if the current enters your hand and exits your elbow. Another story if it passes through your chest."

"So it's the opposite effect of a defibrillator, which shocks hearts back *into* rhythm?"

"Sort of. When this fellow came down through the roof into the attic space, he kicked open the metal grate, which had been electrified by the store owner. The grate was hinged on one side and swung down from the ceiling. When he began to lower himself, as he'd evidently done before, he found it a tighter squeeze, probably due to the tools in his pockets. When he tried to pull himself back up, his upper thighs made contact with the metal rim and the current passed through his torso. Once he was dead weight, he became even more tightly wedged. I understand they had quite a time extricating him."

I drove to Miami Police headquarters, wondering about the man's final moments. Crime accelerates heart rates, sharpens senses. Thieves I know compare it to sex. Heart thudding, on an adrenaline high in the slick dark night, he had listened for footsteps, watched for police, but never saw the killer at hand. Twitching uncontrollably as his muscles contracted, his skin sizzling as he wet himself, he must have smelled the unmistakable odor of burning flesh—his own.

Nobody in the Public Information Office just off the first-floor lobby could give me an update on the charges lodged against Gomez. Detective Levitan didn't pick up his phone in Homicide. I suspected he was in the building and wanted to track him down, but the new police chief frowns on reporters roaming the premises, and security is even more rigid since the terrorist attacks. I was told the top cop had no comment on the Gomez case.

I understood his caution. The job is full of minefields. The last chief lost a war with the mayor over the little rafter boy, Elián González. The chief before him was doing prison time for stealing from a children's charity called Do The Right Thing. The FBI accused him of lavishing the loot on the wife of a convicted cocaine trafficker. The lovers met at police headquarters, where she worked. While reporters were being treated like potential terrorists, she had free access, to the building and the chief.

I left, frustrated after the usual skirmish with the PI officer. Heat rose in waves off the blacktop as I spotted Detective Sergeant Craig Burch striding toward the building. Wearing shades and a dress shirt and tie and carrying a battered briefcase, the eighteen-year homicide veteran had lost the graveyard pallor acquired during long years on the midnight shift and was tanned and upbeat. His current job in a unit that breathes new life into old murder cases clearly agreed with him.

"Hey, Craig, what's new?"

"That's the beauty of the Cold Case Squad." He grinned. "Ain't nothing new. Case we're chasing now is the murder of Virginia Meadows, a nice friendly little old lady, unsolved for twenty years."

The Cold Case Squad is armed with a cop's most powerful weapon: time. Unlike Homicide's chaotic daily routine, responding to murder scene after murder scene while juggling cases, suspects, witnesses, and leads, Burch's detectives have the luxury of enough time to investigate old unsolved cases without interruption.

The small team began with a bang, reopening the thirty-seven-year-old murder of a Miami police officer; they found the killer employed as a New York City elevator operator. They'd closed a string of other "unsolvable" cases in rapid succession.

"Can't beat it," he said. "Better than that, it's done a helluva lot for my home life. The wife loves the weekends off, regular hours, no middle-of-the-night callouts. For me the best part is the expression on the face of some dirtbag who thought he beat the system a long time ago."

"You know," I said, "I've been thinking about pitching a magazine story on your squad to the editor of *Hot Topics,* the paper's Sunday magazine."

I could freelance the story on my own time, I thought. No hardship, given the drought in my love life, and I could use the cash for a diving vacation I yearned to take at Small Hope Bay on Andros Island, a mysterious and unspoiled paradise of pristine white beaches and eerie blue holes hundreds of feet deep.

"Good press couldn't hurt us right now," the detective said. "We've been catching some heat from a few of the brass who think we should be out answering calls with everybody else. And now, with the new lieutenant . . ."

"New lieutenant?"

"Yeah, didn't you hear? Ernie got promoted to captain and went to Special Investigations. We got K. C. Riley from the rape squad."

My stomach did a nosedive.

"Whatsa matter, you don't like Riley?"

"No, it's not that," I said hastily. "K. C. is a good cop. It's just—"

"I know." He nodded. "We hafta deal with that hair-trigger temper every day, explodes at the drop of a hat."

"Right," I said lamely.

Riley and I shared something in common: Major Kendall McDonald, the man I'd longed to spend my life with. Our work created constant conflicts between us, while the job was something he and K. C. Riley shared. Who could compete with that? Lately I'd chosen not to try, but the ache was still there.

As a question formed on Burch's face, I changed the subject. "Hear about the burglar who got zapped this morning? You should see him: black guy, ugly scars like grapes, clustered all over his neck, chest, and stomach. The chief M.E. says they're some kinda old burns."

"Yeah?" He grinned. "Musta thought God threw down a lightning bolt. Hey, would ya look at that?" He removed his sunglasses and lingered in the shade of a sea grape to watch a K-9 officer, a huge German shepherd, scramble easily over a five-foot barricade in a training area west of the parking lot.

"Ain't that something?" Burch shook his head. "The wife and kids always wanted a damn English sheepdog. So we got 'im—big shaggy monster. Face so full of hair he can't see out in front. Got pedigree papers and everything. Costs a bundle to feed, and he's too damn dumb to even raise his head when you call him."

"Work with him. Dogs are happiest when they're trained and know what they're supposed to do," I said, watching the shepherd wheel gracefully on command in the dappled sunlight.

"Lousy watchdog," Burch muttered. "Only thing he barks at is a cat. Only way he'd ever attack a burglar is if the son-of-a-bitch brought a cat with him." He paused, reluctantly taking his eyes off the panting dog poised at alert, awaiting his next command. . . . "Hey!" Burch cocked his head. "Gimme that again."

"What?"

" 'Bout the burglar."

"If he brought a cat?"

"No," he said, exasperated. "The guy electrocuted."

"Oh. Old burn scars, bad ones, battery acid or something, the M.E. said."

"No," he said patiently. "Where'd you say he had them?"

"Lumpy clusters: across his shoulder, the base of his neck, his chest, all the way down to his groin."

"The guy's how old?" he asked, his eyes odd.

"Thirties or so."

" 'Bout six foot?"

"That's right."

"Identified yet?" His posture was no longer casual.

I suddenly felt like a suspect undergoing the third degree.

"No, but I'm sure he will be as soon as they run his prints. Probably has a rap sheet from here to downtown."

"He still with the M.E.?" Burch glanced at his watch.

"I just left there."

Burch used his walkie to inform someone in his unit that he'd be delayed because he was checking something at the morgue.

"See ya." He turned on his heel.

"Wait a minute." I tagged after him across the parking lot. "You know him?"

"No," he said over his shoulder, "but if he's the right guy, I've been waiting fourteen years to meet him."

"Who? Who is he?" I trotted to keep pace with his quick long-legged stride.

"I'm damn sure gonna find out."

"Wait a minute. He's not going anywhere. What case was he involved with?"

"Unsolved," he said tersely. "Don't wanna jinx it. Wait till I get a look at 'im."

"Can I come with you?"

"No." He looked away. "I need to do this solo."

"Okay, Craig," I said reluctantly. "Call me when you know something. Don't forget, okay?"

"Sure." He slid into his unmarked Plymouth, slammed the door, and took off, leaving me standing there by myself in the parking lot. The story of my life.

I'd always liked Craig Burch, despite occasional clashes under deadline pressure. He was reliable, matter-of-fact, and down-to-earth. Unlike some, he'd never lied to me. But I'd never seen him so intense.

I went back into the station and finally dogged Sergeant Joe Diaz in PIO into tracking down what I needed. Gomez would be arraigned in the morning: the charge, second-degree murder. Instead of going back to the paper, I drove the eighteen blocks to the M.E.'s office. Burch's unmarked stood in the parking lot.

A hot breeze blew across the pavement, birds sang, and passing traffic hummed as I leaned against the cannon to wait. The ancient weapon, worn smooth by hundreds of years of ocean waves and tides, had protected the *Santa Margarita,* a Spanish galleon lost with all aboard in a savage hurricane off the Florida coast. Did the doomed ship ever anchor at Andros, a historic haven for notorious buccaneers? I envisioned the ship's crew who had touched this same metal in that era of pirates, sea battles, and exploration nearly four hundred years ago. When overtaken, engulfed by that killer storm, did they see the irony, that no gun is powerful enough to fight off the forces of nature? I wondered if the loved ones who waited for them ever learned the fates of the lost seamen, and I thought of my own father, executed in Cuba when I was three.

As I daydreamed about men long dead, Burch emerged from the building, moving fast, like a man with a mission.

"Hey, hey!" I called, to slow him down. "Is it him? Is it the right guy?"

He broke stride. "Maybe."

"Don't leave me hanging, Craig. I won't write anything until you're sure."

"Right." I could see him considering the possibility that I might do him some good. "There are other suspects," he said slowly. "We don't wanna tip 'em off." He checked his watch. "Got time for a quick cuppa coffee?"

"I'm good to go. La Esquina?"

"Meet you there in ten. Inside."

I drove south on Twelfth Avenue, past a half dozen charming old-fashioned wooden cottages converted into bail-bond offices. Flags were *everywhere*: in yards, on front doors, fluttering from cars, on every street corner, in every window. Since the disasters, Cuban street-corner vendors who normally offer flowers, fruit, or snacks, had been selling small American flags. La Esquina de Tejas, my favorite restaurant, stands at the corner of Calle José Martí and Ronald Reagan Boulevard, a long low building with a red barrel-tile roof and a walk-up window where pedestrians can buy Cuban coffee, pastries, and cigars. I found a table in the back room near an entire wall devoted to autographed photos of President Reagan's historic 1983 visit to Little Havana. The commander in chief dined here on *pollo asado, moros, maduros, flan, y café*—roast chicken, mixed black beans and rice, fried bananas, caramel custard, and coffee—a meal still proudly identified on the menu as *El special del presidente.*

Burch arrived minutes later with two Cold Case Squad detectives—Sam Stone, a flashy, fast-talking, dapper young black guy, and Pete Nazario, a quiet Cuban-born cop. Both watched me with guarded curiosity as they took their seats.

I smiled, trying to look winsome. I knew both men by reputation. Nazario, a sensitive loner, had a gift, a talent that does not provide probable cause for arrest or testimony in court but is priceless to a detective. Fellow cops swore that he could sense when somebody was lying.

A doe-eyed waitress took our orders: *cortaditos,* tiny cups of steaming black Cuban espresso for Nazario and me, and café con leche for Burch. Stone asked for *té frío,* iced tea.

"Okay." Burch planted his elbows firmly on the table and lowered his voice as the waitress departed. "I caught the case fourteen years ago, my fourth year in Homicide. I was the lead. It was big, it was a bitch, and we had up to a hundred people, not counting volunteers, working it at one point. No day goes by, even now, that I don't think of it."

He licked his lips as though they'd suddenly gone

dry. "How many years you on the job?" he asked Nazario.

"Ten."

"So you weren't here yet, but you musta heard about it. You know how there are some you never forget."

The Cuban detective nodded, his intelligent brown eyes attentive, his hands folded on the checkered tablecloth.

"And you," Burch told Stone, "were probably still in diapers."

"Not quite." Stone looked amused. "I was in the sixth grade back then, sarge."

"Your newspaper ran big headlines on it," Burch said to me. "I got 'em all, stapled into the case file. Happened at Christmas. You know the annual Christmas Boat Parade?"

"Sure. Boaters decorate their craft, everything from little putt-putts to millionaires' yachts, and parade the waterways with holiday lights and music on Christmas Eve. I was part of it one year, aboard *Sea Dancer,* a sightseeing boat out of Bayside."

"We had two victims," Burch said, "both teenagers from good families. Richard Lee Chance, white male, age seventeen, a good-looking high school athlete. Kid was straight as they come. Victim number two, Sunny Hartley, white female, just turned sixteen. Real pretty baton-twirler type. Should see her picture. Little pixie smile could tear your heart out. Her mother was a Ford model, big-time, but quit the business when she married Sunny's father, a surgeon.

"Night it happened, the Christmas Boat Parade, was Sunny's first date, if you could even call it that. Pretty well chaperoned. She and Ricky were with her parents, along with her little brother, Tyler, a kid about ten. Had a twenty-eight-foot Chris-Craft named for the girl—called it the *Sunshine Princess*. Had it all lit up, colored Christmas lights, carols on the sound system. But they run into a problem—the engine cuts out and is gonna take some time to fix. Dr. Hartley had taken the boat up to the parade staging area earlier. The wife and kids drove up to join him. So they tell Ricky to go on ahead, take the car, and drive their daughter home while they square away the problem. The kid brother stays with his parents. A blessing, given how things turned out.

"They never get the engine restarted and wind up catching a tow back to the dock behind the house a couple hours later. Santa's still on the roof, Christmas lights twinkling in the yard, everything like they left it, but no Sunny, no Ricky, no car, no note. His parents live a few blocks away. They haven't seen the kids either, thought they were still with the Hartleys. First they're all pissed, then they panic. It's the start of a long night."

I toyed with my coffee spoon and tried to imagine.

"Their worst fear," Burch said, "was a traffic accident. They couldn't even begin to imagine how terrible the truth would be. They start reaching out to cops, troopers, hospitals, tow companies. Nothing.

"We pieced together later that the kids had stopped for ice cream on the way home. It's about ten o'clock on Christmas Eve. Strolling back to their car, no more than a hundred fifty feet from the brightly lit ice-cream parlor, they're surrounded by four or five young blacks.

They're robbed at gunpoint, abducted in a white van, and driven south to a remote farm field. The boy is severely beaten. Both are bound. The girl gets raped every which way by who knows how many, and then she and Ricky are shot in the head and left for dead."

I heard Nazario's sigh—or was it mine?

"Sonsabitches," Stone rumbled.

"Sunny regains consciousness in that South Dade tomato field a couple of hours before dawn. Naked, drenched in blood, she crawls and staggers more than half a mile to the nearest farmhouse." He frowned. "Everything goes against us from the start. Rain starts to pound, soaks the scene, washing away any evidence we mighta found. Meanwhile, the farmer's wife gets outa bed to close the windows, hears the girl's moans, and calls 911.

"She stays with Sunny while the farmer hauls ass out through the rain into the fields in his truck with a searchlight. He finds Ricky dead. Kid took a bullet in the right eye. Went through the orbital plate at the top part of the eye socket and lodged deep in his brain. The M.E. said he was probably alive for hours, leaking blood and brain matter."

The waitress interrupted with our coffee. Eyes downcast, she practically ran back into the kitchen.

"Sarge, you're spooking the help," Nazario said, as she disappeared.

Burch shrugged. "Had no business eavesdropping. She knows we're cops, and this ain't no tea party."

He stirred sugar into his café con leche until it had to be equal parts coffee and sugar, tasted it, frowned at Stone's iced tea, and took a deep breath.

"With all her injuries, it's a miracle Sunny ever reached that farmhouse. Had to be a strong-willed kid. She's mumbling, talking a little. The first responder, a rookie cop, rides with her in the ambulance, asking questions, taking notes. Guy did a good job. She talked about the white van, the scars one-a them had on his body. We're lucky that rookie did what he did, cuz by the time she hits the hospital she's out of it, comatose.

"And that's where I find myself Christmas morning, much to the dismay of my wife and kids, breaking the news to two sets of parents. Merry Christmas: Ricky is dead, and a priest is saying Godspeed to Sunny's soul."

Burch sipped his coffee, grimacing as though the taste was bitter, despite all the sugar. "Some holiday. For weeks I only went home to shower and change clothes. Had to reintroduce myself to Connie and the kids a couple months later. Lucky I got back in the house at all. Damn case drove me to drink. Closest I ever came to getting divorced.

"The manhunt was giganto. Fifty thousand dollars in reward money offered, all the manpower, all the resources, all the OT we asked for. The entire recruit class spent days walking roadsides, searching for the girl's clothes and any of Ricky's belongings that mighta been tossed outa the van. Fifty-man teams worked around the clock, thousands-a hours of overtime."

"Think they lived in the immediate area?" Stone asked.

Burch shook his head. "We talked to the occupants of more than three hundred homes, listed names, ages, everybody who lived there, checked 'em all out."

"Murder weapon ever found?" Stone said.

"Nope. Small caliber, a twenty-two, fairly low-powered. Went through the sales records of every gun dealer in the county, checked out everybody who legally bought that-caliber weapon. Nothing."

"Even though they were young, you think they might have been military or dependents from the air force base down there?" Nazario asked.

Burch shook his head again. "We got help from the military. All personnel and vehicles were checked out. Even had the criminal-court judges release a buncha defendants from the South End without bond, gave 'em promises of leniency if they came up with anything useful. Interviewed more than thirty-five hundred people, all the way from Florida to California and Canada. Fifty or so passed polygraphs."

"Think it was racial?" Stone asked, tight-lipped.

"Nah, black residents were as sick and outraged as anybody. As far as we could tell, the victims just caught the eyes of the wrong people." He pushed his cup away. "I worked that case so hard that when I did sleep I dreamed about it. Still do." He gazed at the two younger detectives. "I don't get it. Never did. Somewhere along the line it should have turned for us. It made no sense that we couldn't solve it."

"Yeah." Nazario stroked his mustache, puzzled. "With that many bad guys involved, you always catch a break."

"Right," Stone said. "There's always a weak link who cuts himself a deal by ratting out his buddies when he gets busted for something else."

"Or they fight among themselves, or drink and run their mouths," Nazario said.

"Or confide in girlfriends who drop a dime on them," I offered.

"You got it," Burch said. "Brothers even fall out and turn on each other. In this kinda case, mothers surrender their own sons. But nothing. It was eerie. Unnatural. Against all the laws of homicide and human nature. It's like they vaporized, fell off the face of the planet. All these years, until today, when this asshole shows up, crawling like a rodent through a hole in a roof.

"And now," he said, teeth showing in an anticipatory smile, "it's time. It's finally time."

"Damn straight," Stone said vigorously. "I say we take a real hard run at this one, sarge."

"I agree." Nazario gave a curt nod. "The Meadows case can wait."

"But," I asked, "how can you ever really know for sure that the man in the morgue was one of them?"

"Hell." Burch rose from his chair and snatched up the check. "We've got us a witness. The girl, Sunny: She beat the odds. She's alive."

2

I blew into the newsroom in a hurry. My editors were impatient to hear more about Gomez and my story for tomorrow's paper.

"They charged the poor guy with second-degree murder," I said.

"As well they should," Tubbs said righteously. He and Gretchen Platt, the assistant city editor from hell, exchanged glances across the city desk. "Take the law into your own hands and you face the consequences."

Gretchen pursed her cotton-candy-pink lips, nodding so vigorously that her perfectly cut shiny-blond hair bounced in agreement.

To them the story was simple black and white. But unlike so many who commute to this fortresslike tower high above the city's steamy streets and siren sounds and drive off at day's end in their air-conditioned co-

coons to gated suburban communities a thousand light-years away, I see shades of gray every day.

I went back to my desk, unable to forget the hopeless look on Gomez's weary face. Sometimes you know at once when a victim will stay with you.

I wondered about the dead man. Medics say that someone who's electrocuted remains conscious for at least fifteen seconds. Enough time to contemplate one's life.

Whatever his past, it would be sad. They always are. The world is full of sadness. Life, like history, is just one damn thing after another. But no childhood hardship could mitigate the evil of what had happened to Ricky Chance and Sunny Hartley.

What a great story it would be if Miami Detective Sergeant Craig Burch solved the crime at long last, suddenly positioned by fate to achieve justice in a case that had haunted him for years. Seek and ye shall find, I thought, tapping out the Gomez piece at my terminal—if you can just live long enough.

Miami's mayor was "unavailable" for comment on Gomez's pleas for help. His Honor was mired in his own soap-opera hell at the moment. Most couples war over sex, money, or in-laws, but when the mayor and his wife skirmished at breakfast over the proper way to brew a cup of tea, the press and the police had reacted as though he were O.J. on a rampage. SWAT sped to the scene, the house was cordoned off, cameramen and reporters ringed the house, news vans blocked the streets, and TV news choppers circled overhead. He blamed his political enemies, among them the police, with whom he had feuded over little Elián.

Elián and Fidel are no longer the chief topics debated over Cuban coffee. Many Miamians who have blamed Fidel for all things *malas* in the world and flown only the Cuban flag for more than thirty years have become fiercely patriotic. Most men and women who crowded recruitment centers to enlist after the attacks on America were not born in this country. Many were in their fifties and sixties, willing but ineligible. The tiny flags they wave from Little Havana street corners are a heartening sight, despite the fact that upon closer inspection they are stamped MADE IN TAIWAN. It is a giant step forward. Sometimes only great tragedy creates unity.

The mayor's secretary fished the shopkeeper's most recent plea from a file labeled NON-URGENT. Police record keepers also found a history of Gomez's complaints. I reported them in my story for the street edition, along with the fact that, if convicted, he faced a possible sentence of life in prison.

I combed my hair and dabbed on fresh lipstick after deadline, then hurried down the long gray hall, past photo and the wire room, to pitch my Cold Case Squad idea to Spencer Morganstern, the editor of the paper's recently revamped Sunday magazine *Hot Topics*.

Morganstern, a small dapper man who favors vests and bow ties, is famous for his creativity and his short attention span. He waved me to a seat amid haphazard stacks of books, files, and newspapers on the leather couch in his glass cage, leaned back in his creaky leather chair, and studied me quizzically through owlish spectacles too big for his face. His unruly Einstein-like hair bristled in every direction, as though electrified by the highly charged ideas, pictures, and possibilities that pervaded his mind, his office, and even the air around him.

"The Cold Case Squad has a terrific cast of characters," I said, launching my pitch. "Good detectives, hand-picked self-starters. They have to be, because they don't get to experience the screams, the blood, or the sense of outrage cops feel at fresh murder scenes."

Morganstern, expression bemused, did not react.

"What drives them is that, unlike other crimes, first-degree murder has no statute of limitations. No matter how old the case, a killer can still be brought to justice."

Morganstern broke eye contact, frowning at a sheet of paper on his desk. My heart sank. Was he already bored?

"I've known Burch since I first covered the beat," I said, voice rising. "Sam Stone, one of the detectives, is an edgy, really sharp young black guy who grew up here, in Overtown. And Nazario was a Pedro Pan kid, one of thousands spirited out of Cuba at the dawn of Castro's regime. The children were airlifted to freedom in Miami. The parents planned to follow but became trapped on the island when Fidel canceled the flights. Nazario arrived alone in Miami at age five. There are a couple of others: Corso, the guy wounded in that bank robbery a couple of years ago, and Acosta, who went on the cross-country gravedigging trip with that serial killer who confessed a few years ago.

"Their new lieutenant," I said, rushing on, "is K. C. Riley. She used to command the Rape Squad."

Morganstern continued to squint at the paper, which

looked suspiciously like an expense account form, then reached for a red grease pencil.

"The team's on a roll," I said, dropping my voice to a confidential tone. "About to tackle another really high-profile old case." He was vigorously crossing out and circling items on the paper. "Their work is dramatic, like time travel. They go back in time to apply new high-tech Star Wars technology—lasers, computers, DNA, and blood-spatter analysis—to murders committed long before such forensic techniques were even dreamed of.

"Everybody loves a mystery, and every one of their cases is a fascinating story in itself," I said, beginning to wind down. "They found the killer in one case but made no arrest. His last address was a cemetery. He'd been there for two years: natural causes."

Morganstern scowled, crumpled the paper, tossed it into his overflowing wastepaper basket, and looked up, as though puzzled to see me still there.

"Will their bosses cooperate, give you access?"

"Sure," I said quickly. "The department has had so much bad press that the brass will be thrilled about a piece on something positive."

The ring of confidence in my words struck an uneasy chord. My pitch for the story made sense, but cops often don't. Police-press relationships are love-hate at best. Lieutenant Riley was notoriously reserved and tight-lipped with reporters. But I babbled on, despite my misgivings, determined to sell Morganstern the idea.

"With so much bad news lately, readers will love the fact that murder victims are not forgotten, even years later. That maybe a bad guy didn't get away with murder after all, that not only does justice still exist in the world, it may prevail."

"Better late," Morganstern said, raising an eyebrow, "than never." His phone rang, but he ignored it.

"Time changes people and circumstances," I went on. "Sometimes all it takes to solve an old case is a few phone calls. Somebody afraid to tell the truth years ago feels free to do so now. The detectives dig up dusty evidence, blitz aging witnesses, travel to track them down, consult with forensic . . ."

"Enough." Morganstern pointed his red grease pencil at me like a weapon. "Don't push it. I was hooked when you said Cold Case Squad. That's catchy." He nodded and leaned back, contemplating the ceiling. "I'm thinking that for cover art, we can get these guys—and what's-er-name, that woman lieutenant with the initials—"

"K. C. Riley."

"Right. Over to the Miami Ice Company. Yeah. Miami Ice Company. Dress 'em all up in business suits, sit them on giant blocks of ice, their jackets open, to expose their guns in shoulder holsters, in front of a sign that says MIAMI ICE HOUSE. You know, Cold Case Squad: Miami Ice?" He lurched forward in his chair. "Whaddaya think?"

"Well," I murmured, appalled at the prospect of personally suggesting such an idea to Riley, "we'll need a really first-rate photographer. Lottie is good with cops."

Lottie Dane, my best friend, with her honeyed Texas drawl, reckless appeal, and flaming red hair, can persuade almost anybody to do almost anything in front of her cameras. Would her down-home charm work on the lieutenant?

"You're right about Lottie." Morganstern stroked his thick mustache. "We'll need photos of victims, perps, crime scenes. A shot of that dead killer's tombstone. We can crop it like a mug shot. Whatever. You know the drill. About time you wrote something for us, Britt," he said.

I left his office both elated and apprehensive. Now I would have to deliver.

I left Lottie a heads-up on her answering machine.

Half a dozen Miami police press releases cluttered my e-mail, including a routine two-line PIO yawner on the gunshot victim I'd seen in the morgue. No mention of chicken feathers or glitter. The shooting, it said, was the result of a "prior dispute."

I beeped Alan Curlette, aka Spiffy, identified as the lead detective. Spiffy, a fastidious and dapper dresser, always stepped gingerly around crime scenes, careful not to get blood, brains, or body fluids on his Guccis. "Hey," I asked, when he returned my call, "how come you never mentioned what the dead guy was and wasn't wearing?"

"Nobody asked," he said sullenly. "I'm still trying to get all that damn stupid shit off of me. All I did was roll the guy over. Now I got little sparkles in my cuffs, on my shoes, in my socks. I go to scratch my head, I see sparkles on my elbow. Is it unreasonable for me to be pissed off that there is glitter all over my goddamn car?

What's more, it don't work. Unfortunately, my goddamn sergeant can still see me."

"Probably because you're dressed," I said. "I think you're supposed to be naked for the full effect."

"How would you know what I happen to be wearing or not wearing?" he asked slyly.

"Somehow, I have a feeling that you're not sitting at your desk in the homicide bureau with no pants on," I said. "Don't ask me why. It's just some sort of sixth sense. Maybe I'm psychic."

"Or psycho. You Cubans are nuts."

"That too."

"Somebody should sue this guy's *santero* for malpractice."

He said witnesses told him the victim never even tried to escape his killer. Instead, convinced he was invisible, he flaunted his naked body, grinning and making rude gestures at the gunman. Imagine his surprise.

Resolving always to ask how all parties to fatal confrontations were dressed—or not—I wrote the story, turned it in, and then called the M.E. office. The scarred man had been fingerprinted. We should know his identity soon.

"A Cold Case Squad detective came by, had quite an interest in this fellow," the chief said mildly. "By the way, I've been thinking about his scars. His burns may have been caused by potash."

"Potash?"

"Haven't seen a case in years, but potash burns used to be quite common in poorer communities, back before guns became so cheap and readily available."

"What is it?"

"Folks used to mix lye, cooking grease, and hot water to make soap. Potash is an old term for the alkaline material used in soap. People buy guns for defense today, but back then lye was the weapon of choice in domestic and neighborhood brawls. Anybody who expected trouble would keep a can of lye behind the door or next to the bed. We'll find out when we learn more about his medical history."

"So you think he might be older than he looks?"

"No, but he may have come from a rural area where people still clung to the old ways."

I began to put notes together on the Cold Case Squad and asked Onnie, who works in the *News* library, for our photo files on Richard Chance and Sunny Hartley.

She brought them out herself a short time later. No longer stick-thin, Onnie is simply slim, even shapely, having gained enough weight to soften the structure of her angular bones. Her simple white blouse contrasted dramatically with her coffee-color skin and short curly hair. In no way did she resemble the desperate, battered young mother I first met. Her son, Darryl, now six, is a survivor like his mom. She is divorced now, her violent ex-husband serving a long prison sentence for an attack on a police officer, among other things.

"Plenty here on the boy." Onnie perched on the corner of my desk, opened a manila folder, and studied a photo. "But nothing," she added, bright black eyes meeting mine, "on the girl you mentioned."

Of course, I realized. The names and photos of rape

victims go unpublished. Sunny's name and face had never appeared in news accounts of the tragedy.

Onnie handed me the folder. Fair hair neatly combed, Richard Lee Chance wore a serious expression in his high school yearbook photo, though his eyes hinted at a subdued mirth. In another picture he knelt on one knee at the forefront of his exuberant varsity basketball team after a winning season.

Snapshots of his short and happy life contrasted starkly with news photos of grim men lifting his covered corpse to load into the morgue wagon. He had been found face up, surrounded by ripening tomato plants that thrived in that fertile farm field. His body had remained on the scene, the caption said, for more than eight hours, as detectives and crime scene technicians painstakingly did their work.

"Unsolved," Onnie said breezily. "No stories on it for years. Is there something new?"

"Could be." I tapped into the library's computer files. "Let's hope."

There had been dozens of stories. Ricky was the only child of Sean Chance, a city planner, and his wife, Heather, who taught school at Millard Junior High. High school students wept and clung to one another at the boy's funeral. Hundreds filled the church, spilling into the street, as Ricky's basketball coach and his pastor delivered eulogies. The family was too distraught to speak.

The wounded girl's parents kept a hospital vigil, their daughter not expected to survive. After ten days, however, her prognosis changed, her condition upgraded from critical to serious, then from serious to fair. Police guarded her room, and as soon as she was able, she cooperated with detectives as best she could.

My phone rang while I was still reading. "Got an ID." Burch sounded upbeat. "Andre Coney, age thirty-one."

"His rap sheet?"

"Dates back to age eleven, mostly petty but some strong-arms, a lotta B and E's, drugs, one lewd and lascivious."

"Was he married? Who did he live with? Parents?"

"According to Levitan, the next of kin's an aunt, one Ida Sweeting in South Miami. She helped raise him. But when he made the notification, she said she wasn't even sure where he'd been staying. Hadn't seen him in weeks."

"Think she'll remember who he ran with fourteen years ago?"

"Hope so, but I gotta do the drill before I talk to her. The team's gonna meet in the A.M., eyeball the file, then vote on whether to take on the case. Only a formality. Everybody's hot to go."

"What about Sunny, she still local?"

"Yeah, made a coupla calls. Lives over on the beach now. I'll look her up tomorrow after the meeting. Meanwhile, if you put Coney's name in the paper, don't mention a connection to this case."

"Right. Think Sunny will talk to me too?"

"It's up to her," he said. "Just don't jump the gun on me. Sit on it until I show her some pictures. I'm digging up Coney's old mug shots from back then."

* * *

Biscayne Bay glinted like broken glass beneath the slanting rays of the late-afternoon sun, as I drove home. No tourist would suspect that beneath its postcard-perfect surface, the bay had become a toilet that couldn't be flushed. Underwater sewer lines had ruptured and water-use restrictions had complicated matters. Power cleaning, car washing, and bubbling fountains had been outlawed. Police were enforcing the bans and Miamians had been warned to limit washing clothes and dishes and to flush only when necessary.

The future seemed grim and increasingly brown. What has happened to the world, to this city, and to me? I wondered, trying unsuccessfully to block out Kendall McDonald, who lingered in my heart and mind like a melancholy refrain. Uneasy and restless, shadowed by a vague foreboding, I yearned to flee, to roam uncharted shores and unspoiled beaches. This *Hot Topics* story, I thought, would finance my brief escape.

There were other benefits as well. Having time to polish a magazine piece is a luxury to those of us who pound out daily news stories. My work wouldn't be mindlessly slashed by an uncaring editor under deadline pressure or forced out of the paper by late-breaking news. This project was something to look forward to in an uncertain world.

Mrs. Goldstein, my landlady, was in her garden, lugging a plastic water bucket that sloshed with each step.

"I'm watering," she explained, "with gray water."

Gray is the term for water discarded after bathing or washing dishes.

"Bathwater," she panted, wisps of gray hair clinging to her neck, her cotton housedress damp with perspiration.

"You can't do this," I protested. The woman is eighty-two years old.

"But look." She gestured, a smile lighting up her face.

The Brunfelsia's pale lavender flowers exuded a heady fragrance. The same delicate blooms were deep purple yesterday. Tomorrow they would fade to white, then fall, like young lives cut short. The wistful beauty of the fragrant flowering shrub, common name Yesterday, Today, and Tomorrow, was worth any effort.

I fetched my own pail. Bitsy, my police-trained tiny mop of a dog, scampered around us as we launched a bucket brigade from the Goldstein bathtub to her garden, pausing only to curse state water managers. Our sea-level city drowned last fall. Homes and cars flooded, sewers backed up, and hapless motorists drowned, their cars submerged after they mistook overflowing canals for flooded streets. State officials reacted by reducing the water levels in Lake Okeechobee—the Native American word for Big Water—far too much. The huge freshwater lake, second largest in the lower forty-eight states, supplies South Florida's drinking water. Now this lake, the planet's most recognizable feature when viewed from outer space, was nearly dry and we faced another water crisis. This time, too little.

I fed Bitsy and Billy Boots the cat, surveyed the unappealing prospects in my refrigerator, and checked my messages. Only one.

I called her back. "You're running with the Cold Case Squad assignment, aren't you?"

"Sure thang," Lottie said. "Any of them bad boys single and hot to go?" Despite a dispiriting string of Mr. Wrongs, she is ever optimistic.

She insisted we celebrate our magazine assignment. So Bitsy and I took a quick walk, Billy Boots trailing at a distance, so he could pretend not to know us if we did something embarrassing. Then Lottie picked me up.

We settled at an umbrella table between the pool and the docks at the Fifth Street Marina. Lottie, the paper's best breaking-news shooter, bitched bitterly about the day's assignments from Gretchen, all local politicians "presenting the plaque."

"Isn't this premature?" I asked Lottie, as I ordered a Painkiller Number One. The sneaky concoction of rum, coconut cream, pineapple, and orange juice is smooth and guaranteed to numb the senses. It's available in various strengths, depending on the severity of your pain. "Shouldn't we finish the project, then celebrate?"

She ordered a lime margarita. "We kin party then too, and again when it's published. Didn't the President say we all should go back to our normal lives?"

"Sure. He also said, 'Watch out, because we don't know when or how but somebody's trying to kill you. Now go on out there and live normally, but stay alert.' "

"Not bad advice whenever," she said, "especially in Miami. I tell that to myself every time I get behind the wheel, especially when I drive the Palmetto Expressway. You ever been to Xochimilco, Mejico?"

"I wouldn't even try to spell it, much less find it. What is it?"

"Little town where they celebrate four hundred twenty-two official fiestas a year!" She wrinkled her freckled nose and grinned. "Them Mexicans sure know how to live."

"Maybe there's nothing to celebrate around here." I sighed, watching night creep along the western horizon. "Lately, Lottie, especially after what happened in New York and DC, life feels like a long winter with no Christmas." I told her about Sunny Hartley and Ricky Chance.

She shook her head at the terrible details. "Gonna talk to the poor little gal?"

"Sure. But Burch has to break the news first, find out if the dead guy really was one of her attackers. No point in me intruding on her if he wasn't."

"We're gonna be working with Riley on the Cold Case gig," Lottie said cheerfully. "Still suspect she and McDonald have the hots for each other?"

I took a healthy swallow of my Painkiller and shrugged. "Nothing I can do about it if they do." The lack of trust, the misunderstandings and regrets all came back to me. I stared in dismay at my drink. So far it wasn't doing its job. "I don't even know if he's back from New York yet," I said. "Haven't heard a thing since he left with the contingent of Miami cops who volunteered for the assistance mission. Isn't it strange that he'd find Riley attractive? You'd think she'd be the last woman he'd lust after. We're nothing alike. She's such an obnoxious bitch."

Lottie squinted and cupped her ear, as though she

hadn't heard right. "Sure. And you're a real little Miss Congeniality, so shy and sweet."

"What do you mean?" I asked, incredulous. "Riley is a superbitch."

"And what are you like when some fool gets in your way on deadline?"

"That is *so* different," I said. "You do what you have to on deadline. All that matters is the story. So you do things you'd never do normally. You know how it is. The job gives you tunnel vision. But I'm not really like that, am I?"

"Then why do some people swear you have a tail and horns?"

"How can you say that?" I snapped, irritated. "I'm in no mood—"

"What I'm saying," she said earnestly, "is that K. C. Riley is probably a whole lot like you: tiger on the job, pussycat at heart."

"Oh, puleeze." I rolled my eyes in exasperation.

"Why not give McDonald a call when he gets home?" she said. "He'll probably need lots of TLC after Ground Zero. Be sweet, check it out. Maybe nothing's going on there. Maybe they're buddies. You know cops. How they like to hang out with other cops, live in the same neighborhoods—"

"Yeah, and they tend to intermarry. I never returned his last message," I confessed glumly.

She frowned. "You need a blood test," she said, "to see if any is getting to your brain. I thought you and him were—"

"So did I, Lottie." I sighed impatiently. "So did I."

"What about Fitzgerald?" she asked. Dennis Fitzgerald is an investigator for the Volusia County state attorney's office, and we had hit it off when an old case brought him to Miami.

"A great guy," I said, "but in Daytona Beach, three hundred miles away."

"He'd be here in a heartbeat if you'd show a little interest."

"My heart just isn't in it, Lottie."

Mercifully, she changed the subject. "So this gal Sunny survived, but did she recover? Living a normal life?"

"I guess so," I said uncertainly. "As if anybody could after what happened to her. You remember what sixteen was like. Everything was a big deal. A date for the school dance was a matter of life or death. She's grown up now, must be twenty-nine or so. I wonder if she has a life, or just therapy three or four times a week."

"People are resilient," Lottie said quietly, "especially kids. We see it all the time. Even close to home, look at little Darryl."

"Right." I couldn't help smiling. "He couldn't be better. In fact, Onnie gave me one of his new crayon drawings the other day. It's on my refrigerator; I love it. I think he's got a real talent, even though he's only six." I lifted my glass. "I hope Sunny's life is happy. Maybe she's married, with kids of her own. Strange, isn't it, for us to be here, talking about her like this, knowing something she doesn't?"

"Like what?"

"That even if she has put that terrible night behind

her, it's back. Nobody outlives the past." We watched a quarter moon emerge in the darkening sky. "Wherever she is, whatever she's doing, I wonder if she feels something in the air, senses that her life is about to change."

"If that barbecued bandido was one of 'em, she'll be happy to hear he's on an elevator ride straight to hell and the rest of 'em may soon git what's coming to 'em." She smiled sweetly and winked back at a hunk at the bar.

An apprehensive chill rippled up my spine. What was Sunny's life really like? I wondered. How would she react to the news?

The man at the bar, a smiling sun-bronzed yachtsman named Brad, zeroed in on Lottie like a heat-seeking missile. He was eager to buy us drinks, dance with us to the island music, and whisk us away on a moonlight cruise. She was ready to go, but I wanted an early start in the morning.

Lottie gave Brad her phone number as he walked us back to her company car, still cajoling us to stay. As we rolled out of the parking lot, her dashboard police scanner crackled to life. Typical Miami night: shots fired in Wynnwood, a hit-run driver fleeing east in the westbound lanes of I-95, and an out-of-control fire at 224 Northwest 14th Street.

My heart sank. I wanted another Painkiller. "Hear that, Lottie? Fourteenth Street. Let's go." I fastened my seat belt.

"Only one engine company so far," she protested. "Don't sound big to me."

"It's big," I said, a bitter taste in my mouth.

She shrugged, stomped the gas, burned rubber in a U-turn, and we streaked west.

"Dammit." I locked the scanner onto Miami's fire frequency. "Hear that? Fully involved, out of control." I groped in my purse for a notebook. "You got your camera gear?"

" 'Course, in the trunk." The eight-cylinder engine whined as she swerved around a slow-moving jitney and floored it. She pouted. "Thought you was dead set on gettin' to bed early."

"I was," I said somberly, "but now I need to get back over there."

"Over where?"

"Gomez Watch Repair."

3

Hoses snaked through the streets and alarms howled like wounded animals. Flames savaged the night sky until firefighters knocked down the blaze, too late for the shop or its contents. Crucial time had been lost initially because illegally parked cars blocked all the nearest fire hydrants. Stolen cars, I was willing to bet. Certain people didn't care about Andre Coney's long rap sheet or that he was a thief who probably preyed upon them as well. They wanted Gomez ruined, run out of their neighborhood with nothing to salvage. My Aunt Odalys says it best: *Las calles estan duras, hija.* The streets are hard, girl.

"It wasn't enough to see him in jail," I told Lottie. "They had to destroy him. I bet the torch is a face in that crowd."

She discreetly photographed the jeering, hooting

spectators while I asked questions. None of the strangers enjoying the flames reflected in their eyes admitted to knowing anything. A fire captain said the presence of an accelerant was suspected and pronounced the blaze one of "suspicious origin." Surprise.

We returned to the *News,* parked under the building, and scrambled through a rear door into the deserted lobby and onto the elevator. We split up on the fifth floor, Lottie to process her film while I inserted the fire into a new top on my Gomez story for the final.

Later, at home, I took Bitsy out for a last look at the quarter moon sailing like a pirate schooner through a dark sea of night. Good things do happen on my beat, I thought, I just hadn't seen any for a long time. After we returned and I went to bed, Billy Boots purring beside me and Bitsy curled up at my feet, I prayed not to see the woman again.

But there she was in my dreams, among hundreds of terrified people fleeing a towering all-consuming tornado of debris and smoke from a collapsing tower. They ran for their lives, the hellish billowing blackness in pursuit. As always, since I first saw it live in my living room, I focused on one face in the crowd: a young woman in a blue sweater, her flowing brown hair pulled back. Despite the people streaming around her, she did not run. Instead, she walked, more and more slowly, until she finally stopped and turned to face the rapidly advancing darkness. "Run! Run!" I cried from my living room. But to my horror, as the surging humanity parted around her in flight, she slowly began to walk into the oncoming blackness.

I searched all the footage that followed but never saw her again. Why did she go back? Did she survive? Who was she?

My eyes ached and my sinuses felt scorched when I awoke. I blamed the dream on last night's fire scene, but it was something else, something real in the air. I pulled on shorts, a T-shirt, and sneakers, snatched up my Walkman, plugged in the earphones, and trotted the two blocks to the beach.

The morning tasted acrid. Smoke stung my nostrils and the horizon shimmered in a hazy blur. I didn't need news radio to know the Everglades was burning again. Wildfires were raging up and down the state, three hundred thousand acres blackened so far this year.

I jogged the boardwalk at a labored pace, gasping in the polluted air as my footsteps thudded on the weathered boards, the news of a surreal war washing over me. Sword-swinging soldiers on horseback, backed up by Stealth bombers and spy satellites. Unfriendly skies, airport lockdowns, and bad mail—really bad mail.

Locally, lightning had sparked dozens of new blazes in Dade and Palm Beach overnight. Smoke from two thousand acres of burning saw grass was threatening posh Boca Raton neighborhoods. "And locally, fire destroyed . . ." The newscaster read the first few graphs from my Gomez story almost verbatim. A few callers reacted to it on the talk show that followed. Most sympathized with the jailed shop owner.

Like a good omen, a treat waited on my doorstep when I returned, a plump grapefruit freshly picked from one of Mrs. Goldstein's three trees. So far, they had escaped the chain saws of the canker police, state agricultural inspectors on a search-and-destroy mission to protect Florida's commercial citrus groves. They cut down both infected trees and every healthy tree within a third of a mile as well. Backyard citrus, another joy of life in South Florida, would soon be just a memory. I cut the grapefruit while my English muffin toasted. Yes! My favorite, ruby red, sweet and bursting with juice. I devoured half with my muffin and tea, planning to save the rest, but couldn't resist and ate that too.

I set out on my beat feeling better. Despite the roller-coaster ride that is my job, I love being a journalist. There is something noble and exciting about venturing out each day to seek the truth. And my beat has it all, comedy and tragedy, sex and violence. Shakespeare in the raw—Macbeth, Othello, Hamlet, King Lear, Romeo and Juliet—I meet them all on Miami's steamy streets.

I kept an eye out for Sergeant Craig Burch during my usual rounds but had no sightings. He did not respond to a phone message or calls to his beeper. A good sign, I thought. I imagined him seated across from Sunny, dealing out mug shots like playing cards in front of her. Her features were a blur in my fantasy but I saw Burch clearly, poker-faced, alert, sharply observing her reactions.

A two o'clock bond hearing had been scheduled for Hector Gomez, but I didn't cover it. Andy Maguire, the courthouse reporter, was as territorial about his beat as

I am about mine. Just as well, as it turned out, since breaking news intervened.

Jerry, an intern who monitored police radios in a cubbyhole niche off the newsroom, called me to report that something unusual seemed to be happening deep in south Dade farm country.

"I don't know if it's anything," he said hesitantly. "I can't get a handle on it, Britt."

"What does it sound like?" I said.

"I dunno, but there's a lot of radio transmissions."

"Such as?" I gazed at the murky haze beyond the newsroom's big picture windows. The horizon was white with a yellow cast.

"Sounds like a scene in a farm field."

An image flashed through my mind: Richard Chance's sprawled body; Sunny, covered with blood, staggering to her feet.

"I checked the map," Jerry was saying. "Looks like the middle of nowhere. The call went to police, then fire rescue dispatched on a three, and now they're asking for drilling equipment—"

"Oh, no!" I blurted.

I told him what it was, exited what I had on the computer, and gathered my things.

He called back less than a minute later. "You were right," he said breathlessly. "There's a baby down a well!"

Four toddlers had tumbled into uncapped irrigation wells in U-pick-'em farm fields in the past two years. Each frantic rescue attempt had ended the same way, with the recovery of a small lifeless body.

The field, southwest of the old Homestead Air Force Base, was forty-five minutes away if I was lucky. I told Tubbs on the city desk and rushed for the elevator.

"Britt!" My instinct was to make a run for it, but the slow-moving elevator hadn't arrived. Too late. I was trapped. Gretchen had seen me.

"Wait," she said. "We'll want two people on this."

"I can handle it." Fidgeting like a racehorse at the starting gate, I willed the elevator doors to open. They didn't.

"No. Too many angles here for one reporter." She positioned herself between me and the elevator, her gleaming blood-red fingernails resting lightly on her crossed arms, her stance confrontational. "Take Ryan," she said, cocking her head in her detestably perky way.

"I don't need help, Gretchen. It's a long drive. I need to get down there ASAP."

Ryan Battle works general assignment and is my friend, but I didn't want help.

"You two can go together." Gretchen's take-charge attitude would impress anyone who didn't know she was clueless, mean-spirited, and homicidally ambitious.

She hailed Ryan, as though he were a cab, from across the huge newsroom. He sprang from his desk at her summons, eager to please, soft brown eyes alight. I sighed and tried to zone Gretchen out, focusing on her chunky gold earrings, winking cheerily beneath the newsroom's fluorescent lights. I always lose mine when using telephones somewhere on deadline. I save the singles, in the futile hope of one day finding their missing mates, or a deserving one-eared person, or that I will someday take up crafts and convert them to meaningful pieces of art in my spare time. But like me, I thought glumly, they will probably remain single, without a mate. Forever. Perhaps I could pierce my belly button and wear the orphans like ornaments, I thought, dangling from my navel.

Ryan is a gentle soul, sweet, handsome, and impossible to resent. But I tried my damnedest. I hate too many reporters on a story.

We descended to the lobby in silence.

The white-hot light was blinding and the heat took my breath away as I charged out onto the pavement, three strides ahead of him.

"Let's take my car," Ryan offered.

What did he mean by that? Was he referring to past events, the times my cars and Lottie's were totaled?

"It was never our fault," I said, with a sharp look.

"What?" He blinked, as though puzzled. "My car's in the west lot."

"You must be joking," I said. "You almost got us killed last time." The jagged scar across his forehead was barely noticeable now.

"But that was a riot," he protested. "A brick through the windshield. But if you want to drive, Britt, that's okay. I'll ride shotgun."

He held on without comment as I blew an amber light to escape a stampede of aggressive window washers at the Dolphin Expressway ramp, where the winos were in bloom and the bums in season. We hurtled west, then south to the Don Shula. Local street names leave no doubt as to what takes priority in Miami.

Traffic resembled a presidential motorcade, with flags mounted on nearly every vehicle.

"Makes you feel good to see that, doesn't it?" Ryan said.

"Sure," I said. "if you think it makes sense to fly American flags from huge gas-guzzling SUVs."

I thought of the two-year-old girl whose mother had decided to surprise her husband with a shortcake dessert that night. Their toddler stumbled into an uncapped well in a strawberry field and suffocated before rescuers reached her.

After that tragedy, the county ordered that wells in fields open to the public be capped and marked with red flags.

They must have missed one.

After farmers' commercial harvests, entrepreneurs lease farm fields and open them to the public. Families on outings or tight budgets pay to pick their own produce.

"It must be fun," Ryan was saying dreamily. "I've always wanted to go down there and spend a day picking fruits and vegetables. You can really experience what it's like to be a migrant worker. Like Cesar Chavez—"

"Oh, sure," I said. "It must be so enlightening when you go home to your air-conditioned condo to relax in the Jacuzzi with a glass of wine."

Ryan gazed at me fondly, all soft eyes and long lashes. "Are you in a bad mood, Britt?"

"Who wouldn't be?"

"Want to talk about it?"

"No." How could he remain so together, so relaxed, on deadline, when my every pore oozed adrenaline? I hit the gas to pass a lumbering cement truck, then apologized for being so snotty.

"That's okay," he said. "It's healthy to vent."

I told him about the squad, the old cold case they were hot to pursue, and my lackluster love life.

Farm fields stretched as far as the eye could see as we neared our destination. Was this the route the killers took with their captives that Christmas Eve? I wondered aloud. Did Richard Chance die here? Over there? Or had the crime scene been lost forever, obliterated by one of the new subdivisions we had passed?

"The maps are all different now," Ryan said.

"Right." I sighed. "The middle of nowhere is a lot farther south and west than it used to be."

Luckily my scanner picked up police transmissions from the scene, radioing directions to incoming emergency crews. Soon we were trailing a convoy of flashing red, blue, and yellow lights.

Badges and sunglasses glinted amid precise rows of tomato plants. Florida Power and Light and Bell South drilling equipment arrived when we did. Far from the wildfires, there was no haze here, only brittle blue sky and an unforgiving sun.

My stomach clenched like a fist as a distraught young woman in a cotton blouse and blue jeans struggled with a fireman and another man who were trying to lead her away from a small opening in the ground.

"Look," I told Ryan, "I don't need any help. I can handle it. I like working solo."

"Sure," he said. "I don't feel so good anyway. I think I'm coming down with something. I'll go find a cold drink. Want one?"

The man's becoming a hypochondriac, I thought, as I stumbled through stubble and loose dirt.

The weeping woman was in her twenties, with honey-colored hair and little makeup on a face ruddy with emotion. "It's Justin!" Her voice teetered on the edge of hysteria. "He's only sixteen months old! He was right behind us."

She turned, sobbing, against her husband's chest. Tourists from Findlay, Ohio, they had stopped to see the farm and buy fresh vegetables.

"He was tagging along about three rows behind us," the father said, eyes wet behind the lenses of his glasses, "sort of talking to himself and singing like he always does. All of a sudden, we didn't hear him."

When they turned, Justin had vanished, leaving only his strangely muffled wails, as though from an echo chamber.

"He's scared," his mother sobbed. "He's so little." She clenched her fists helplessly. "It was covered by grass. You couldn't even see it!"

Rescue crews moved in heavy equipment, wheels spinning in the dirt. "They're the best," I assured them. I didn't mention that, so far, the best had never been good enough.

Reggie Handleman, the fire department's information officer, took off his orange hard hat and steered me away from the parents. "It's an irrigation well," he said, "about twenty-five-feet deep. The hole is nine inches across. The kid slid down feet first and got wedged about ten feet down, in water up to his chest."

The child's father had run to the farmhouse for help. A twelve-year-old boy came running with a rope, as his mother dialed 911. The boy wriggled into the well but couldn't reach the child. When his shoulders got stuck, they dragged him out.

The first police officer who arrived managed to hook the child's T-shirt with a fruit picker—a wooden pole with curved metal claws at one end—to keep him from sliding any farther as he squirmed and struggled.

"After the last kid," Reggie said quietly, "the guys worked out a plan, Britt. They think we've got a good shot at saving this one."

I wondered how long the tot could survive his watery claustrophobic prison. I said a silent prayer, as drilling equipment rumbled loudly into action, and wondered why it had been so long since my prayers, or anyone else's, seemed to make a difference. Was anybody listening?

Firefighters began to dig a parallel shaft but struck solid coral rock just beneath the sandy loam. Progress was painfully slow as the sun climbed higher, melting the air around us into liquid heat. Gasping workers drilled a connecting tunnel to the well, wading in waist-deep water as the baby wailed.

The media pack had arrived. TV crews ran amok, trampling adjacent farm fields. News choppers churned up huge clouds of gritty dust, increasing the discomfort. My sunglasses kept skidding down my sweaty face until the bridge of my nose was rubbed raw. I could feel the tan on my arms darken and wished I could wring out my underwear.

I interviewed firefighters, cops, the man who had leased the field, and the stouthearted twelve-year-old who'd made the first rescue attempt. Villanueva, a

News photographer dispatched by Gretchen, had also arrived.

Ryan reappeared to steer me toward a witness. "She and her husband own the place," he said in my ear. "Her son, Burt, attempted the first rescue. She remembers the murder you were just talking about."

"My husband's up in Tallahassee lobbying for farm aid," the anguished woman told me. "I want to go over to talk to the mother; I'm a mother myself. But I don't know what to say to her. . . ." Her voice trailed off. They had never had an accident like this one in the three generations the farm had been in her husband's family.

"I'm surprised you still remember it," she said, when I asked her about the teenagers abducted and shot fourteen years earlier. "I haven't heard talk about that for years. A terrible thing. They never caught them, you know." Her eyes flooded. "Seems like nobody can live a normal life anymore. We haven't had a good year in so long I can't remember when. You just survive." She stared tearfully across the fields at the emergency equipment, reporters, and their vehicles. "You just try to get through one disaster after another—fires, floods, hurricanes, drought. If not for bad luck we'd have no luck at all."

The field where the boy and girl were shot still existed, she said, about five miles south. "The Pinder place, real nice piece of property."

"The Pinders are still there?"

"Not for long," she said. "I hear they're packing it in. They're inside the new district. Used to be no more than one house allowed for five acres. But the county changed the zoning. They're selling out to developers.

They got lucky, the Pinders did. Somebody's paying big bucks for their property. Wish it was us." She covered her eyes with her hand.

Microphones suddenly appeared over my shoulder, thrust in her face. TV reporters are relentless when they smell tears.

The pounding air hammers were giving me a headache. The baby must be deafened and terrified, if he's still alive, I thought. But when the hammers stopped, the sudden silence made my heart pound.

"It's too dangerous," Handleman said. "The connecting shaft is only inches away from him. They'll work by hand now, chip the coral rock away with chisels."

Justin began to wail again, his cries music to our ears.

But as the tunneling slowly continued, his cries faded, then stopped. His mother's eyes closed, lips moving.

"He's whimpering!" a firefighter shouted from the mouth of the well. Those of us still braving the shadeless heat breathed a collective sigh of relief.

My underarms felt sticky, my clothes soggy, as sweat made a snakelike spiral down my spinal column.

Twenty minutes later, a fireman in the shaft cautiously broke through the final few inches of rock.

"I see his face!" he shouted. He carefully enlarged the opening, then tugged Justin through it.

Like being born again, the child emerged from darkness into the light. Handed up to a husky deputy, he howled and waved his tiny fists amid the cheers, applause, and whir of the cameras. A happy ending.

At last! Tears stung my eyes. Glare from the sun, I told myself. But burly firefighters also wiped away tears.

Squinting at the light, his face a grimy pout, Justin was embraced by his parents and then bundled in a blue blanket for a helicopter ride to county hospital.

Ryan returned, sunburned and loaded down with enough cartons of tomatoes and okra for us both. We piled into the T-Bird and raced north to Miami. He was already off for the day, so I left him at his car in the *News* parking lot.

I conferred with the art department on diagrams of the successful rescue effort and then began putting the story together. Villanueva's color photos had captured the glorious moment of rescue. The hospital said Justin was fine, only a few minor scrapes and bruises. I wished I could say the same for myself. Gretchen hovered over me like a vulture as I wrote.

"No." She peered over my shoulder, tapped a polished finger against her chin, and frowned. "That's not the right lead."

Gingerly exploring the raw spot on my nose, I squinted at the racing hands on the newsroom clock and wondered what cruel twist of fate had put her in charge of my story.

"How about," she said, in singsong fashion, slowly rolling her eyes, "leading with the fact that, despite passage of the well-capping ordinance, no county inspection program was ever implemented to enforce it." She snapped her fingers. "That's it! There's your lead!"

"I don't think so, Gretchen." My overheated body began to shudder in the icy air-conditioning. The transition from farm field to newsroom had the effect of heatstroke followed by frostbite. "I think the human drama of the rescue should lead, with the ordinance and inspections coming in at about the third graf."

"TV will report the rescue," she said, shaking her head emphatically, her bouncy hairdo swinging like a model's in a shampoo commercial. "We need a second-day lead."

"But people want to read about the joy of that moment," I said. "They need it; we all do. The firefighters, the rescuers, are heroes. After the other tragedies, they devised a new plan and made it work. Unlike TV, we can describe it in depth, on a personal level."

"This is not the time to be a prima donna, Britt." She frowned, pursing her lips.

"I'm not a prima donna," I protested, echos of air hammers beginning to pound in my head, "but I'd be embarrassed to turn in a story that ignores the human element, the most important point."

"It won't be ignored," she snapped. "Report the rescue farther down in the body of the story, as tight as you can make it." Lowering her voice, she leaned so close that her perfume made my eyes water. "I will be editing your copy," she said crisply, "so if you don't change it, I will. And, Britt, I hate having to bring this up again, but for God's sake, will you try to remember that, when in public, you represent this newspaper."

I squinted up at her, dehydrated and thirsty. "What?"

"Appearances," she hissed, eyes wandering disdainfully from my limp sweat-soaked hair to my rumpled clothes and muddied shoes.

"I'm busy," I muttered, gritting my teeth. "If you decide to rewrite it your way, you can just take my name off it."

"Fine." She shrugged and stalked back to the city desk.

There are editors whose orders I will follow like a marine. Gretchen is not one of them. I wrote the story with the strongest stuff at the top and hit the SEND button, and it was out of my hands.

My first stop was the water fountain. Then, chilled to the bone, I dug an old yellow cardigan out of my locker. Gretchen was busy at her editing screen when I returned. I couldn't bring myself to look. "Any questions?" I inquired from a distance.

She shook her head without looking up.

When Andy Maguire returned from criminal court, he said a $75,000 bond had been set for Gomez. The shopkeeper and his pregnant wife, devastated by the charges and the fire, had wept in court. The Reverend Earl Wright, a fiery local black activist, was now involved. He had organized a noisy demonstration outside the Justice Building before attending the hearing with a number of protesters, all seeking justice for the dead man and harsh punishment for Gomez.

All I was seeking was a cool shower, a hot meal, and bed. The phone rang as I cleared my desk. I thought about walking away but didn't. I never do.

It was Craig Burch. I slid back into my chair, the neurons in my brain so fried by the sun that it took a moment to remember why I'd been so eager to reach him earlier. Right, I thought, and announced we had a green light on the story for *Hot Topics* and asked about his progress on the Chance case.

"Don't ask." He sounded bummed.

"Uh-oh," I said. "You mean Sunny couldn't identify Coney as one of her attackers?"

"Shit, worse than that, Britt. I've had a helluva day."

"Tell me about it." I commiserated. "I've got this editor who—"

"We need to talk."

"Go."

"No, I mean face time, me and you."

"When?"

"Whatcha doing now?"

"Oh, Craig, I'm a mess."

"This ain't a date."

I made an exasperated sound. "I know that, Craig, but I've been melting in the hot sun all afternoon. You should see me. I'm gonna have to burn these clothes."

For a moment I thought he'd hung up, but then I heard him breathing.

"Where are you?" I said, resigned.

"The boat ramp up at Pelican Harbor. Buy ya a beer."

I massaged my stiff neck and wondered if I had any aspirin.

"Ten?" he asked.

"Give me twenty."

I stared in dismay at my reflection in the ladies' room mirror. Worse than I thought.

I had never seen anyone use the locker room shower.

I unearthed a washcloth and a free shampoo sample from my locker, along with a change of clothes stashed for emergencies—fresh underwear, a T-shirt, and an old pair of jeans. Sure, this was no date, but Gretchen's slurs had stung. I gingerly touched a bare toe to the tiled floor of the narrow cubicle, grimaced, and wished for shower shoes. Who had bathed here last? It had not been recent. The cold, rusty spray of water looked blood red in the dim light. The color eventually cleared but the water never grew warm.

I trembled as it cascaded over me, teeth chattering as I thought of the young life saved today and of the other youngster, Ricky Chance, who had lost his years ago.

Once wet, the plastic shampoo packet was too damn slippery to tear open. Frustrated, I finally tossed it aside and, knowing I'd regret it, washed my hair with a dried-out bar of unidentified soap someone had left behind.

I blotted myself roughly with brown paper towels from the rest room, pulled on the clean clothes, and tried unsuccessfully to drag a comb through my wet, tangled hair. Gretchen walked in as I applied a lipstick named Torrid, the only shade in my locker. She shook her head in amused disbelief.

"I see you have a date, Britt," she said smartly. "One of your policeman friends?"

I drove with the windows open to dry my hair, but all the damp, smoky air did was make me sneeze. The temperature, slightly cooler after sunset, was still in the eighties.

I rolled up behind Burch's Chevy Blazer. He waved

from a rough wooden picnic table that overlooked the dark waters of Biscayne Bay. His jacket and tie were gone, along with the jaunty look he'd worn the day before. A six-pack of Coors sat in front of him. He had started without me. It was half empty. He did a double-take as he rose to greet me.

"You look half drowned," he said. "You swim here from the *News*?"

"Took a quick shower at the paper." I paused to sneeze again. "Thank you very much. I'll probably wind up with pneumonia and athlete's foot."

"Thirsty?" He reached beneath the table. "Didn't know if you were a beer drinker. Some girls aren't. So I got you these." He proudly plunked down a six-pack of assorted sweet wine coolers with names like strawberry blush, mango tango, and peach surprise. The names alone made me queasy.

"I'll have a beer, if you don't mind."

"Sure thing. Help yourself, there's more in the car."

He cracked open a can and slid it across the table, along with a plastic cup. A thoughtful touch, since he was drinking straight from a can. Normally I am no beer drinker, except with pizza, but this was ice cold and tasted good.

I sipped, suddenly comfortable in this free and open place, in the heat of the night, as breezes whispered over rushing water, sharing the moment with this man. Strangers might see Burch as an ordinary guy, a beer can in his fist, but I saw him as a soldier on a mission. What pursuit is more important than justice?

"What happened?"

"The squad met this morning," he said carefully.

"Corso's on his way back from England, interviewing a witness in another case. But we called 'im and Acosta, who's still up at Ground Zero with the city's other volunteers. Made it unanimous. We decided to run with it."

"Great. So what's the problem?"

He paused, elbows resting on the table in front of him. "The problem? Riley told me to forget it."

"What do you mean?"

"She's the boss." He cracked open another can and took a long drink. "She said no way."

"Why?"

"Lot of reasons, none worth crap if you ask me. Said even if we could put Coney there that night, he's dead and beyond prosecution."

"But the others. What about them?"

"Sez we don't have a snowball's chance of IDing 'em now, and even if we did they're probably dead too—or in prison."

"Hell, you could say that about every cold case. This one's high-profile, it would be a coup to close it."

"Tell me about it," he said bleakly. "But there ain't no talking to her. Doesn't want us spinning our wheels, wasting time. Says we got to 'prioritize.' Target cases with higher possibilities of prosecution. The brass wants stats, results."

"How much time would it take to talk to Sunny and to Coney's family?" I asked indignantly. "Did you give Riley an argument?"

"Got into it big-time. You know what a short fuse that woman's got. Says she don't have to explain. She's the supervisor," he said bitterly. "Said to focus on Meadows and half a dozen others we've been looking at."

"Can you go over her head?"

"Sure. Let's see now," he said sarcastically. "Which future do I want? Busted to patrol on the midnight shift and never seeing my family, or still working regular hours with a normal happy family life for the first time in twenty years?" He weighed the options, using his hands as scales. "Midnight shift? Family life? Crappy life? Happy life?

"I shouldn't have pushed it," he said, with regret. "Then she wouldn't have got pissed and issued me a direct order to leave it alone."

"Don't beat yourself up, Craig. It was a good catch. You were doing the right thing. It would be different if Ernie was still lieutenant."

"Damn straight."

"What are you going to do?"

"Off the record? That's where you come in, Britt. We were thinking maybe you could help us out."

"Me?"

"You're already on top of Coney getting zapped. You've got a rep for digging, checking things out. What if you started looking at it, asking questions? The lieutenant hears about it and has to react so we don't look bad in case you start coming up with answers. You know how it is. When the press starts looking into something, that always blows a case wide open."

"But the Sunday magazine editor wants to make the Cold Case Squad a cover story. If I piss Riley off, she could make it really difficult for—"

"Neither one of us do what we do cuz we wanna be

loved. If we wanted that, we'd be firemen. Me and the guys talked about it. Stone and Nazario thought it could work. You'll just have to protect us, make it look like you nosed out the story on your own."

"Craig, I don't know. . . ." A sudden chill swept over me, and despite the night's heat I hugged my arms.

He popped two more beers. I sipped mine, then sipped again. Burch raised his eyes to mine.

"There was dirt in that girl's lungs," he said. "They pushed her face into the ground while they were raping her."

I closed my eyes, and we sat without speaking across the scarred boards of the picnic table.

"I used to go out there at night," he said softly. "I'd turn off the car lights and walk out there with no radio, no flashlight, and just stand there, in the silence of that dark remote field, in the same place, at the same time that it happened, trying to get a sense of what those kids felt, what they saw or didn't see as they were being forced out into that field to be brutalized and shot."

"Did it work?"

"It ain't solved, is it?" He got to his feet, walked heavily to his car, and took another six-pack out of the trunk.

He crushed an empty beer can in his fist, then lobbed it into a wire trash can six feet away.

"Bull's-eye." He cracked open another.

"Hey." I shook my head. "No more for me. You either. It's ten o'clock. Does your wife know where you are? You want *two* angry women on your case, your wife *and* K. C. Riley? Then you'd *really* wish you were dead. Hey, I thought you quit a long time ago."

"Beer is proof that God loves us and wants us to be happy," he said simply.

"You really believe that?"

"They ain't my words. Benjamin Franklin said that. What's the matter, you don't like beer?"

"Sure," I said. "I mean the part about God."

"Lately," he said, eyes hidden in shadow, "I'm not even sure He exists."

We gazed across the dark deep water at the stars, the glittering city lights, and the moon racing through misty swirling clouds.

"Look," I said. "I can ask Coney's friends and family a few questions—and maybe talk to Sunny. But I don't know how much good it will do."

"If the victim wants it looked at and starts raising hell, it'll make a big difference," he said confidently. "I told the guys we could trust you, you wouldn't burn us."

He dug a manila envelope out of his jacket and a ten-year-old mug shot of Coney, taken after a drug bust. "Show it to her," he said, and handed them to me, "but make sure you mix it in with the rest." A half-dozen other mug shots, all men, approximately the same age and description, were in the envelope. Burch wrote Sunny's address on the outside.

"I hear she's some kinda artist now," he said, as we walked back to our cars, pausing for a last look at the Miami Beach skyline winking in the haze. "You know, Britt," he commented, as I climbed into the T-Bird, "you're a pretty girl, but you really oughta do something with your hair."

My landlady, Helen Goldstein, and her husband, Hy, were out in their patio chairs, enjoying the late evening. "We couldn't take the TV news anymore," she told me, when I stopped to share some of my fresh-picked vegetables.

"But isn't it too smoky out here?"

"It's chased away the mosquitoes," she said cheerfully, then peered more closely in the dim porch light. "Britt, what happened to your hair?"

I left the frozen pizza in the oven too long, nibbled some anyway, and went to bed. Frustration burdened my dreams. I searched in vain for the brown-haired girl in the blue sweater, then tried and tried to make an urgent call, but the phone would never work. I was trapped, on deadline, in impossible, impassable traffic. Then I had to pee but never could find a rest room. The digital face of my bedside clock glowed in the dark when I awoke—3:24 A.M. Part of my dream was real, I thought, and climbed out of bed to visit the bathroom. I blamed the beer.

Unable to go back to sleep, I wondered why some women, like Gretchen and K. C. Riley, don't know or care that we should help each other, especially in times like these. Loneliness and fear are always more acute in the wee small hours. Was Lottie right about Fitzgerald? I wondered. Maybe . . .

I groped for the TV remote and flicked fitfully, hoping for something to occupy my restless mind. A startling image caught my eye. Mesmerized, unable to take my eyes off it, I watched. Finally, knowing I shouldn't, I reached for the phone. He answered on the first ring.

"Hey, Fitz," I murmured.

"Do you have any idea what time it is, young lady?"

"Sorry, did I wake you?"

"No, sweet thing. Matter of fact, I was thinking 'bout you."

"Imagine that. I was thinking about you too."

"Just get in?"

"Nope," I said. "Couldn't sleep."

"Me too. Just watching the tube."

"Me too," I said. "Wait a minute! What are you watching?"

He chuckled evasively.

"The History channel!" I accused. "You're watching it too! Shame on you. So am I."

"I'm missing you, baby. Big-time, right about now."

I laughed aloud, surprised at the sound in my dark bedroom. "Did you see what those Greeks were doing?"

"How about those Roman frescoes?" he said. "Who'da thought? Say, when are *we* getting together?"

"Wish you were here right now," I said, voice dropping to a seductive whisper.

"Me too. How about Tuesday? I've got an early deposition in a homicide case, but I can drive down right after. I'll put in for the time tomorrow."

"Can't wait to see you, gorgeous."

"Hey," he said, "I can get dressed right now, hop in the car, and be there in time for breakfast."

"Don't tempt me," I said, voice husky. "You know we both have to work tomorrow."

"The Volusia state attorney's office and the *Miami News* would manage fine without us."

"See you Tuesday," I said.

4

"How could I have known he'd be watching *The History of Sex* too?" I said, phone to my ear, as I brewed coffee the next morning.

"I'da stayed up to see it myself," Lottie said. "Why didn't you call me?"

"It's so easy to flirt at a distance," I said, with remorse. "But now we have a date."

"You won't be sorry," she predicted. "I'd bet the Ponderosa on it."

The morning was already a scorcher, I discovered, standing barefoot on my front stoop. Billy Boots did figure eights around my ankles and Bitsy chased a lizard through the shrubbery as I picked up the newspaper. The protective plastic sheath slid like an oversized condom off the giant phallus upon which my life revolved. Damn, I thought, I've got to swear off late-night TV.

I settled at my kitchen table to devour the morning paper with juice and coffee. The headline over my story was huge: FIREFIGHTERS RESCUE TRAPPED TOT in 48-point Bodini. They ran Villanueva's picture, five columns, in color. The young mother's expression as she reached for her child was poignant and unforgettable.

The subhead read:

CHEERS, TEARS END SIX-HOUR DRAMA
by Ryan Battle
NEWS STAFF WRITER

I nearly spit up my orange juice. Gretchen had called my bluff. But why? She hadn't changed the copy. The story read just the way I wrote it.

The phone rang minutes later. "Did you see?" Lottie asked.

"Just now."

"Didn't you—?"

"Yes! Every word."

"That bitch," we chorused.

Irritated and dispirited, I showered and shampooed. The directions said to leave the hot oil conditioner on my hair for two minutes. I left it on for ten. Still far from perfect when I rinsed, it looked a bit better than the night before. Hopefully it would be back to normal before Dennis Fitzgerald arrived.

* * *

The building I was looking for was a few blocks from the ocean, light-years away from the phony glamour, glitz, and glitter of South Beach. North Beach is still real, but it won't stay that way long if the city and the developers have their way.

The address, a small two-story hotel, appeared to have been converted to apartments. An ornate wooden front desk, unmanned and dusty, still dominated the front lobby. Clearly, no guest had checked in for years. A worn stairway to the left led to the second floor. The hotel dining room must have been to the right originally but appeared to have been partitioned off. A door built into the partition was marked 1-A, the same apartment number Burch had given me.

Because her parents were well off, I found it hard to believe that Sunny Hartley lived in the dining room of an old hotel in an aging North Beach neighborhood still untouched by the building boom. I knocked, then knocked again. No response. But a door slammed upstairs and a bearded man descended, his flip-flops slapping the soles of his bare feet. He wore shades and an open shirt over a pair of baggy bathing trunks and carried a beach towel and a magazine. He paused on the landing, startled to see me.

"I'm looking for Sunny Hartley. Does she live here?"

"You've got the right place," he said.

"I guess she's not home," I said. "I'll leave a note."

"You have to knock loudly." He tapped his ear as he reached the lobby. "She's probably in there. She's almost always home."

He left for the beach.

I rapped louder and called, "Hello, is anyone home?"

I sensed movement behind the peephole.

"Who is it?" a woman finally asked.

"Britt Montero, from the *Miami News*."

"I'm not interested in subscribing."

"I'm looking for Sunny Hartley. Is that you?"

"What do you want?"

"To talk for a moment."

"Reference?"

I looked around the lobby. "A private matter."

"Can I see your identification?"

"Here's my card." I slid it under the door. "And I can show you my press ID."

I waited, fanning myself with my notebook, my hair damp with perspiration.

"Did you find my card?" I called eventually.

I heard the metallic sounds of a chain lock disengage. The door inched open. I don't know what I expected, but certainly not the woman who stood there.

It was difficult to determine what she looked like. All I could see was her red nose and cheeks, as though painted by Jack Frost himself. She wore a ski cap with woolen ear warmers, goggles, a fleece headband, thermal gloves, an insulated snowmobile suit, and fleece-lined boots. She looked as though she were about to scale Mount Everest. But this was Miami Beach, where the temperature was 96 in the shade. Furthermore, she held a knife in her gloved hand. Light glinted off its odd blade, curved in the shape of a half moon.

"I guess you're on your way out," I said stupidly, reacting to her attire. I tried to appear friendly, one eye on the blade. Why is it that whenever I think I have met every possible sort of Miami Beach screwball, eccentric, and mental patient, a new variety turns up?

"No, of course not." She reacted as though *I* was crazy, then took off her goggles and gestured with them. "Come in," she said.

I stepped inside, cautiously. There was little furniture in what once had been a large high-ceilinged dining room. Bright light poured through big picture windows designed to overlook a tropical garden that had withered long ago, falling to the ravages of wind, weather, and neglect. Its centerpiece, once a sparkling art deco fountain, stood chipped and dry, the rusty piping corroded and exposed. The view now consisted of passing traffic, a Kentucky Fried Chicken outlet, and an Amoco service station across the street.

The big windows were tinted so no one could see into the huge space, which had been converted into a studio. Dining tables set with crisp linen, silver, and fine china had been replaced with well-braced wooden work tables constructed of sturdy six-by-sixes stacked up like log cabin walls. Tools and sharp blades of various sizes were arranged on smaller tables. There were stone shapes and figures of polished marble, some sheet-covered, along with an air hammer and a compressor motor mounted on a tank with air hoses snaking out.

"I'm a reporter," I began. "I cover the police beat for the *News*."

Something flickered for a millisecond in the cold depths of her eyes.

I could see her better in the studio's natural light. Her pale eyebrows and lashes, nearly invisible without makeup, made her deep-blue eyes look even more intense. Her hair, straight and pale blond, hung down beneath her cap in a single thick braid that reached nearly to her waist.

"A thief named Coney was killed breaking into a downtown shop. You may have seen or heard about it on the news."

She shook her head, her expression distant. "I don't watch much television news or read the paper. I'm too busy."

"He was thirty-one years old, a criminal, with terrible scars on his body from old burns."

She paused. "I have to get back to work," she said, and turned abruptly, face unchanged.

She stepped briskly through double doors into what had been the hotel kitchen. I followed. The doors were framed with an overhead hoist, like a giant IV with chains. Huge ovens, stoves, a grill, and double sinks stood to the left. A pop-up toaster, a blender, and a small microwave oven appeared oddly out of place among the culinary relics. An open pantry at the far end of the kitchen had been converted to personal living space. An alcove where rows of shelves once held food supplies or kitchenware was now lined with books and potted plants. A small four-drawer dresser and a chifforobe flanked a daybed with a crocheted coverlet. A canvas smock, a green rubber face mask, a hat, and a heavy leather apron hung from an old-fashioned brass coatrack.

"There is a possibility," I said, trailing her uncertainly past a garagelike delivery door that opened out onto a loading dock surrounded by mini-gantries, like those used to load cargo at the port of Miami, "that the dead burglar may have been one of those responsible for the crime in which you were a victim fourteen years ago."

Acting as though she hadn't heard me, Sunny adjusted her ear warmers, put on her goggles, and yanked open one of two wide metal doors to our immediate right. A frosty cloud emerged as she stepped inside. I followed. The sudden icy blast made me shiver. We were in a huge walk-in freezer. But no sides of beef hung from above; there were no cases of frozen vegetables. Instead, another sturdy worktable stood front and center, reinforced by stone and metal supports. A lighthouse appeared to be emerging from a half-carved six-foot block of blue-white ice atop the table.

I stood in awe, mouth still open, stung by the cold and the sight of my own breath, a phenomenon that always revives wretched memories of my J-school days at Northwestern and the gut-wrenching miseries of cold, snow, and being homesick for Miami.

"You're an ice sculptor!" I exclaimed, relieved that she might actually be sane.

"It pays the rent," she said curtly, "and buys me time and material for more serious work." She stepped back, studied the unfinished sculpture for a moment, and began to work, ignoring me as her knife blade skimmed the ice, sending showers of icy crystals erupting into the air.

Something about the sculpture began to look familiar. "Is that . . . is that the lighthouse at Cape Florida?"

Startled, she paused to stare at me for a moment as though impressed. "I'm surprised you recognized it at this stage. You must know it well. Actually, even when the piece is finished, the form you want isn't there yet. That doesn't come until about a quarter of the way into the melting process. You should see it then. There'll be a prism at the top, with a light wheel focused on it from a distance."

"Who's it for?"

"The South Florida Historical Society, an event this weekend at Vizcaya."

Made sense. The restored lighthouse is one of South Florida's few surviving historic sites.

"Who do you work for?" I asked, beginning to shiver.

"Myself," she said. "I freelance pieces for hotels, restaurants, nightclubs, private parties, weddings, bar mitzvahs, engagements, and lots of conventions. As my own boss, I can pick and choose my jobs. So many just want their company logo." She wrinkled her nose. "That's like painting by number. I like to find out about the event and the people and then present a concept, my own ideas and sketches. If they like it, fine; if not . . ." She shrugged.

"Cool!" I said.

"Exactly." She waggled a gloved index finger at me. Did I detect a hint of warmth in the eyes behind the goggles? "Most ice sculptors have no art training," she said solemnly. "They're chefs who learn the basics at culinary school. They don't mind the routine, repeating the same things over and over: a swordfish for the seafood buffet, twin hearts for a wedding."

I hugged myself in the cold, secretly pleased. We seemed to be hitting it off.

"You're wrong," she blurted, without looking up from her work.

I thought she'd read my mind.

"It won't be fourteen years until December." She cut her eyes at me in a brief sidelong glance. "How did you find me?"

"We had lots of old stories on the murder case." The frigid temperature was becoming increasingly uncomfortable.

"My name was never in the newspaper." She sprayed the lighthouse with a fine mist of some icy cocktail, chose a straight wide blade, and resumed work.

Strike two, I thought, as tiny icicles formed in my damp hair.

"Sergeant Craig Burch, the lead investigator, believes the dead man fits the description of one of the suspects. I brought some photos for you to look at."

She reacted slightly to Burch's name; then she averted her eyes and skirted the sculpture to work on the far side.

Fingers numb, I opened the manila envelope containing the mug shots. "Would you take a look?" I quavered, my nose running.

She picked up a heavy mallet and swung it with surprising power, breaking away chunks of ice at the base.

"Here." Shoulders hunched involuntarily against the cold and the sounds, I looked for a place to spread out the pictures. "Maybe you could just—"

"Careful," she warned suddenly, "that tank is liquid nitrogen; I use it to fuse the ice when I'm finished. It's almost four hundred degrees below zero. You don't want to knock it over."

I gave the tank a wide berth as she continued to work, her chisel grating on the blue-white ice like fingernails on a blackboard, her demeanor as frigid as the air.

"Ms. Hartley." I raised my voice, my teeth actually chattering. My thighs felt frozen together, like drumsticks in a freezer. "You may not be aware that first-degree murder has no statute of limitations. The men responsible for the crime can still be prosecuted and punished." I shivered uncontrollably, my words slightly slurred. I was freezing to death in Miami Beach.

She continued to work as though I wasn't there.

"Look," I croaked in desperation. "I am really, really cold right now. Can you please just take a moment to look at these?"

She ignored me.

"All I need to know is whether you recognize—"

She looked up suddenly from behind the clear blue ice, the same color as her wide expressionless eyes.

"You must be cold," she said, as though concerned for my health.

"Yes!" Frost had formed on my eyelashes, and I couldn't feel my toes.

"You should leave," she suggested, selecting another razor-sharp tool with a narrow blade.

I left a second business card and, taking the mug shots with me, practically bolted out. I wasn't sure her front door locked behind me, but I didn't bother to check as I plunged headlong out into South Florida's wonderful, soupy, steamy hot bath. Now I knew what it felt like to be a Pop-Tart, going straight from a freezer into a toaster. Sinuses aching, I closed my eyes and lifted my face to the sun's warm embrace.

Was the woman crazy, I wondered, or as cold as ice?

5

Burch and I rendezvoused in mid-beach, at the Fisher monument, an elevated bronze bust of Carl Fisher, the pioneer who carved this resort city out of a swampy mangrove jungle. Like so many others whose vision imprints the world forever, he died alone and broke.

"Hey," Burch called good-naturedly, as he walked up to my car. "You're all sunburned."

I glanced in my rearview mirror. My face was bright pink.

"That isn't sunburn," I snapped, stepping out of the T-Bird to join him. "It's frostbite."

"What?"

"You didn't say I had to wear goddam thermal underwear to talk to that woman! Why didn't you warn me?"

He looked bewildered.

I filled him in, temper flaring, as my body temperature inched toward normal. "I was thisclose," I said, illustrating with thumb and index finger, "to being the first reporter frozen to death on the job in Miami."

"How the hell was I to know?" He wore a puzzled frown. "I don't remember her being into anything like that when she was a kid."

"Of course not," I said. "Teenage girls don't aspire to futures in freezers, chipping away at giant blocks of ice for banquets and bar mitzvahs. It's her day job while she's a struggling artiste."

"What'd she say about the mug shots? Did she pick 'im out?"

"Wouldn't even look at them." I wriggled my toes, hoping to restore feeling to my feet. "All she wants to talk about is her work. When I brought up the case, it was as though she didn't even hear me. Kept working, wouldn't listen—"

Burch reacted with a wince.

"What?" I demanded.

"Oh, jeez," he said.

"What?"

"Sorry, Britt. I guess I forgot, or figured that after all this time it mighta gotten fixed. You know, her dad's a doctor, big time plastic surgeon, with access to all—"

"What are you talking about?" I demanded.

"The bullet Sunny took to the head. It shattered the mastoid bone, left her deaf in one ear. They said it was permanent, but that was a long time ago. She can hear fine with the other one."

"Which ear was damaged?"

"Let's see." He paused. "The right. Yeah, that's it, the right."

I visualized the scene, as Sunny turned away and continued to work.

"Oh, fine. She just tuned me out," I said, voice rising. "Talk about turning a deaf ear. Thanks, Craig. What else didn't you tell me?"

"Sorry. Guess this was a lousy idea from the start." He sighed. "Is she okay? How'd she look?"

"What little I could see of her looked fine, if setting up housekeeping in the dining room of a crumbling old hotel is okay." I paused to reflect. "A little reclusive, maybe. Neighbor said she's always home. Doesn't look like she entertains a lot. Windows all tinted. She sees out, nobody sees in. Mucho hardware on the doors."

Burch paused, arms folded, at the foot of the coral rock steps that descended from the bust of Carl Fisher. The pioneer, sensitive about a receding hairline, historians say, wore his trademark fedora, brim turned up. Both men, one dead, the other alive, gazed bleakly at passing traffic.

"Look," I said, "I have to follow up the Gomez story anyway. I'll try to talk to Coney's relatives, see if I can size up his boyhood compadres."

Burch's head shot up in surprise. "Thanks, Britt."

"A little background might help, so I don't waste more time talking into a deaf ear. I'll drop by your office, shoot the breeze with your lieutenant."

"Okay," he said, eyes wary, "but don't let on we talked about the case."

* * *

Riley was tied up at a meeting, according to her secretary, so I stopped by the office of Public Information Sergeant Joe Diaz to break the good news about the *Hot Topics* story. He regarded me with suspicion, as always.

"Sounds okay," he said guardedly, "but I'll run it by the chief."

Always better to start at the top, I thought as I left. When you start at the bottom, somebody on the way up the chain of command will find a reason to object.

An unexpected sighting in the lobby took my breath away: Major Kendall McDonald. Lean, long-legged, in uniform. *Muy macho.* Strong jaw. Cleft chin. *Guapismo.*

"Hey, Brenda Starr." There was warmth in his smile, but his eyes looked weary. "What's new?"

"I didn't know you were back," I said casually.

"Got in last night," he said hoarsely. "Drove straight through."

"How bad was it up at Ground Zero?"

"Devastating. Worse than you could imagine. Still is. What news are you chasing today?"

"*Hot Topics* wants a cover story on the Cold Case Squad."

He nodded. "Excellent. Our squad's a model for other departments."

I looked into his silver-blue eyes, remembered our times together, and got lost in the moment.

"How are you, Britt?" His voice dropped to an intimate tone. "Is everything all right with you?"

"Busy as ever," I said airily.

"Tried to call you a few times, before nine-eleven.

When you didn't return my messages, I figured you were busy."

"Oh?" I said, flustered. "My answering machine must have fouled up again—or maybe I did."

What did I just say?

He grinned, his eyes catching mine. I blushed and grinned back. A pair of gangly young public service aides stopped chattering to eyeball us both as they went into the PIO office, and the moment was gone.

"Good luck with your story," McDonald said. "I'll look forward to reading it."

My eyes still locked on his, my jumbled thoughts focused inanely on the bullet scar high on his right inner thigh. What if he could read my mind? "Put in a good word for me," I managed to say primly. "Diaz has to run it by the chief."

"Sure thing," he said. "The chief'll be pleased at recognition for something positive—for a change."

Considering that Miami police were currently under fire for shooting too many civilians, among them an unarmed seventy-two-year-old grandfather killed in his home by cops who fired 122 bullets at him, a homeless Vietnam vet, and a man who'd been standing on a street corner holding a portable radio (they mistook it for a gun, they said), he was probably right.

I willed McDonald not to walk away from me, but he did. My stomach did a double back flip with a triple twist when he turned. "You're doing something different with your hair, aren't you?" he said, squinting at my sorry coiffure. "Nice," he added, instantly reading my reaction, then fled.

Knees rubbery, I hurried out into the scorching heat

of the parking lot to cool off. Chemistry, I thought. Nothing lasting. It's only chemistry.

Coney's current address was still the morgue. His family either wasn't interested or was too poor to bury him and therefore hadn't claimed his body. I'd find out from the next contact on my list.

There was no green at Green Gardens, a government-subsidized low-income housing project. Two gray box-shaped buildings with no discernible character faced each other across a grim cement courtyard where swarms of children cavorted noisily with a dozen stripped-down shopping carts strung together into a clattering snakelike contraption—their improvised version of playground equipment.

Ida Sweeting, Coney's aunt, wore shapeless pull-on slacks, a flowered blouse, sandals, and wire-rimmed spectacles. She appeared to be in her seventies, hair iron-gray, eyes gentle.

Many people who suffer loss react to strangers with hostility. To my relief she was not one of them. She invited me into her second-floor apartment without hesitation. A well-worn family Bible lay open on a small table next to the threadbare couch where we sat. Her apartment had at least three bedrooms and was impeccably neat, despite a small red tricycle and other signs of children.

"We went on down to Rawlings Funeral Home this morning. They're working with us on it," she said, nodding. "We hope to have Andre's service next week."

"I'd like to know more about him," I said, notebook open on my lap.

"Not much left to say," she murmured, eyes watering.

"I understand you raised him."

"I tried," she said, right hand over her heart. "The good Lord knows I tried, but somewheres along the way I stumbled and failed that boy."

"I doubt it," I said. "He made his own decisions. I'm sure you did everything you could. I'm so sorry."

"I don't hold nothing 'gainst that other fellow, the man who owned the store. And I'm sorry 'bout the fire." Her words were in a mournful monotone. "Andre had no business being there. I keep thinking that maybe if I'd let him stay here. . . ." She studied the dull beige walls around us. "But I couldn't," she said regretfully. "I got my daughter, my niece, and their babies to think about. We'da lost this place. Rules here are strict, you know. We're held accountable. Anybody goes to jail or gets caught with drugs, they evict the entire family. Everybody. And Andre, he was always in trouble."

I knew about the zero-tolerance policy, designed to improve the quality of life among public housing residents by instilling responsibility and pride.

"That boy, rest his soul," she said, gazing at a picture among clusters of framed family photos on a shelf, "he got off to a bad start."

I felt a stab of guilt. Part of my reason for being there was to establish that Andre was far more evil than she or the world knew and most likely deserved his fate or worse.

"Are his parents alive?" I asked gently. "Was he born here in Miami?"

"No, ma'am. We're from Jesup, up in Georgia. My late husband, Franklin, and I came down here in nineteen and seventy-six. Andre is my baby sister Annie Mae's boy, her oldest. A beautiful child, but he done took after his daddy."

"Andre's scars," I prompted. "His old burns. What happened?"

"His daddy drank," she said, eyes swimming now, "and when he did, he'd beat up on Annie Mae something terrible. I always thought he'd kill her someday. By the time Andre was five or six years old, he'd try to stand up to his daddy, try to make 'im stop hurting his mama. He'd wind up gettin' whupped too. Annie shoulda left 'im, but she had four littler ones and she'd dropped outa school in seventh grade, had trouble readin'. He kep' threatenin' to put her in the ground if she called the law on 'im. He'da done it. I know he would.

"Finally, she just had enough, I guess. One night he come home drunk, cussin' and arguin' like always, and she was waitin', had the potash on the stove just like our grandma always did. When he started in on her, she snatched up that pot by the handle and throwed it all at 'im.

"Andre was nearly eight then. He darted in between 'em, tryin' to stop the fightin'. Most all of it splashed onto 'im. He run right out the door, screamin', the potash just eatin' away, burnin' the flesh right off his little body, smoke risin' off his skin. Annie Mae tried to catch him, runnin' after him, screamin' as loud as he was. Finally he just fell thrashin' on the ground. My godmother lived acrost the street, said she heard the most godawful screams. The kind that freezes your blood and makes your hair stand straight up on end."

Ida Sweeting closed her eyes and heaved a great shoulder-sagging sigh. After a moment, she rose and went to the sink for a glass of water. When I declined her offer of something to drink, she returned to the couch, the plastic tumbler in her shaking hand.

"Andre's daddy panicked. Run to a pay telephone at the service station on the corner, askin' for the ambulance. But I guess he got scared cuz he'd been drinkin' and beatin' on his family, so he run off. Man always was a coward."

"The poor little boy," I said, hating it. I wasn't here to feel sympathy for an evil man, to see more shades of gray. "What happened then?"

"The po-lice arrested his mama; his daddy, too. Found 'im at the same bar where he always drank. The state took the other kids, sent Andre to a special burn hospital way up in Atlanta. When he got out months and months later, they sent 'im on down here to me. Annie Mae went to jail." Her face softened. "We was thinkin' she'd come to git 'im when she got out. Sent her bus fare, but she never came. Heard she went to New York. Had a postcard from Detroit back in 'eighty-eight. Said she was sick. Nobody's heard a word from her in years. Andre's daddy left a bar drunk one night, walkin' home along Route 301. They found 'im dead next mornin' at the side of the road. Mighta been a big rig hit 'im. Whatever it was, it never did stop."

She sipped from her glass and pursed her lips.

"It musta been the wrath of God, sent down to smite 'im. Kin in Georgia took Andre's brothers and sister, but when they got too much to handle, they sent 'em on down here too."

"You raised them all?" I said.

She nodded, the Bible on her lap now. "But Andre—that boy was never right again. I tried to get 'im help, but he was always in trouble."

"You must have been the only good influence in his life." I reached for the worn hand resting on the Bible. "You had no control over all that damaged him before he came to you. Or the peer pressure—you know, the boys he ran with.

"Who," I asked, pencil poised, heart skipping a beat, "were his buddies back when he was a boy, maybe sixteen, seventeen?"

Ida Sweeting searched my eyes for a long moment. "Andre didn't make friends in school," she said slowly. "Didn't like physical education, any kinda sports or swimmin'. Said everybody stared at his scars in the shower. Called 'im names, like Lizard Man and Monster. Same thing with girls. I tried to tell 'im we all carry some kinda scars, whether people can see 'em or not. But he dropped out, wouldn't listen. Not much point in 'im stayin' in school, cuz I couldn't make him go most times anyway. It was after that when he started makin' friends, boys from the project where we were livin'. But I knew they were trouble."

"Who were they?"

"A boy used to call hisself Mad Dog and his cousin Parvin. Cubby Wells was another one. In trouble, one thing after another."

"What's Mad Dog's real name?"

"I think—" The front door opened and a young woman, her hair braided in a wild array of beribboned cornrows, maneuvered a stroller and two little girls inside. One was about three, the other looked to be five.

She saw me and did a double take.

"Who are you?" she demanded. She wore a T-shirt, jeans, and an attitude.

"Britt Montero. I'm a reporter for the *Mia*—"

"A reporter? Mama?" she pleaded, wheeling to face the older woman. "What you doing talking to a reporter?"

"She's asking about your cousin Andre—"

"You have a lot of nerve showing up here!" the younger woman said, refocusing on me. "You the one wrote that story? Didn't anybody ever teach you to show respect for the dead?"

"Did you object to something in the story?" I asked. "If there were any factual errors, we—"

"That bullshit 'bout all his arrests! The man's not even cold in his grave, and the auntie who raised him has to read all that shit in the newspaper? Then they repeat it on TV! Over and over again," she said, raising her voice. "Way you wrote it made it look like he deserved what happened. You hear what Reverend Earl Wright axed on TV? 'Since when do they execute people for burglary?' Since when you get capital punishment for that? You don't know anything about Andre!"

"That's why I'm here," I said. "To find out."

"You did enough already!" she said bitterly. "You better get the hell out of here before I kick your scrawny white ass!"

The two little girls watched wide-eyed as their shouting mother shook her finger at me. So did I.

"Lakisha," the older woman entreated.

She turned on her mother. "Why did you let her in here?"

"I'm sorry," I told Ida Sweeting, and rose to leave.

"You better be!" Lakisha screeched, as the smaller girl screwed up her face and began to cry. "You be a lot sorrier, I catch you bothering me or my family again!" In my face, full of fury and outrage, she herded me unceremoniously out the door, slamming it hard behind me. Not the first time I'd been cursed at, threatened, or given the boot—and certainly not the last—but I regretted Lakisha's lousy timing. Just as I was getting somewhere. Damn.

She continued to shout, her voice carrying down the hall as I trudged to the stairwell. Ida Sweeting had known a lifetime of grief, and I regretted bringing her even a moment's more.

Mad Dog, his cousin Parvin, and Cubby Wells, I thought. Not much, but it was something. I called to bounce them off Craig Burch as I drove back downtown.

Ryan was at his desk, directly behind mine.

"Britt?" he said softly, as I checked my messages. "My name is on your story."

"I saw," I said crisply.

"How did that happen?"

"An unsolved mystery," I said.

"Well, it's a great story," he said. "I've had nothing but compliments all morning."

Villanueva stopped by my desk minutes later, dark eyes perplexed, the A-section in his hand. "I thought you wrote this." His big voice turned heads.

"I had nothing to do with it," Ryan piped up, face flushed.

"What the hell's going on?" the photographer asked.

I shrugged. "Life is cheap and editors are treacherous," I said. "Great picture, by the way."

Ryan answered his phone. "Hi, chief," he said cheerfully. He shrugged as Villanueva and I turned to stare. "You're welcome, glad you liked it." He rolled his eyes at us. "Anytime, chief, your guys did a great job."

"The fire chief," he announced, hanging up. "He loved the story."

Lottie arrived a short time later with the 411 from her buddies on the national desk. Gretchen had altered the story, but the front-page editor didn't like her changes and had restored the original copy.

Having a bad hair day, nearly frozen while being ignored by Sunny, given the boot by Andre Coney's cousin, unappreciated by my editors and the world at large, my psyche already bruised and bleeding, it seemed a perfect time to call on K. C. Riley.

We first met when I was a rookie reporter. K. C. had rescued her husky, seriously injured male partner by shooting his attacker in the knee. The headline writer had dubbed her a Hero Cop. Yet she'd reacted angrily to my story. How was I to know? Kathleen Constance Riley seemed a perfectly good moniker to me, and *News* style is to use full names rather than initials. But she took offense and warned me in no uncertain terms to never *ever* use her given name in print again.

Like most female cops, K. C. Riley had to fight for rank and respect, but her macho attitude always struck me as over the top.

I went to headquarters and called from the parking lot. Her secretary checked with Riley, who agreed to see me briefly, between meetings—in ten minutes. Her usual MO. Agree to an impossible appointment, forcing the reporter to risk death or dismemberment, desperately racing through traffic only to be—too late.

"Great," I said sweetly. "I'll be there." A PIO officer escorted me to my approved destination, no detours allowed. What would happen, I wondered, if I suddenly broke into a run? Would they lock down the station? Set off a terrorist alert? Call out the dogs to hunt me down?

The Cold Case Squad's small office—several desks, computer monitors, and three metal filing cabinets—was adjacent to Homicide on the fifth floor. The lieutenant's glass-enclosed office on the north wall provided a view of Overtown, a rundown high-crime neighborhood sliced in two by the expressway.

Neither Nazario, on the telephone, nor Stone, at a computer terminal, acknowledged me or my no-nonsense escort as we exited the elevator. The usual banter, good humor, and camaraderie that characterizes most detective bureaus was absent here.

"How is the lieutenant today?" I asked the tiny middle-aged secretary. "In a good mood?"

She rolled her eyes, then tapped gingerly on Riley's door, standing aside, out of the line of fire, the same technique cops use when knocking on the front doors of deranged homicide suspects holed up with shotguns. I winked at her and breezed into the lion's den.

"Montero!" Riley checked her watch, startled by my prompt arrival. I smiled instinctively as our eyes connected. All cops' lives are tough, but they're far tougher for the women. I respect those who succeed at it.

She cocked her head and motioned me to a chair without returning my smile. "Sit," she ordered.

Her straw-colored hair was shoulder length, with a slight natural wave. Tanned, fit, and sleek as a Thoroughbred, she didn't have an extra ounce of weight on her athletic frame. Her cream-color blouse was crisp and sharply tailored, and she wore her gun at the waist of her fitted beige slacks. A matching jacket hung from the back of her chair.

"So," she said. "You're planning a story about us."

"For the Sunday magazine."

"And to what do we owe this honor?" She lifted her eyebrows and regarded me the way she would a hostile suspect. "You won't find any scandal in *my* unit."

"I don't expect to," I said. "The editor agrees that the Cold Case Squad's success is a good story."

"I didn't know you covered good news."

"Every chance I get," I said deliberately. "Too bad there's so little around here."

"Touché." Her smile was ironic. "Given the current state of the department, you know the brass will buy anything that may improve our image. But you've written a lot of the stories that have made us look bad."

"It was news, Lieutenant. Not designed to make anybody look good or bad, just news. If something or somebody looked bad it's because they were. I had nothing to do with it."

"That's debatable," she said. "You and I have butted heads enough times that you know exactly where I stand. My job is closing cases, not selling newspapers. If it was up to me, we wouldn't be here right now. But it's not up to me. The chief wants to cooperate, so that's what I'm doing, one hundred percent."

"Great," I said earnestly. "It'll be a good read."

"I'll settle for accurate," she said, with an odd smile. "Since I'm the supervisor, I thought it strange that you didn't come to me first." She toyed with a metal paperweight in the shape of a hand grenade. "Why was I last to know?"

Oh, shit, I thought, an ego thing. I hate it when women professionals act like men.

"You know how the department is," I said, a hint of exasperation in my voice. "They insist that everything go through PIO first. I assumed they'd call you."

"They did," she said softly, "but not until after I heard it elsewhere." She smiled slightly. "Kenny Mac—you know, Major McDonald—he happened to mention it."

Kenny Mac? Where did that alias come from? A pet name?

"Oh, right," I said. "I ran into him outside PIO and told him that Diaz planned to bounce it off the chief."

"Just don't screw around with my unit, Montero." She leaned forward, eyes intense. "My guys don't need any heat, any problems generated by the press. This is the best team I've ever worked with. Dead files speak to them. If an old cold murder case still has a faint pulse, these guys can detect it. They can get into the minds of people they've never even met and do it better than anybody."

"They deserve the recognition," I said.

"Sure." She sighed. "All I need is for my detectives to believe their own press, grow big heads, and turn into a buncha prima donnas.

"But all right," she said, as though resigned. She leaned back and gave me the spiel. "Unlike other units, time works in our favor. Frightened children have grown up, once-intimidated spouses are divorced, lives have changed, or there's been a death. We look at letters, leads from other sources, and requests from victims' families, and we evaluate old cases. Team members read the files, reread them, and then vote on which have the best potential for closure."

"How were the detectives selected?" I asked.

"Each has his own story." She narrowed her eyes slightly. "I'm sure you already know most of them."

She pushed back her chair abruptly and stepped to the window to stare out over the bleak rooftops of Overtown. "Hard to believe anything good ever comes out of there. But that's where Sam Stone grew up. Where you come from doesn't mean shit." She turned to face me. "What matters is who you really are.

"He was hot for this job, wanted it bad. But they turned him down every time. Sure, he was a flashy patrolman, savvy and street-smart. But the brass said he was inexperienced, definitely not detective material.

Everybody else up here had years of homicide experience.

"After he gets turned down for the third time, he's so pissed off on the way out that he rips an eight-year-old WANTED poster off the squad-room bulletin board. The damn poster had turned yellow. Hung there so long it left its outline on the board. The son-of-a-bitch in the picture was still wanted for murdering his wife. First degree. Man had a rap sheet longer than I am tall. For him, getting busted was a lifelong habit. How, Stone asks himself, could this asshole not be arrested in the eight years since he killed his wife? Something's wrong here.

"He calls Records. They show nothing in their computer, but the warrants division still shows he's wanted. Evidently, nobody ever bothered to send a copy of the warrant to Records. Or if they did, somebody slipped up and never filed it.

"Stone asks ID to transmit the man's fingerprint classification to the FBI, asking if he's been arrested anywhere since the murder. And guess what? The FBI responds with the news that the guy's been arrested twenty-seven times under another name during the past eight years. Mostly minor; drunk driving, shoplifting, assault and battery. Most recent arrest? Six weeks ago, up in Ocala."

I took notes and watched her as she went on. K. C. Riley had always worn a world-weary veneer, as though shell-shocked and tempered by the brutality and tragedies encountered on the job. But she was different now, speaking freely, almost enthusiastically.

Was it her current assignment—or a happier personal life?

"Stone calls the Ocala police chief," she was saying. "Says, 'Here's the real name of a man you arrested three months ago. We want him in Miami for murder,' he says. 'Think he might still be up there somewhere?' The chief calls back an hour later. 'We've got him for ya,' he says. 'Come and get him.' "

Riley slid back behind her desk, her features alight with approval. "When Stone was rejected again, he didn't punch the wall, hit the bars, go home to kick the dog. Instead he got motivated, decided 'I'll show them!' and found that fugitive in less than two hours with a few phone calls. Not bad, huh? It got him the job."

"Great story," I said. There I was, chatting civilly with K. C. Riley. I should have quit while I was ahead. "So the team members vote to take on a case?"

"Right."

"Do you always support their decision?"

She chewed the inside of her upper lip, as though deciding how to answer.

"In almost every case, yes," she said carefully. "But, as supervisor, I take responsibility for our productivity. I'm the one accountable. The buck stops with me."

I opened my mouth but caught the challenge in her eyes and abruptly swallowed my next question. So far, so good, I thought. Don't spoil it now.

"I'd like to talk to the detectives."

"Sure," she said, eyes guarded. "Just don't screw with us, Britt. We're not playing games here."

"Right." I smiled, got to my feet, and turned to leave.

That's when I saw several framed photographs atop a bookcase I had passed on the way in. One stood out.

Two people aboard a boat. Blue sky above, liquid sky below. A K. C. Riley I had never seen before, sunshine in her hair, wearing cut-off shorts and a bathing-suit top. Laughing as she held up a puny grouper. The grinning man beside her, right hand on her shoulder, wore a Florida Marlins cap, one I had insisted he buy at a game one hot and sultry afternoon. I remembered the searing sun, the lush green field, and McDonald and me, intoxicated by the cheers of fans, the music, and each other. For a moment I forgot to breathe.

K. C. Riley's sharp eyes had followed mine. "The department's annual fishing tournament," she said. "I guess you can see—we didn't win a trophy."

6

"You look like you've been shot at and missed," Stone said.

"Or shit at and hit," Burch said.

"You sure know how to make a girl feel special." I attempted a jaunty smile. "I'm fine. Your lieutenant was all giggles and grins, promised a hundred percent cooperation."

"Good." Burch rubbed his hands together briskly. "Glad you two hit it off. Listen, those names you gave me paid off. Nothing so far on Cubby Wells, but Stone found an old field interrogation card on a Ronald Stokes, street name Mad Dog. Age and description fit. He and Coney got busted together twice, accomplices in old burglary cases."

"Bingo. He still around?"

"In a matter of speaking." The detectives exchanged glances. "He's a guest at the Graybar motel, serving ten to twenty upstate. Guess what for?"

"Sex offense?"

"Rape and robbery."

"Jeez, Craig, you are gonna solve this one!"

"We've got a helluva long road," he cautioned, "but I have a good feeling. When I saw that body in the morgue, I knew in my gut this was it."

"Are you going up to talk to him?"

He shrugged. "Not yet. Hell, he ain't going anywhere. We know where to find him. With the lieutenant breathing down our necks, it's tough to take half a day to drive up there right now."

I called Lottie, who said she'd join us, as Burch checked to confirm that Riley had left for the day. Then he dragged a bulky storage box from beneath his desk. "I've got three more like this one," he said, lifting the lid. "More than a thousand typewritten pages, index cards on every one of the two hundred and fifty suspects we talked to in the Chance case."

"Today, this would all be computerized from the get-go," Stone said, scowling. "Let's ask Karen over in Intelligence to program the cards into a database that's easy to cross-check."

"Yeah, she's the best analyst we've got. Send 'em to her along with the names in the Meadows case," Burch said, "that elderly widow, murdered in 1981. Clue her that they're separate cases, but log 'em under the same number so Riley doesn't pick up on it."

The detectives exchanged conspiratorial glances.

Joe Corso had joined us, just returned from London where he'd been chasing down a suspect in an old bombing case, I'd been told.

Burch pawed through the box, then thrust a file folder at me. A photograph was stapled to the cover. Ricky and Sunny, smiling shyly in front of a brightly lit Christmas tree, moments before embarking upon their first and last date.

"I kept that one out, to remind me," Burch said, his intensity so electric that it charged the air around us.

The slender sweet-faced girl smiling from the photo in no way resembled the icy young woman I'd met, bundled up against the cold of her freezer.

The Hartleys and Ricky appeared in other photos aboard the *Sunshine Princess*. The teens, her parents, and little brother, Tyler, all wore holiday colors and smiles of anticipation. Sunny's father, the distinguished physician, wore a jaunty red Santa hat with a white pom-pom. Their faces, illuminated by bursts of flashbulb brilliance, were painful to see, knowing that before the next sunrise young Ricky would lie dying in a field and life, for the others, would never be the same. Official crime-scene photos displayed from all angles the lanky boy-man body of Ricky Chance, battered and blood-soaked in the dirt.

Nazario's dark eyes glistened as he studied them.

"*Que linda,*" he murmured at Sunny's picture.

"A stand-up kid," Burch said. "Got more *cojones* than half the people we got wearing badges. Shoulda seen the way she worked with us—no tantrums, no tears, polite—even when she was hurting, after all she'd been through. Well brought up, everything anybody could want in a daughter. Those people are damn lucky they didn't lose her that night."

"Her folks," Stone said thoughtfully, "might persuade her to cooperate. Maybe you or Britt should talk to them."

"Worth a try," I said. "I'd like to meet the boy's family, too."

"Haven't heard from the parents in years." Burch looked wistful. "Was a time we talked every day."

"Musta figured they hadda get on with their lives," Corso said.

The elevator doors opened, spilling out Lottie and the same public information officer who had escorted me. He no longer wore his stern no-nonsense expression. They were laughing like old friends. Leave it to Lottie, I thought. Even the detectives perked up in her presence. Her red hair wild and frizzy from the ever-present humidity, she wore her usual faded blue jeans, hand-tooled leather cowboy boots, and western-style shirt, expensive cameras dangling like accessories from leather straps around her neck.

"Hey!" she greeted Corso, her freckled nose wrinkled, teeth flashing in a wide grin. "You sure look a damn sight better. First time I made your picture you were horizontal, being loaded into the air-rescue chopper, headed for the trauma center. Bet that's a Kodak moment you'd like to forget."

We had both covered the bank robbery in which Corso was wounded.

"Damn straight." He grinned. "All I was thinking about was staying alive."

"What don't kill you makes you stronger," she said. "Heard you went to jolly ol'."

"Couldn't wait to get back here," he said. "No decent Italian food in that whole damn country, no pasta, no pizza, no *pasta e fagioli*. And those people drive on the wrong side of the road. I almost got wiped out half a dozen times in London traffic. Kept looking the wrong way when I stepped off the curb."

"Did you book the Jack the Ripper tour?" I asked. "Takes you to the crime scenes, shows you where he left the bodies."

"Why'd I want to see that? We ain't got enough crime scenes here? That bastard only killed about eight; we got guys on the loose here that put him to shame."

"Jack the Ripper." Stone leaned back in his chair. "Now that's a cold case."

"Bite your tongue," said Burch, still digging through his box of old files. "Lieutenant hears about it, she'll give us that one too. Bad enough she wants us to solve Meadows, more than twenty years old."

"Some people believe Jack the Ripper was a member of the royal family," Stone said.

"Speaking a them," Corso said, sipping from a coffee mug bearing the advice DON'T LET THE BASTARDS GET YOU DOWN, "I seen the Queen Mother herself. I'm standing on a street corner, and she passes right by on some local holiday, gives me the royal wave."

"Hah." Lottie wrinkled her nose. "Don't tell me you buy into that."

"Inta what?"

"That whole Queen Mum scam. Hell-all-Friday, I made pictures of that woman two–three times when I was based over there. What is she now, a hundred? Out there in high heels, spry as a mountain goat, posing for photographers. That ain't her, can't be. No way. That woman was old during World War Two. The original musta bought the ranchero years ago. Like Lassie."

"What on earth are you talking about?" I said.

"How many Lassies have there been?" she drawled, cutting her eyes at me. "Some-a those collies weren't even females. Or Morris the cat. There've been a couple dozen Morris the cats."

"No way," I protested. "It makes worldwide headlines when a royal dies."

"Think about it." She plopped into a desk chair on wheels, rolled back several feet, and continued. "Today's royal family is a joke. Too damn much inbreeding screwed 'em all up. Cost the country a fortune. An embarrassment in the scandal sheets, a drain on the economy. The Queen Mum is the most popular one-a the bunch. They got to keep her for public-relations purposes. There'll always be a Queen Mum. Count on it. She's all that's keeping the monarchy alive. Without her, the Brits would've abolished it a long time ago."

She pouted at our hoots of derision. "Okay, be naive. Think it can't be done? What about Fidel?"

Nazario and I reacted, as all Cubans do, to the mere mention of the name.

Lottie smiled archly, now the undisputed center of attention. "You think he really survived all them assassination attempts, outsmarted ten presidents, the CIA, *and* the Eyetalian mob? God knows how many Fidels've been used up."

We stared at her in amazement as she casually picked up a stack of eight-by-ten black-and-white pictures from Nazario's desk.

"Where'd you git these?" she said, squinting at them. "Didn't know you still used black-and-white."

"We don't," Stone said. "We use video, living color, digital cameras, and three-D. We even have virtual reality that re-creates crime scenes for juries. Those, unfortunately, are circa 1981, the Meadows case."

I peered over her shoulder as Lottie turned a picture sideways, frowning at an elderly woman, dead in her bed. She appeared to be sleeping, pink plastic curlers in her thinning hair, the sheet and a flowered bedspread tucked up neatly beneath her chin.

"Virginia Meadows," Burch said. "Age seventy-nine. None of us were even on the department yet when that case went down."

"But what do you want to bet that we solve this sucker?" Stone replied, pacing the small office. His lean body exuded energy. "I feel it in my bones. The son-of-a-bitch is out there somewhere. Thinks he got away with it. Thinks his secret's buried deep in the past. Well, his worst bad dream is about to come true. We're coming for him."

"Nice to see you thinking positive," Burch said. "But it ain't gonna be easy. We got a helluva lot better shot at the Chance case."

Lottie snapped candids of the detectives at their desks, on the phones, and poring through old reports while I studied the Chance files and Burch located addresses for the victims' parents.

"Any physical evidence that could tie Coney to the

rape?" I asked, thumbing through a supplemental report. "DNA?"

"Nada," he said. "All they focused on at the hospital was trying to save her life. It was clear what happened, but nobody did a rape kit or collected evidence. DNA wasn't in the picture yet. If we had her clothes they could be tested, but no chance of finding them now."

We dined on pizzas the detectives ordered in as they filled us in on the Meadows case.

"Another sad story," Nazario warned.

Widowed and childless, lonesome after her husband died, Virginia Meadows, age seventy-nine, befriended strangers who seemed lonely too. She took in runaways, AWOL servicemen, and other lost people. A stranger she met on the bus or in the park would be invited for a home-cooked dinner. Sometimes she lent money to these new friends, who neglected to pay her back. Neighbors said later that she often appeared depressed. Some of them warned her, and for a time she listened. But loneliness took over. She began to take in strangers again.

At about 10 P.M. on an October night in 1981, a neighbor dropped her off at her house after a trip to the supermarket. She was found dead at about five the following afternoon by a boarder. He was a man she'd met in Bayfront Park. He'd asked her for a dime and she'd invited him home for dinner. He had lived there for about three weeks. He passed a polygraph.

The killer had arranged her body in a sleeping position after strangling her, so as not to arouse suspicion. He took nothing else, only her life.

"The original detectives spent a whole lotta time on the case," Burch said, reaching for another slice of pizza. "Kids who had crashed there were traced to Tampa, Panama City, Key Largo. Most didn't know she was dead. Every last one asked the same question."

"What's that?" I asked, wiping mozzarella off my chin.

"Why would anybody kill her when all she did was help people down on their luck?"

"She'd be a hundred years old if she were still alive," I said.

"Like the Queen Mum," Lottie said, eyebrow lifted.

"Would have been nice if she'd had the chance," Nazario said solemnly.

"Sad," I said, "what loneliness can do."

Thoughts of loneliness and the faces in the photo in K. C. Riley's office almost overwhelmed me as I drove back to the office.

In the library, Onnie had hit pay dirt. She'd found a *News* file on Ronald Stokes, aka Mad Dog. An enterprising reporter covering courts back then had featured him in a project on juvenile justice, documenting a violent felony record that began at age nine. I checked the dates. Stokes had been released from a youth detention center just two days before Ricky and Sunny's abduction.

Beginning to share Burch's excitement, I faxed a request to the Department of Corrections. This investigation could be the centerpiece in my Sunday magazine project. I'd follow it from the start, a minute-by-minute account, then be there for the arrests. Lottie could shoot the suspects being handcuffed. This story would be bigger and better than I anticipated. I needed to work on it full time.

I asked Fred, the city editor, for comp time. Howie Janowitz could cover my beat. I promised to be available if all hell broke out and I was needed, and to follow developments in the Gomez case, which was related, but otherwise I'd be off the schedule.

"When do you want to start?" Fred asked doubtfully.

"Now," I said. "Eight o'clock."

He checked his watch. "It's already nine."

"I know," I said.

He gave the nod and I nearly danced out of his office, free from the city desk and daily deadlines. I confirmed a visit with the Department of Corrections by phone, checked a map for the most direct route to the prison, and went home.

Next morning I slathered a toasted bagel with cream cheese, dropped it in a sandwich bag, and filled a thermos with Cuban coffee. Provisions for the long drive north on I-95, then west through West Palm Beach to Belle Glade, a farm community of migrant workers on the fringe of the Everglades. The detectives might not be able to take the time now, but I could. And Lieutenant Riley could never accuse Burch of putting me up to it, because he didn't know.

My car radio reported news of war, shadowy enemies far away and among us, and smoke rising like the souls of the lost from still-smoldering wreckage. I tried to focus on the mysteries at hand. What became of the killers' white van sought by police for so long? Probably rusting, I thought, at the bottom of some deep Everglades canal or rock pit. Most mystifying was how such youthful killers had successfully kept their secret without cracking throughout the long high-profile investigation.

I still had some coffee left when the prison gates loomed before me, a world of concertina wire, steel mesh, and low-slung buildings surrounded by farmland and Everglades swamp.

The population here was adult male, a mix of high-, medium-, and low-risk inmates. Mad Dog spent most of his time in "closed management," due to disciplinary problems, according to the captain who checked my ID and had me sign the logbook.

The veteran guard who frisked me even checked my shoes to ascertain whether I was smuggling any contraband into the facility. He made no attempt to conceal his disapproval that out of 70,000 inmates in Florida's prisons I had chosen to visit this one.

As we awaited Mad Dog's arrival, the guard loosened up enough to discuss a recent controversy that arose when state officials decided to cut costs by eliminating recreational television in prisons. Inmates were there for punishment, not entertainment, the state said. However, the decision was swiftly reversed when it became clear how many more corrections officers would have to be hired. Prison officials use twenty-one-inch ceiling-mounted sets the same way many parents use the tube—as a baby-sitter. TV keeps their charges occupied and out of mischief. The most-watched shows here, the guard said, were *Cops* and *America's Most Wanted.*

The sounds of automatic locks and the clanging of steel doors heralded Mad Dog's arrival. Two keepers accompanied him. I hadn't seen the shackle shuffle done with a swagger before. With his thick neck, broad chest, and bulging biceps, his muscles had muscles. He looked as though he worked out daily with his own personal trainer. Perhaps he did.

Several cigarettes and a Snickers bar, prison currency, were casually displayed in his shirt pocket, the way a player on the street would flash a roll of cash. Something behind the surface of his oil-slick eyes made me grateful for the sturdy wooden table between us. I wouldn't have minded bulletproof glass.

Slowly and deliberately casual, he eased himself down into the chair facing me, cocking his head first to check out my legs.

"Whu's up, mama?" He showed off a few decorated gold teeth with his grin.

I refrained from explaining that I was not his mama.

"A man was killed the other day," I said. "An old friend of yours."

Mildly interested, he nodded casually.

"Yeah." He rocked back in his chair, as though he found it humorous. "Heard ol' Andre bought it. Dude got hisself fried. Always warned him 'bout those nickel-and-dime burglaries. Dude never listened."

"Lots of things get people in trouble." I smiled sweetly. "Look at you."

"A-live," he said, relishing the word. "I'll be walking free, outa here one day. Never shoulda been here to start with. Police framed me. You looking at an innocent man."

"Interesting," I said, "but I understand you were caught at the scene and they had DNA evidence against you."

"DNA don't mean nothing," he crowed. "Look at O.J."

"Yeah," I said. "Well, I'm not here about that. I'm interested in something that happened on a Christmas Eve—"

"Right, right." He sounded impatient, nodding like one of those little doggies in the back window of a car. "You don't have to 'splain it to me, mama. I know all about it. When they tol' me 'bout the reporter, they didn't say you looked so sweet."

"So you remember the case?" My heart thudded.

"Sure." His eyes fixed on mine. "Some blond bitch and her boyfriend. Everybody knew about it. People talk."

"I heard it was you there that night, with Cubby Wells, Andre, Parvin, and some other guy."

Something sparked in his eyes, as though about to ignite, but then it was extinguished, as quickly as it had appeared. He wagged his head, curling his lips in a beatific smile.

"Other guy? You think you know something, but you don't know shit. Tell me a name."

"You tell me."

He clapped his palms together, a sharp retort that startled his guards and made me blink. His laugh was a rude high-pitched bray. An officer shifted uneasily on his feet. "Hear that?" Mad Dog said, turning to him. "Woman thinks she knows it all but don't know shit."

"Four out of five is a good start," I said serenely. "It's just a matter of time. Murder has no statute of limitations. And this will probably be a death-penalty case, a minimum of life without parole. So I thought, if you really want to walk away from here one day, you might like to talk about it. Somebody will tell the truth, and the one who does first might catch a break."

He laughed again, an unpleasant sound, too loud and long, his smug glee conveying that he knew much more than I did.

"No way they can prove we did it, now or ever," he sang out. His words echoed off the dreary walls as he leaned forward, eyes bold. "Cuz I didn't shoot nobody that night; they didn't shoot nobody; we didn't shoot nobody. I'm an innocent man. We're all innocent men. But thanks for stopping by." He jerked his head at the guard, as though the man were his personal chauffeur, and stood up.

As he was led away, he turned back to me. "Say hello to the blond girl," he said. "Tell her she be seeing me again. Look forward to it." He nodded again, his grin bone-chilling. Then the metal door clanged closed behind him.

Burch was surprised and not thrilled to hear where I'd been. "He as much as admitted it," I told him, via cell phone, as I rode my wave of indignation back to Miami. "But he's so hard-core, he'll never cooperate. Mad Dog still insists the police framed him in his last case.

"I'm telling you, Craig, this guy is the poster boy for capital punishment. Thank God he still has years to serve on his last conviction. You should see the shape he's in. Looks like he's in training."

"Maybe he is," Burch said grimly. "Look, don't tell Sunny about this. He thinks he'll see her again? Hell, when we make this case, he'll never see daylight again."

7

I hit the road again early the next morning. Sunny's parents, Donald P. Hartley M.D., plastic surgeon to the rich and famous, and his wife, Maureen, now lived in Weston, an affluent southwest Broward County community studded with football and baseball stars. Posh gated neighborhoods where the crimes were low and the property values high.

The couple's sprawling Spanish-style hacienda, nestled among lush gardens and shaded brick terraces on a private cul-de-sac, was in stark contrast to their daughter's dining room digs.

Maureen Hartley greeted me with a serene smile, despite her uncertainty when I called. She wore white, the classic cool blonde type that Alfred Hitchcock loved. Tall and slender, she still dressed and carried herself like the elegant top-flight model she had been.

"I'll fetch Donald," she said softly. "He's in the shade house."

I waited in a room with a massive staircase, oil paintings, and a huge stone fireplace until the doctor appeared, silver-haired and imposing, dignified in steel-rimmed glasses, expensive slacks, and a sport shirt.

"Well, now," he said, smile engaging, as the three of us settled in the library with floor-to-ceiling bookshelves, a mahogany desk, and comfortable overstuffed furniture.

"Maureen said you mentioned the . . . incident. I believe she explained when you called that there have been no new developments for many years now."

His wife's smooth brow was furrowed, and her eyes had taken on a look of sadness.

"Frankly," her husband said, "we'd prefer that nothing more be written. With all that's happening in the world today, there's little point in resurrecting old tragedies."

I explained about Andre Coney, adding that if he was one of those responsible, the others might still be identified and brought to justice.

"You really think that's possible, after all these years?" He sounded dubious.

"It's never too late in a murder case," I said. "But the police—Sergeant Burch—would need help from Sunny."

Both reacted to Burch's name.

"I remember that policeman," Dr. Hartley said quietly.

"He'd like her to look at some mug shots," I said.

Maureen Hartley stared without seeing, her thoughts roaming somewhere in the past.

"Sunny doesn't live here. You'd have to take that up with her," her father said.

"Right. She didn't seem interested when we spoke."

The parents exchanged glances. "You saw her?"

"Yes."

"Our daughter is extremely independent," he said.

"You're not close?" I frowned. Not exactly what I'd hoped for.

Maureen Hartley said nothing.

"Not as close as we'd like to be. We love her dearly," the doctor said, hands clasped in front of him, "we always have, and we're here if she needs us. But, as I said, she's an extremely independent young woman."

Maureen's face brightened at footsteps in the hall.

"Here's Tyler." She sprang to her feet to kiss the cheek of a young man who loomed tall in the doorway.

Sunny's little brother would have been movie-star handsome, except for eyes set a tad too close together.

"Doc," he said, "I need to borrow the Navigator."

"What's the matter with your own car?" Hartley said gruffly.

His son had an interesting, slightly dissipated look for one so young, as though he needed the discipline of a tough drill sergeant, basic training, or regular workouts in a gym.

"You know how it is." He flashed a charmingly sheepish grin.

"Can't say that I do." His father removed a set of car keys from his desk.

"The convertible got towed last night from South

Beach. You know how they are down there. You go to a club, come out, and your wheels are gone. It's a racket."

Hartley tossed the keys.

His son snatched them smartly out of the air. "Thanks. Sorry I interrupted, didn't know you had someone here." He looked me over curiously as Maureen introduced us.

"A reporter? They printing a story about you, Doc?"

His father shook his head.

"It's about Sunny, sweetheart," his mother said. "She's looking into what happened to Sunny and Ricky."

Tyler wheeled and left the room without a word, his face sullen. A door slammed moments later.

Maureen stared after him.

"The whole business was hard on him," the doctor said. "As it was on all of us."

"Of course." I picked up my pen. "Do you keep in touch with Ricky's parents?"

Both looked pained.

"We grieved for one another after it happened," the doctor said, "but we'd relive the . . . event every time we saw Sean and Heather. I'm sure they felt the same way. Our friendship couldn't survive what happened to our children. Lifestyles changed. We sold, moved away from the water. We haven't seen or heard from them for years.

"If you and Sergeant Burch assumed we could persuade Sunny to assist, I'm afraid you're wrong." He sighed. "Parents seem to be the last people in a position to influence the young these days.

"By the way," he asked, in an afterthought, "why isn't Sergeant Burch here himself?"

I explained that I was researching a story on Burch's squad and that he was tied up. I left out the office politics.

"Frankly, as much as I'd like to see justice done, as much as I'd give anything for just five minutes alone with those men," the doctor said softly, "it seems unfair to ask our girl to go through it all again now. Sunny tried so hard to work with the police then. If you knew. . . ." He sighed, then consulted his gold watch. "If you'll excuse me, I have office hours."

I lingered in the hallway, trying to strike up a conversation with a pair of brightly plumed African parrots perched in an elaborate cage, and then asked to use the bathroom.

Maureen showed me the way. When I stepped out, I heard fleeting voices in the foyer, then caught a glimpse of Hartley's black Mercedes as it rolled down the driveway.

"How is Sunny?" Maureen murmured, as she showed me to the door. "We haven't talked in months; she's always too busy. How did she look?"

"She seemed fine, too busy to spend much time with me either. She seems dedicated to her work."

"I hope she's eating right." She looked troubled. "Sunny became a vegetarian years ago. I thought it was a passing fad but she kept it up. I worry about her. Is she getting enough protein in her diet? Is she taking care of her skin? She's as fair as I am. Is she still spending time on the beach?" She scrutinized my tan and did an excellent imitation of my own mother.

"Women your age have no idea how damaging the sun can be. You must use a good sunscreen, at least SPF twenty, every day. Take care of your skin now, and it will take care of you later."

Sunny was more likely to suffer freezer burn than sun damage, I thought. But I was reassuring.

"Sorry," she said. "I must sound like your typical neurotic mother."

"How did you know I have one?"

We smiled at each other. "Would you like a cup of coffee?" she asked.

"I'd love it," I said.

Their cheerful breakfast nook looked out on flowering trees and tropical plants. Water burbled from the mouth of a huge stone dolphin into a manmade pond. Beneath its surface, tropical fish darted, flashes of bright orange, gold, and silver in the dappled water.

"It's by design," she said, when I admired the soothing effect. "Donald's job is very stressful, so I worked hard to make this house an oasis of serenity in a hectic world."

She poured richly brewed coffee and served a plate of fresh-baked scones gracefully while carrying on our conversation, a woman accustomed to being the perfect hostess.

Not only was her husband a surgeon with his own outpatient facility, she said, he owned several converted luxury motels where patients recuperated after face-lifts, tummy tucks, and breast augmentations.

"It upsets him that Sunny refuses our help," Maureen said. "She did accept some money her grandmother left her. Her grandmother never knew what really happened. She lived in New York and was in poor health, so we never burdened her with the terrible details. We let her believe that Sunny had been seriously injured in an auto accident."

"Did Sunny always plan to be a sculptor?"

Maureen laughed. "No, not at all. Donald's youngest brother owned a well-known restaurant in Chicago. When Sunny's doctors suggested that a change of scenery might do her good, we sent her out there for a while. She liked to spend time behind the scenes at the restaurant, of all things. Her uncle taught her how to make ice carvings for special events. We thought it was good therapy for her. She'd always liked art, and it just escalated from there. Later, she went off to Italy to study. Her father didn't approve, but she had the money from her grandmother and used it."

"You must be so proud of her," I said.

She didn't look proud; the blue eyes clouded.

"We had her in therapy for years," she said, "but all it ever accomplished was to make her more distant, more eager to be alone, on her own."

She averted her eyes.

"I had such mixed emotions when you mentioned Sean and Heather Chance. What happened to them was tragic. They went through hell; they lost their son. But no one realizes that we lost a child that night too. It was worse for us, in some ways. Sunny was just beginning to blossom. We sent our darling girl off with their son that night. We got back a total stranger. She returned to us silent, moody, and morbid. She'd look at us as if we were strangers. She refused to go back to her old high school.

"Ricky's parents, and everyone, kept telling us how lucky we were that she survived. I didn't feel lucky. I wanted my baby back the way she was, full of fun and laughter. I live with our loss every day. Yes, we have a daughter, but not the daughter we knew. I guess that sounds terribly crass and selfish, doesn't it?"

"No," I said. "The crime changed your lives forever, through no fault of your own. You were innocent victims. Perhaps if the case is solved, you'll feel some relief and a sense of healing."

"Those monsters are still out there," she said bitterly. "They should have to pay for what they did. Look at what they've cost us all. Lord knows how much damage they're still doing to others."

We strolled out into the morning heat together. She slipped behind the wheel of a midnight-blue Jaguar, bound, she said, for a charity board meeting.

She called out, as I turned to leave. "How is Sergeant Burch?"

"Good. Still giving it his best shot."

"And his family?"

"Thriving. He finally has regular hours and gets to spend a lot more time with them these days."

She nodded.

The car's automatic window rose, its tinted glass obscuring her face, and she drove off as I ambled on down the drive to my T-Bird. Not until I pulled out onto the street did I realize my left rear tire was flat.

Damn, I thought, looking up and down the shaded

street for help. There was none. I'd have to change it myself, in the suffocating heat. The situation could be worse. At least I was in a safe, shaded place. Better than a high-speed blowout on hot highway pavement. I opened the trunk to remove the spare, one of those damn little rubber doughnuts. The instructions warned not to drive more than fifty miles on it, which wouldn't get me back to the paper. I'd have to stop at a service station anyway, so I called AAA. They said a truck would arrive within an hour.

A bronze Lincoln Navigator slowed to make the turn into the driveway as I waited. Tyler stared from behind the wheel.

He rolled down his window as I approached.

"You still here?" Behind dark shades, he looked as sullen as before, but the cool air escaping his car's interior felt good.

"A flat," I said. "I'm waiting for Triple-A."

He looked amused, shut off the engine, and headed for the house.

"Tyler, I know you're pissed because they towed your car, but give me a break," I said. "Keep me company while I wait for the tow truck?"

He turned to me angrily, lashing out, his rigid body hostile. "Leave us the hell alone! What's the fucking point of stirring up ancient history?"

"Justice is the point," I said. "They might be able to close the case."

"Says who?"

"The police. Sergeant Burch."

"Him." His eyes squeezed closed, as though he was in pain. "Oh, swell. Goddamn déjà vu all over again."

"Look," I said patiently. "Wouldn't you like to see the people who hurt your sister go to jail?"

"As if there is a chance in hell of that happening. Listen—" He took a ragged breath. The anger behind his dark glasses verged on tears.

"I know it was terrible for Sunny," I said, "but—"

"Yeah-yeah-yeah! Sunny-Sunny-Sunny. What a swell Christmas that was. I was ten years old, *ten fucking years old*. That was the year I lost my sister *and* my parents. From that night forward everything was Sunny: Sunny's doctors, Sunny's therapy, cops coming to see Sunny. I was the little kid in the corner, wondering what the hell had happened."

"I can imagine how you felt—"

"Guilty! That's how I felt. You can't know how guilty I felt." His voice shook. "I used to cry. I thought it was all my fault, that if I'd only gone with them, I could have stopped it; I could have saved her somehow."

He paused to catch his breath. I just stood there. What could I say?

"She looked right through me after she came home from the hospital," he went on, "like I wasn't there. She'd flinch when I tried to hug her. I hardly ever saw her; strangers, cops were always taking her somewhere. She'd scream at night. 'Go back to bed,' they'd tell me. 'It's nothing. Sunny just had a bad dream.' Nobody would talk to me about it. They wouldn't even tell me what happened. Other kids, at school, told me she got gang-raped. I didn't understand what the hell that meant. Nobody even knew I was there anymore. It was all for Sunny who, in a nice little O. Henry twist, never wanted a damn thing more to do with any of us. Let me tell you, it got old fast." He took a deep, ragged breath.

"Well, you're here now," I said quietly. "I'm sure your parents appreciate that."

"Yeah, and you show up, writing a story to bring it all up again. Sunny-Sunny-Sunny."

He practically dashed away from me, fumbled with his keys, finally got the front door open, then slammed it behind him.

The AAA truck came twenty minutes later. Why wasn't I surprised when the driver said my tire could not be repaired because the sidewall had been deliberately filleted with a razor-sharp object?

8

I cursed Tyler's name all the way back to Miami and police headquarters. The poor little rich kid who'd clutched the keys to a $60,000 luxury car, while whining he'd been ignored, neglected, and forgotten, had definitely lost my sympathy. Instead, I worried about how to finagle the price of a new tire onto my expense account.

At PIO, I cheerfully signed a release absolving the city of all liability should I be crippled, killed, or maimed while accompanying or observing police officers on the job.

Escorted up to the Cold Case office, I waved merrily to K. C. Riley as I passed her cage, ignoring the sharp little stabs of jealousy. Craig Burch was at his desk.

"I'm working on this story full time!" I told him.

He failed to share my excitement but showed considerably more interest when I described my visit to the Hartleys and my encounter with Tyler.

He frowned. "You sure the kid did it?"

"My car was in their driveway, in a gated community with security patrols, no street crime, no graffiti, and no vandals, unless some wealthy scion decides to slash tires after a bad round of golf at the country club. Was Tyler always such a nasty son-of-a-bitch?"

Burch shrugged. "He was a little kid, out of the loop. I don't remember much about him."

"That seems to be his gripe."

"Surprised he still lives at home," Burch said mildly. "Guys his age usually can't wait to strike out on their own."

"I gather he's still dependent on Daddy Warbucks."

The detective looked preoccupied. "How's the mother, Maureen?" he asked.

"Classy," I said. "Blond and beautiful. Her husband still practices. Apparently he's put out because Sunny wants to succeed on her own. Looks like they don't have much contact with her—or influence."

"Good for her," he murmured.

"But not for you if you want her cooperation."

My next stop was Sunny's studio. I was prepared for freezing temperatures this time. I'd dug out an old down parka, a red wool muffler, and a pair of fuzzy moth-eaten earmuffs, packed away since my college days in Chicago. I put them all on in the lobby. It was deserted, as usual, but the decibel level broke the local sound ordinance. Upstairs, somebody played jazz riffs on the saxophone. Downstairs, a demolition crew was apparently dismantling Sunny's apartment. The noise reminded me of the machinery that had hammered through coral rock to free little Justin from the well.

I pounded and kicked and bellowed like a banshee, until the air hammer or whatever it was finally stopped.

"It's me, Britt!" I cried, several times.

Expecting Sunny to be in Sherpa togs, I was startled by the person who opened the door.

Perhaps it was the green rubber face mask or the snout, a filter cartridge, that protruded from its center. Her huge round plastic safety goggles resembled alien eyes. Her hair was hidden by a scarf, then covered by a hat. A sturdy work glove exposed the fingertips of one hand. She wore a thick wrist support on the other, which, again, held something sharp and shiny. Overalls and a leather apron completed her ensemble. A thick chalk-colored dust storm swirled in the room behind her. We stared at each other.

"Sunny?"

"Britt?"

She quickly motioned me inside and slammed the door to keep the sand storm from escaping into the lobby. The dust around us was dense and gritty, the sort that rises when demolition crews implode old buildings. Pressing my muffler to my face, I followed her through her studio and the double doors to the kitchen/living area.

My eyes stung and I was gasping for breath by the time she closed the kitchen doors behind us. She removed her safety goggles, peeled off her rubber mask and breathing cartridge, and removed a foam plug from her good ear.

"You aren't allergic to dust, are you?"

"Not until now," I said, amid a paroxysm of coughing. "What on earth are you doing?"

"Working. It makes a lot of dust," she acknowledged. "That's why I wear protection, to filter out the silica released by the marble."

"Thanks for warning me," I said, trying unsuccessfully to clear my sinuses.

"I didn't expect you. Do you ever call first?"

"I have a message from your mom."

She studied me suspiciously. "Why are you wearing earmuffs?"

"Don't point fingers," I said. "The fashion police are probably looking for both of us." She didn't smile. I took off my earmuffs.

"Okay," I said apologetically. "I'm sorry I interrupted your work again."

She shrugged. "I'm overdue for a break." She glanced at a school clock on the wall. "Way overdue. OSHA advises people working with pneumatic tools to stop every twenty minutes." Reluctantly, she loosened the Velcro wrist straps and removed the heavy glove.

"I wear it on my hammer hand," she explained, flexing her fingers as though they were stiff. "It's filled with an absorbent gel that supports your wrist but frees your fingers to work." Her long graceful hands were as slender as a surgeon's.

"I didn't realize art could be so like construction work," I said.

"You do need lots of upper-body strength," she said,

splashing cranberry juice into a blender. "On your feet, your concentration is high, you're swinging the hammer, using the chisel." She added scoops of yogurt to the juice. "But I think the fatigue is more mental than anything. It's easier with the pneumatic hammer. Once you get a rhythm going, it's just a matter of guiding the hammer." She took a plastic bag of sliced bananas from the freezer, and they too went into the mix. "It's so easy to lose track of time," she said, as the blender whirred. "It's hard to stop work until you're at a place where you're able to leave it."

She poured the thick creamy concoction into two tall glasses and handed me one. Icy cold, sweet, and delicious, it was probably good for me but it lacked . . . something. Caffeine, I realized.

I hung my parka and my scarf on her coatrack and pulled a wooden stool up to her little table. "Those tools are dangerous to work with, aren't they?"

"You have to know what you're doing," she agreed, "and even then you get hurt. I had a cut on my thigh that needed twenty stitches. Tools get stuck and kick, a block of stone can topple onto your foot, your fingers get pinched, stone chips will hit you in the eye."

"Why do it?" I asked. "I never could."

"I could never do what you do." We eyed each other warily across the table.

Upstairs, the saxophone still wailed in a melancholy melody.

"You don't mind the serenade?" I asked, rolling my eyes at the ceiling.

"I'm in no position to complain," she said, with a hint of a smile, "but I don't mind at all. He's a musician and a good neighbor, works nights and weekends at a club in South Beach. If his music bothered me, I'd just wear the earplug. I have great neighbors, they're almost never here: flight attendants and a troupe of cruise ship entertainers." She paused. "You spoke to my mother?"

"Right. Your dad too. I even met Tyler."

She bit her lip. "You said she sent a message?"

"She worries. Wants you to take care of your skin, SPF twenty, so you don't regret it later. She also wants you to eat right."

"So typical," she said softly.

Up close, without the rubber mask and plastic goggles, I saw that Sunny had inherited her mother's flawless bone structure, the classic nose, the high cheekbones. "She didn't say all that in front of my dad, right? Or ask about my work."

"True. How'd you know?"

"He's a very strong personality." Sunny sighed. "How *is* my mother?"

"Sad she doesn't see more of you."

"I'm very involved in my work," she said with a shrug. "And my mother is into Gucci, Pucci, and Chanel."

"Tell me about it," I said, secretly delighted at what we shared in common. "My mom is also into high fashion, while I insist that any initials on my clothes, my purse, or my shoes should be mine, not some rich stranger's."

Sunny laughed, a sudden girlish peal, framed by flashing white teeth. "My sentiments exactly." She cautiously touched her dusty hat. "If she saw me . . .

Even with all this I can't keep the dust out of my hair. It just settles into the scalp somehow. I have to wash it every day. My work leaves layers of dust on my clothes, my shoes, everything. That's why I have an industrial-strength vacuum cleaner and sleep out here instead of in the studio."

"How did you ever get into it?"

"Studied art as part of my therapy program. I *was* in therapy, you know, for some time." She gazed at me over the rim of her glass.

"Who wouldn't be?" I murmured.

"I highly recommend it," she said lightly, "even for those who aren't raped, shot, and left for dead."

She had my attention.

"Your mother mentioned your uncle's influence."

"He owned a wonderful restaurant in Chicago, and I'd watch him make ice carvings. He taught me. I loved the creative aspect but wanted to do more permanent things that didn't just melt and disappear. So I began working with alabaster. It's softer, lighter, and you do pieces by hand. My doctors and my parents seemed delighted that I'd found a therapeutic way to express myself. Nobody took it seriously except me. I'd found what I was always meant to do. I'm lucky," she said solemnly. "Some people never do."

"You're right," I said. "It's a blessing."

"I'm sure I would have found my calling anyway." She averted her eyes. "It might have taken a little longer and perhaps the medium would have been different. . . ."

She paused, as though reminiscing.

"In my early twenties, over huge objections from

my parents, I went to Italy alone, to Pietrasanta, near Carrara, an international center for marble work. I rented a small space in a marble-carving studio. You have a table and a hookup to the air compressor—and you learn. I stayed for eighteen months, even learned some Italian."

"Sounds romantic," I said. "Italian men—"

"—love blondes. They hit on me like crazy. The ones I studied with were all macho and competitive. You know: 'I am carving a three-ton piece.' 'Oh, really, I am working on a *four*-ton piece.' " She imitated a male Italian-accented voice. "I was just another art student. No one there knew about my . . . past. I was focused. I only wanted one thing. My time there was short; the work was my passion. It still is. They finally wrote me off as unapproachable, a bitch. They called me *una ragazza di ghiaccio,* an ice maiden. Lots of other young Americans were there too, but most of them weren't as serious as I was. They wanted to drink wine and hang out with artists, you know, while I went out to the quarries, picked up scraps, and worked all night."

"I can relate," I said. "Sometimes a passion for work takes over your life."

"Then I got lucky," Sunny said. "I met a team planning the restoration of a twelfth-century cathedral in Lyon, France. They invited me to work with them, replacing rotted blocks and the heads of gargoyles. It was wonderful."

I nodded, imagining how exciting it must have been.

She paused, her soft smile fading into a somber expression. "You didn't come here just to deliver a message from my mother. Why did you bother my family?"

"A new development," I said. "The police think they've identified a second suspect in your case. If so, it's only a matter of time before they find the others. I hoped that if I couldn't convince you to cooperate with the detectives, maybe your parents could."

She stared at the tabletop. "So what did they say?"

"That they have no influence; it's up to you. Except for your kid brother, Tyler, of course, who went postal, cursed me out, and slashed my tire."

"Your tire?" Her brow furrowed. "Poor Tyler," she murmured. "That doesn't sound like him. He usually doesn't lash out at others, only himself."

"He was upset. His convertible had been towed."

She chuckled. "Now *that* sounds more like my brother. He keeps my father busy bailing him out of trouble."

"Too bad," I said.

"Not for my father. He likes it that way; it keeps him in control. So you came back here to twist my arm."

"Not at all," I said, jealous that she had a father she chose to ignore, while I would have given anything for some time with my dad. "I live on the beach too. This is more a social call—though I was hoping you might talk to the detectives."

She took our empty glasses to the sink. I followed, making sure to stay on the side of her good ear as she turned away from me.

"Listen, I paid my dues. They stole a lot of my life, and they took Ricky's." She sighed. "Now you've done it," she whispered, eyes suddenly moist. "I hadn't spoken his name in years."

She rinsed the glasses in the sink and dried them briskly with a terry-cloth dish towel. "Life is short. I won't let them steal any more of mine."

"Even to achieve justice for yourself and Ricky?"

"It won't work." She shook her head. "No one can ever retrieve time lost. Can I simply demand my life back? Will anything bring Ricky back? They took enough." Her back to the sink, she hugged her arms. "It's easy for you to tell me what I should do. You weren't there. Did they tell you I had no hair in the beginning? They shaved it off when I had surgery. I was sick; the headaches were horrible. I had a problem with my lungs. You don't know what it was like. Riding endlessly through parking lots with the police looking for the killers' van, examining photo after photo, viewing lineup after lineup, my head aching, sick to my stomach, answering the same questions over and over, giving statement after statement, looking at pictures of other people's nightmares. They even hypnotized me, hoping to retrieve details I might have blocked out.

"In spite of the bad dreams, in spite of everything, I did it all, whatever they asked. It was so hard." Her hands kneaded one another, eyes pleading for understanding. "But it was even harder when I wasn't with the police. Facing Ricky's parents was worse. And my parents. I worked with the investigators for more than a year. Finally I realized that I had to try to live, if they would only let me. All I remember is looking up at the sky and begging God. . . ."

She paced the room still clutching her arms as though cold. "It's not that the police officers weren't decent, good people," she said quietly. "They thought the murderers might come back to eliminate the only witness. Me. Some nights I would lie there and wish they would. A young policewoman stayed with me, trying to help me remember. She was like a big sister. We really became attached. And I know how much Detective Burch cared. But eventually you have to leave the trauma behind, along with the detectives who are part of that trauma. How can you heal when they keep making you relive that terrible night? You understand?"

She sat on the stool across from me again, her expression earnest.

"They were part of what I had to leave behind in order to go on, to have a life. The time finally came when I never wanted to see any of them again."

"I hear you," I said. "But don't you think putting those men away for good would stop the nightmares, the bad dreams? I've seen it happen many times."

"But, Britt, what I'm trying to tell you is that I'm well now. I'm good. Doing what I love. I don't *have* bad dreams. You want to know what I dream about every night?"

She told me, hands folded on the small table, blue eyes aglow, features serene.

"I dream about seeing incredible sculptures. I dream about visiting Mayan ruins, seeing ancient works. I dream about Michelangelo." She paused. "Oh, my God, Britt. Can you imagine what he could have done with a pneumatic hammer?"

"You've grown up," I persisted. "You're strong

enough to look back on it all from a distance. There's nothing to be afraid of."

"Yes, there is," she said softly. "I like my dreams now. I don't want the old ones coming back."

"You wouldn't even have to see the same faces. The Cold Case Squad detectives weren't even cops when it happened. Why not talk to them? Once. See how you feel."

"I'll think about it," she said, seeing me to the door, her expression frozen, eyes already distant. "I'll call you."

As I tried to brush the dust off my clothes outside her apartment, I thought, Sure, she'll call me—the day hell freezes over.

9

"Can't blame 'er," Burch muttered gruffly as I sat at his desk and described my visit with Sunny. "You gave it your best shot. How about going back over there tomorrow, take one of my guys, whichever one is available, introduce 'im to Sunny, and see what happens. Worst she can do is slam the door on 'im."

"Okay," I said, watching a Kodak moment taking place behind the glass walls of K. C. Riley's office. She pored over papers, McDonald leaning over her shoulder. I blinked and looked away.

"Got it bad, huh?" Burch said.

"No way." I feigned surprise. "She's not my type."

He guffawed. "Come on, Britt. I've been there myself and it's a bitch."

Like hell. Who is he kidding? I thought, married to his high school sweetheart all these years. It made me uneasy that he'd noticed. Cops are notorious gossips, and station-house rumors fly faster than speeding bullets.

I left Burch busy on the phone, hating myself for deliberately timing my departure with McDonald's. He was on the elevator, door closing. He saw me and hit the button, just in time.

"Thanks." I stepped primly aboard. "I forgot what fast reflexes you have."

"How's the story coming?" He stood against the far wall watching me. What the hell was his body language saying?

"Still reporting," I said.

"I'm jealous. Those Cold Case guys are monopolizing your time." Was he teasing?

"Surprised you noticed. I thought you were too busy breathing in K. C. Riley's ear."

He reacted, then grinned. "So we're both jealous. Well, a little jealousy is only human."

"But not always attractive." I sighed.

Was the magnetic pull I felt one-sided? Was the sizzle still there for him too? I wondered, as we descended in silence.

"They say the best way to love anything is to know you might lose it," he finally said. He'd stopped smiling.

"Pretty profound for a cop," I said softly.

The door opened too soon, spilling us out into the busy lobby. I wanted to continue, to ride up and down for a while, to prolong this conversation.

"I have a meeting," he said reluctantly.

"So do I."

We exchanged hot looks, then parted. As usual.

* * *

I drove south to the scene of the abduction. But even the address was gone, obliterated by a new manmade lake surrounded by a sprawling industrial complex. It was as though the ice-cream shop had never existed.

I continued past the Parrot Jungle, the Orchid Jungle, then west past the Metrozoo, lost in thought about McDonald, love and life, and how brief everything can be. If life were fair, Ricky Lee Chance would be alive, a grown man now. What if the *Sunshine Princess* hadn't stalled that night on the Intracoastal? What if Sunny's parents hadn't let the teenagers drive on ahead? What if the ice-cream store had shuttered early on Christmas Eve like most places? Minor events and seemingly insignificant decisions, weaving together to intersect life with sudden death, always haunt me.

Because of the traffic, it took another twenty-five minutes to reach farm country. On that dark Christmas Eve fourteen years ago, the drive would have taken less time, but it still would have been an eternity in which to be terrified. With two abducted teenagers held at gunpoint in their van, the killers probably drove carefully, well within the speed limit.

Soon I was passing rustic roadside stands offering sweet corn, eggplants, and pyramids of fat red vine-ripened tomatoes fresh off the farm.

I finally located the right mailbox and turned onto a rutted unpaved road through the fields. The bumpy ride branched off in several places: One led to an old barn, another disappeared into vast fields, the third took me to the house.

The roof had been repaired with mismatched shingles and the front porch sagged. A yellow and green John Deere tractor and an ancient gray Chevy pickup were parked alongside. Half a dozen empty barrels stood lined up like soldiers on the wide wraparound porch. Two dogs, a big yellow Lab and a German shepherd mix, came tearing around the side of the house barking furiously, loving the raucous sounds of their own voices, tails wagging madly. I would have stepped out, but they were young and large and they propelled themselves off the ground like missiles, hurling themselves at the side of my car, bouncing off the hood out of sheer exuberance.

I'd decided to wait until they wore themselves out when a raspy voice began to shout. A tall figure had appeared behind the front-door screen. "Tigger! Bear! Git down! Stop it! You crazy critters! You hear me? Go lie down! Lie down!"

They continued their assault with gleeful abandon, thudding off my car, with occasional guilty glances over their shoulders at the woman. But as she continued to shout, they slowly simmered down. Finally, they just stood panting in the heat, pink tongues lolling.

I exited the car gingerly, one eye on the dogs, the other on the woman, who had pushed open the screen door. Nearly six feet tall and rangy, with a wiry, too-curly salt-and-pepper permanent, she wore a shapeless cotton housedress, stockings rolled down to mid calf, and sneakers.

The dogs followed curiously as I approached the porch. I patted the yellow Lab.

"Don't mind them, they's all bark," she called. "Kin I help you?"

"Mrs. Pinder?"

She nodded and I handed my card up to her, introducing myself. She held a section of newspaper, a good sign. I twisted my neck to confirm, with a touch of pride, that it was the *News*'s local page. A subscriber. Perhaps she'd just been reading one of my stories.

"Thought you were from the real estate company," she said. "What kin I do for you?"

The dogs padded happily up the porch steps after me.

"Weren't you the one who called the police when two teenagers were shot and left for dead in a field a long time ago? On Christmas Eve? Do you remember?"

Her expression changed, face somber. "I'll remember that night till the day I die."

She held the creaky screen door open and I followed her inside. "Excuse the mess," she said. "Me and my husband been here thirty-four years, my husband's family afore that. This was his father's place originally. We're fixing to move out soon, a job I wouldn't wish on anybody. I was just packing the good china."

I saw she hadn't been reading the newspaper after all. She was using it to wrap the dishes she was packing into two wooden barrels like those waiting on the front porch. A stack of newspapers sat on the wood floor in front of a half-empty china cabinet.

"We don't close till next month, but there's too much to do. Can't leave it all for the last minute." She led me into the living room, where old-fashioned Bermuda-style shutters blocked out the sun.

"Didn't know anybody else still remembered."

She sat, her feet resting on an old-fashioned footstool. Her ankles looked swollen.

"That poor young girl still livin'?"

"She's an artist now, a sculptor."

"Praise be to God. Night she left here in that there ambulance, I thought she'd never live to see another day."

"I'm writing a Sunday magazine story about some homicide detectives who are working new leads in the case."

"After all these years?"

I nodded. "They think a man who was killed recently might have been one of them, a second suspect is in prison, and they're attempting to identify the others."

"They should hang them," she said abruptly. "By the neck, until they are dead."

"Sounds fair to me." I opened my notebook. "I'd like to talk to you about that night."

"I believe I still have it all here, somewheres in the sideboard." She struggled to her feet. She opened one drawer, then another, sorting through tablecloths, napkins, and place mats, and then lifted a cardboard box out of the bottom drawer. "Knew it hadda be here somewheres. Good you came today, probably woulda thrown it out when I started the packing in here."

She sat heavily on the couch next to me and lifted the lid. The box on her ample lap was full of musty old news clippings. Most I had read in the *News* files, but these were in their original state, photos and headlines still attached, yellowed newsprint jagged and crumbling at the edges. A few were stories from other papers that I hadn't seen.

"Who's this?" I asked, studying a picture that accompanied one story.

"That there," she said, pointing, "is my husband. It

was after sunup then. All the police and their people were here, and reporters had started showing up. After a while when they got too pushy, the cops got tired of it and pushed 'em back to where they couldn't take pictures. But reporters, they don't take no for an answer. Don'tcha know, some of them came back by helicopter, started shooting pictures from the sky. Nothing the police could do about that."

The news photo, shot by one of the competition, showed half a dozen crime scene trucks and police vehicles. In the foreground, a younger Craig Burch and a South District police lieutenant were deep in conversation with a man wearing a baseball cap, windbreaker, and jeans. Clyde Pinder was sharp-featured, with a prominent nose and chin. He wore glasses, and his raised right arm pointed toward some far-off object beyond camera range. The eyes of the two cops followed his gesture.

"We go to bed early," she said. "Planned to load up the truck early next morning. Had a fresh ham, a Key lime pie, and a couple of jars of my mango chutney. Taking it to my sister's in Florida City for Christmas day. I thought it was the storm that woke me up. A real gully washer, it come on with no warning, just teeming, pounding on that roof, which needed fixin' at the time. Clyde was dead to the world, so I got out of bed to close the windows and set a pan under a leak in the upstairs hall. The squall was comin' out of the east, hammering right acrost the fields, through the screens, gettin' the floor all wet. That was when I heard the moans. It was eerie. I thought it was the wind. You know how sometimes the wind has a voice?"

I nodded, recalling fierce tropical storms I had heard, their voices ranging from the deep bass rumble of a freight train to the high-pitched wail of a screaming woman.

"But this time it had words to it. Half asleep, going on back to bed, I stopped to listen. It was saying *Help me, oh, God, please, help me.* Then it faded. I opened the window again, to listen. Rain hitting me in the face, spraying cold water on my bare feet, and I didn't hear nothing but the storm. But when I started to close the window again, the wind said *Please. Don't let me die.*

"I run down those stairs like a crazy woman, barefooted, in my nightgown, throwed open the front door, and she was laying there at the foot of the steps. Naked as the day she was born, half drowned, facedown, had long hair, one hand pressed to a bloody hole in the side of her head. I just blinked for a minute. I couldn't believe she was real. We had an old collie then, name of Lady. Used to be a good watchdog, but she never barked that night. The dog was just standing there beside her like a ghost, whimpering in the rain.

"I run down the front steps, scared to touch her, scared that somebody hurt her and was still hiding out there in the dark somewheres. But I couldn't leave her laying facedown in the rain. So I drug her up the steps onto the porch and into the front room, threw an afghan over her, dialed 911, and started screaming for Clyde. About then she started shaking, teeth chattering, like she was having a fit. Blood and water was streaming out of her hair onto my clean floor. I thought she was dying. She looked so young.

"Clyde couldn't believe what he was seeing when

he come down those stairs. Thought he'd have a stroke and I'd have two dead bodies on my hands. She stopped shaking, started talking 'bout a boy named Ricky. Said he was out there, hurt. Needed help. I held a dish towel to her head, trying to stop the bleeding, telling her to hang on, the ambulance was coming and yelled for Clyde to get his ass on out there, somebody else had got hurt too. He pulled on his pants and a yeller rain slicker, got his shotgun, put the big spotlight on the truck, and run on out to look.

"Young policeman got here first. He was radioing for them to put a rush on that ambulance, when Clyde got back, white as ashes. Said he found a boy, but he was dead. Next thing you know the whole front yard looked like a carnival, full of flashing red and blue lights.

"They carried her off in the ambulance, that young cop holding on to her hand. Had a notebook like yours on his knee. Never saw her again. Detective brought my afghan back next day, had blood on it. I couldn't bring myself to look at it, finally threw it in the trash. Thing took me half a year to make."

She paused. "The mother wrote me a nice note later, to thank me for helping her daughter. Are the parents still living?"

"Up in Broward County," I said.

"The girl must be growed up by now. Did she ever marry, have children of her own?"

"She lives in Miami Beach. Not married."

"And she's okay, up here?" She tapped a thick forefinger to her temple.

"Fine," I assured her. "The shooting cost her the hearing in one ear, but that's all that's noticeable."

"Amazin'," she said, in disbelief. "A miracle from God she ever found this place. It's pitch black out here at night. Ordinarily the whole house would be dark. It was raining, no stars, but, you see, I had a little Christmas tree up in the front window, had sparkly lights blinking on and off. It was Christmas Eve. Only time I let the tree lights burn all night. She was lucky."

"To survive," I said. "But if she'd been really lucky it wouldn't have happened."

She showed me where Ricky's body was found. Rebecca Pinder sat in my T-Bird, directing me, as the dogs barked madly and scrambled after us.

The field itself, with its tidy and uniform rows of plants, looked no different from all the others, apparently chosen by the killers only for its proximity to the unpaved road that ran by it. I stood out there for a time, imagining what it had been like, remembering what Burch had told me about his visits there in the dark.

The farmhouse seemed much too far away to walk. I wondered what it had been like for a young girl, wounded and bewildered and bleeding, in a dark and unfamiliar place, naked in a cold and driving rain. How long had she wandered before seeing the lights?

I drove Rebecca Pinder back to her home, silhouetted against the big sky, surrounded by drifting clouds and endless sunlit fields. If I had been an artist, I would have liked to paint the scene.

"It must be difficult to leave a home you've lived in for so long," I said.

"Pshaw," she said. "Truth is, I can't wait to walk out of this hellhole. Glad we're sellin' it. Nothin' but hard work and heartbreak here. Farmers are screwed. Can't make a living anymore. Nobody can. The government favors foreign imports, cheap produce from Mexico and South America. They give foreigners a break. And what do we get? Flood and fire, hurricanes, droughts, and tornadoes. Farmers don't stand a chance. If that's what people want, cheap fruit and vegetables from places where the workers pee and poop right in the fields and use dangerous pesticides and fertilizers banned in this country, well, they can be my guest."

The new owners, the Catholic archdiocese, planned to subdivide the property, she explained, for a retirement complex: a townhouse village with a golf course, an assisted living facility for those unable to maintain their own residences, a nursing home for the sick, and a hospice for the final stage, all in one huge development.

"We're damn lucky," she said. "We got us a good deal. After all the sweat, all the labor we put into it, this is the end. No more crops will be growin' on this land."

Another crime scene would be paved over, its ghosts erased from the map, more farmland swallowed by concrete, asphalt, and contrived landscaping, I thought, as the T-Bird lurched down the unpaved track. The two dogs followed me halfway to the main road.

10

"Wait till you see her," I said, sotto voce, as we approached apartment 1-A. "She'll either be bundled up like an Eskimo or behind a green rubber mask with what looks like an elephant's trunk. You may freeze to death or cough your brains out in a dust storm. And if the woman speaks at all, it will be about her work. Exclusively. There is nothing else. Zilch. She's always alone, like a recluse. And, oh"—I warned Nazario—"did I neglect to mention that she's probably armed? Most likely with a knife, but it could be anything from a chisel to a sledgehammer to a chain saw. The place is full of power tools.

"This could take time," I explained, hammering on the wood paneling. There were no sounds of demolition under way or major construction work inside.

"She's probably taking a break," I said. "Or she's in the freezer."

He lifted a wary eyebrow.

"I forgot to tell you about the walk-in freezer. Big as the coolers at the morgue. She could stack two, maybe three dozen bodies in there."

The door inched open. No one seemed to be there until I looked down.

The huge eyes of a small boy, age five or six, gazed up at us.

"Jonathan, remember what we learned? We never open a door until we know who's there." It was Sunny speaking, a Sunny I hadn't seen before.

Hair long and loose around her shoulders and down her back, she wore a white T-shirt, sleeves rolled up, white Capri pants, and sandals that accentuated her long tanned legs. She had a box of Crayolas in her hand and two little girls clinging to her as though they were attached. She looked beautiful, wholesome, normal. Not at all like the weird recluse I had described.

Nazario gave me a quick puzzled look.

Sunny caught it, taking a startled step back.

"Hi, Sunny," I said cheerfully. "When you didn't call, we decided to stop by. This is Pete Nazario, from the squad."

A bigger boy, about ten, and a sad-faced small girl scrutinized us inquisitively from their seats at a worktable. Not a knife, hammer, or razor-sharp tool in sight. Only colored pencils, crayons, and bright-hued children's drawings scattered across the tabletop.

"Hey," squealed a high-pitched voice. A pixie

peeked from behind the leg of the other worktable. Pink barrettes in frizzy hair, eyes big and dark. I glanced around. Where did all these munchkins come from? How the hell many were there? Not an icicle or speck of dust in sight. Nazario must think I'm crazy, I thought. He smiled at Sunny, then at little Pixie-face.

"Hey, yourself," he said. "What's your name?"

"Rosie." The child preened and posed.

"I asked you to call first," Sunny said, ignoring Nazario, her voice cold.

"Sorry. It's my fault." Nazario apologized for us. "Didn't know you had company. Look at all this fabulous artwork!"

The children flocked around him as he examined their drawings. He held up a crude picture, crayoned orange palm trees silhouetted against a hot pink sky with a large purple blob in the center. The blob had big round eyes and sported whiskers.

"Excellent!" The detective turned to Sunny. "This must be yours. I knew you were an artist, but they didn't tell me you were this good."

She didn't smile, not even when little Pixie-face, literally spinning with excitement, screamed, "No! No! I did it! It's mine! It's mine!"

"Lookit mine! Lookit mine!" the other kids chorused.

"We were just leaving," Sunny said.

"To see manatees!" shouted the child who had opened the door.

"Not you. You're not going. You in trouble," the bigger boy said with authority.

The smaller boy's face crumpled. Sunny didn't look

much happier. "Now, Carlos," she said softly, "of course we wouldn't go without Jonathan."

"You're all so lucky." Nazario turned to me. "We love manatees too, don't we?"

"Absolutely," I said. "They're so cool."

"Can you eat them?" the smaller boy said.

"No!" everyone else cried.

"Sea cows are our friends," Sunny told them. "We have to help save the manatees. Remember the book we read?"

"Can you come with us?" Rosie coyly asked the detective.

"We'd love to, if we're invited." Nazario looked hopefully at Sunny.

"Yes, yes!" the children cried.

"We can help," I offered. "I'm sure you have your hands full."

Sunny shrugged reluctantly.

"Great!" Nazario boomed, as though she had welcomed the idea.

"Everybody goes to the bathroom before we leave," Sunny told the children. "No, no. One at a time, not all together. That's right, let Jonathan go first."

"But I don't have to," the boy protested.

"All right, let the girls go first. But Jonathan," she whispered, "remember last time? Just go in there for a minute and try before we leave. Okay?"

"Where are we headed?" Nazario said, as the children got their things together.

"The Seaquarium," Sunny said frostily, without looking at him. The children, she explained, were from a South Beach shelter for battered women. Another volunteer, a former ballerina, taught them dance steps and took them to performances. A local writer read to them and helped them write stories and poems. Sunny was introducing them to art.

"You'd be surprised how many of these kids miss the normal cultural activities most children are exposed to," Sunny said softly. "Their mothers are busy just surviving."

We were rolling across the Rickenbacker Causeway in Sunny's eight-year-old van, the kids all strapped in and singing "Over the River and Through the Woods." I wished my editors could see me. I love this job, I thought. I never know what the day will hold. I might find myself at an inner-city murder scene, aboard a police helicopter whirling high above the bay, clinging to the back of an airboat skimming across the saw grass headed for an Everglades plane-crash site—or in a van full of happy children bound for discovery and adventure. The earlier scenarios were more usual for me. Was this a glimpse into how normal people lived? No, I thought. Sunny was damaged. These kids had probably already seen more strife and violence than many people do in a lifetime. And though Nazario seemed to be enjoying himself, this was certainly out of the ordinary for a homicide investigator. We were all outsiders, our noses up against the glass, wistfully seeking glimpses of real life.

I caught an occasional puzzled look from Nazario, but he sang along, learning lyrics from the children, pointing out rare palms, gliding pelicans, and out-of-state license tags. But mostly he looked at Sunny like a puppy coveting a bone.

The kids clamored to see who would spot the Seaquarium's distinctive round dome first. This was their second visit. Last week's was fun. Today's would focus on manatees. Later, in Sunny's studio, they would fashion manatees out of quick-drying clay, paint them with acrylics, and bake them.

"We're working with a new clay that bakes at three hundred fifty degrees in your own home oven," Sunny said.

Carlos, the oldest, age ten, held the exalted post of Sunny's assistant, age apparently his sole qualification. The sad-faced girl was his little sister, Pilar. The other two girls were sisters, ages five and six.

We navigated the turnstiles holding hands, then clustered around the huge manatee tank. Several gentle thousand-pound sea cows were in residence, one a mother with her calf. The unique white patterns, visible on the backs of all, were deep scars, cuts, and gashes from boat propellers. The endangered slow-moving vegetarians munch aquatic plants in shallow waters where they are unable to avoid speeding watercraft.

"I wouldn't want to be a manatee," Rosie said. "They don't have arms."

"How can they hug?" Pilar asked. "Do they kiss?"

"That's what they're doing now," Sunny said, as the mother nuzzled her calf with a whiskery snout.

"If the state would only enforce boating regulations," Nazario added, "manatees could coexist with people."

I resolved to take Onnie's son, Darryl, to the Seaquarium soon. I wished he were with us today. These children were learning more than just art.

"Are daddy manatees bullies?" Rosie wanted to know.

"No, sweetheart," Sunny said, her hand on the child's shoulder. "They just like to swim in warm water and nibble on plants. We're their worst enemies."

"Right," Nazario said. "All these manatees were injured, but good people rescued them, and when they're well enough they'll go back to their old homes in the wild."

Sure, I thought. Until the next drunk or hopped-up speed-crazed boater runs them down. My heart ached for the slow, lumbering sea creatures.

"How do they get hurt?" Rosie said.

"Boat propellers cut them," Sunny said, "and sometimes they get crushed in floodgates or in the locks of drainage canals."

"Or poisoned when people throw trash in the water," I said. "Careless people leave fishing lines, hooks, and plastic bags floating among the plants manatees eat."

Sunny nodded. "That's why we never ever throw garbage in the water," she said.

"Did you know that early sailors and explorers thought manatees were mermaids?" Nazario said.

Carlos hooted skeptically. "They must have needed glasses."

"Maybe they did." The detective shrugged. "Or maybe they'd just been at sea too long."

"They never saw *The Little Mermaid,*" Rosie said, stretching into a ballet pose.

"Can we pet them?" Jonathan asked.

"No," Sunny said. "We mustn't pet or feed them because they'll lose their natural fear of us and be more likely to be hurt later."

"Why are they that color?" Rosie grimaced. "I'm painting mine pink."

Jonathan suddenly grabbed his crotch and demanded a bathroom—*now!*—and Nazario hustled him off to the men's room.

Sunny watched in alarm. "Is he . . . I'm responsible. Their mothers all sign releases."

"For God's sake, Sunny," I said, "the man's a police officer, one of the good guys."

Still, she looked as relieved as Jonathan when the two rejoined us minutes later.

"You ever notice," Nazario said later, as Rosie interrupted her ballet stretches to comfort Jonathan, now whimpering over some imagined slight, "how little girls are born knowing what they're supposed to do—"

"But little boys *never* know what they're supposed to do," I said, finishing his sentence.

Sunny was quiet until we were ready to leave the manatee tank.

"Take a good look," she told the children. "Remember what they look like, because by the time you grow up there might not be manatees anymore."

She sure knew how to take sunshine out of a day, I thought.

* * *

During the drive back, Nazario spun the children a story about his adventures with a volunteer rescue team on a mission to save an injured manatee in the Alligator Hole River on the south coast of Jamaica. Despite dense tropical vegetation, hidden caves along the riverbanks, and hordes of nesting Jamaican crocodiles, they succeeded in hoisting the 900-pound manatee out of the river onto a specially designed stretcher.

"Did you come from Cuba too?" Carlos asked Nazario.

"Sí," the detective said, nodding. "A long time ago. I was five years old, smaller than your little sister."

"Did your *mami* and *papi* bring you?" Rosie asked.

"Nope. I came to Miami all by myself."

"No way," Carlos said.

"Oh, *sí, amigo,*" Nazario said. "My parents sent me on a plane. They were going to follow later but they couldn't, because of Fidel. So here I was in Miami, all alone. Lots of parents sent their children then. They called it Operation Peter Pan."

"When did you see your *mami* and *papi* again?" Rosie asked, as Sunny steered the van into northbound traffic.

"I never did."

"Never? Who did you live with?" Carlos asked.

"Lots of families. The church put me in foster homes up in New Jersey for a while. Then they sent me back here and I stayed with some other people."

"Why wouldn't Castro let them out?" Sunny asked, speaking directly to Nazario for the first time.

"My dad wound up in prison, a political prisoner. My mom wouldn't leave Cuba without him. She died waiting for his release. So did he, still in prison, a few years later."

"Castro killed my father too," I said. "A firing squad."

"It must have been frightening," Sunny said, "to be a little child, alone in a foreign country, orphaned."

He shrugged, expression nonchalant. "It was tough in the beginning. I spoke no English and they kept placing me with families who spoke no Spanish. After my parents, I missed the food the most. I can't complain." He turned to Carlos. "So, *amigo,* I hear you went to the ballet last week. How'd you like it?"

"I can't complain." The boy shrugged, mirroring the detective's nonchalant expression. "It would've been okay, if it wasn't for all that dancing."

"I hope they have Mickey Mouse next time," his little sister said.

Rosie skipped, holding tight to Nazario's hand, as we trooped across the lobby to Sunny's studio. She must have thought we'd never leave. She'd planned to fix soup and sandwiches while the children worked on their clay models.

Instead, Nazario ordered pizza.

"Sunny?" Jonathan looked up from his shapeless blob of clay.

"Yes?"

"Can I have a kiss?"

"Of course." She kissed his cheek.

Smiling sweetly, Rosie looked up from her hot-pink manatee, dripping paintbrush in hand. "Sunny?"

"Yes, sweetheart?" She turned her good ear toward the child.

"My mom says you bleach your hair and had a boob job."

Sunny's cheeks colored, as the little girls giggled.

"Mothers are always right," Nazario commented, with a straight face.

"Sometimes they're mistaken," Sunny murmured.

With the clay sea cows finished and in the oven, the tables were cleaned off and set. Somehow I wound up at the kiddy table, leaving Nazario and Sunny at the other. They didn't seem to eat much but they were talking quietly, a hopeful sign. I tried eavesdropping, but it was difficult with the kids all chattering. The only snatch of conversation I heard was Sunny saying, "You have to study the stone, let it speak to you and tell you what it wants to be."

"Then you carve," he said attentively.

"No, not yet. You do lots of drawings. Then you make clay models of the piece—much smaller, of course, but proportionate. After that, you do a plaster cast."

Nazario nodded, impressed. "All that before you even start carving?"

Then Jonathan spilled his juice, the kids got noisy, and I heard no more. I'd warned him that all she'd talk about was work. How, I wondered, would he calculate the right moment to whip out a fistful of mug shots? And how would she react?

He and the kids were still there when I left.

I had a date with a dead man.

11

The viewing for Andre Coney was set for 7 to 9 P.M. The Reverend Earl Wright and his demonstrators marched up and down the block, his voice chanting the loudest, as they waved signs that read MURDER! and JUSTICE NOW! Which came first, I wondered, the TV crews covering them or the protesters eager to perform for the camera?

The Liberty City funeral home resembled a large, comfortable, slightly rundown private residence, except for the wide gravel parking lot at the rear, the shiny black hearse at a side door, and the parade on the sidewalk out front. A funeral-home employee in a dark suit greeted visitors at the door, solemnly distributing leaflets memorializing the deceased. Andre Coney's black-and-white picture on the front seemed a bit informal for the occasion. He was grinning, clad in

T-shirt and jeans, the photo cropped in a way that hinted it had been a group picture and he'd apparently been holding a drink. The only other choice was probably a mug shot, I thought. His brief biography, printed inside, along with biblical verses, poems, and a list of relatives, made no mention of his accomplices.

"Andre faced many trials in life," the bio stated. That was true. They left out his impressive string of arrests.

Lingering in the red-carpeted foyer, listening to piped-in organ music, I wondered what this fine send-off would cost Ida Sweeting and her family.

When it was my turn to sign the guest book, I pored over all the other names. Bingo! A Mr. and Mrs. Charles C. Wells. Could that be Cubby, the boyhood friend Andre's aunt had mentioned?

I scanned the crowd of mourners for a possible candidate. Many wore black T-shirts bearing Coney's same slaphappy snapshot, his name, the dates of his birth and death, and the words IN MEMORIAM. Wayman Andrews from Channel 7 was trying his best to stir up some action among them at the back of the room.

Ida Sweeting, the dead man's aunt, was front and center in the first row, clutching her Bible as friends paid their respects. She grasped my hand and thanked me for coming, despite her daughter, who shot me daggers.

The star of the show lay in pious repose, hands folded over a small black Bible. Mourners kept saying how "good" he looked. It was true. His scars covered, Andre Coney did look good in his casket, probably better than he'd looked in years. All cleaned up, shaved, hair neatly trimmed, he was manicured and well dressed in a new suit clearly bought for the occasion. His appearance had improved vastly since I first saw him.

I sidled up close when one of Andre's cousins cried out a greeting to "Cubby."

The young man wore a suit, dress shirt, and subdued silk tie and had an attractive, vivacious young woman on his arm: the picture of someone who'd escaped the projects and prospered. Coney's sister and cousins welcomed him like a long-lost friend.

Keeping the couple in sight as I mingled, I saw him hug another young woman and introduce her to his companion.

Moments after they parted, I caught the second young woman's eye. "Wasn't that . . . ?"

"Cubby Wells," she said affably.

I asked about Ronald Stokes as we chatted. "I thought he, Andre, and Cubby were old buddies," I said, "but I didn't see his name in the guest book."

From her reaction, she knew him too.

"He'll probably be at the service tomorrow," I said innocently.

"No." She shook her head. "He won't. He's . . . away."

"Oh, right," I said. "He had some trouble years ago, so he's still . . ."

"Yes, he's . . . away," she said softly.

Her name was Shelby Fountain, formerly Stokes, Mad Dog's sister. It didn't seem to make her proud.

"I'd like to meet you somewhere, so we can talk," I said.

"Why would you want to talk to me?" When another mourner turned to stare she lowered her voice. "I hadn't seen Andre in years."

"I'm trying to piece it all together," I said. "You know, the whole picture. The history, all the things that happened back when Andre, your brother, and a few of their other buddies were teenagers."

Her eyes widened.

"I hear they were a tough crowd," I said.

Something in her face made my heart beat a little faster. Her hand flew to the silver cross on a chain around her neck. She knew what I was saying. We were on the same wavelength.

"People got hurt," I said.

Her eyes darted nervously, as though uneasy at being seen with me.

"Let's talk somewhere in private," I said. I reached for a business card, but she demurred. She didn't want to be seen accepting it.

"Take my number," she said softly, "but don't let anyone see you write it down." She recited the number softly, under her breath. Before I could repeat it, a man in a black T-shirt interrupted, scowled at me, and whisked her away.

I jotted down the number and then lingered until Cubby Wells and his companion said their goodbyes. They left first, me right behind them. He held the door open. "Aren't you Cubby Wells?"

He hesitated, but the young woman flashed a friendly smile.

"I was," he said reluctantly.

"His childhood nickname," she explained. "He hasn't used it for years."

"It's Charles," he said.

"My husband is *such* a stuffed shirt," she said fondly. "I don't know why he minds so." She held out her hand. "I'm Abby Wells."

She taught fourth grade, she said, and he was a social worker who counseled troubled teens on probation.

"Cool," I said casually. "Too bad Andre didn't have someone like you to turn to when he was that age. You guys were pretty wild back then, weren't you?"

He didn't answer as we three strolled back to the parking lot. The evening fell soft around us. The sun had set, leaving just a glimmer of orange above the horizon.

"Andre couldn't stay out of trouble," I went on. "Mad Dog is doing time. How did you manage to rise above it all and become a success?"

He shrugged, face solemn.

His wife giggled and gave him an affectionate nudge. "Come on, sourpuss, answer the nice lady."

"I don't know if you could call me successful," he said tersely. "You don't get rich counseling kids in trouble."

"You're not dead," I said. "You're not in prison. You're a success."

His wife frowned. "Charles, what has gotten into you this evening? Of course you're successful. We're a success. We do what we love. We're making a difference." She turned to me. "We made that our mission statement when we got engaged, to make a difference."

They had reached their car, a blue Buick Skylark.

"It's still early," I said. "Can I buy you two a cup of coffee or a drink? It's important," I added, as they hesitated, "for the press to show the positive side, the good that can emerge from the same neighborhood where these things"—I jerked my head toward the protesters and the funeral home—"attract all the media attention."

Wells shook his head, mumbling, "We've got to pick up the baby—"

"Oh, let's stop for coffee," Abby persuaded. "The baby's fine. My mother doesn't expect us for hours. I thought I'd finally get to meet all his childhood friends," she told me, "but he rushed me out of there like he's embarrassed to be seen with me."

He denied it and apologized. The man didn't stand a chance. We met at a diner on Twenty-seventh Avenue and sat in a booth. He and I had coffee while Abby ordered a glass of milk and blueberry pie à la mode with vanilla ice cream. "I'm hungry all the time," she whispered. "I'm not showing yet, but we're expecting another one."

She was four months pregnant, she said. Their first child, a little girl, was three.

"Charles isn't really like this," she told me, as he looked uncomfortable. "I think the death of this childhood friend is affecting him more than he admits."

"We weren't all that close," he protested. "I don't even know why we came tonight. I was just . . ." He shrugged, momentarily at a loss for words. "I was curious. I hadn't seen anybody from the old neighborhood for so long. I hadn't even seen Andre since I was fifteen."

"But you and your buddies were tight then, weren't you?" I said.

Eyes troubled, he reached for his wife's hand. "Half a lifetime ago. I was the youngest in the group."

"What happened? What made you break away from them?"

"My grandmother happened. My mother sent me up to Fort Lauderdale to live with her, right after the New Year. That's what saved me," he said.

Apparently it was the only good thing his mother had ever done for him. The intent was not to save him, though that was the result. His move out of Miami and out of her life was a matter of convenience: hers. A troublesome teenager, running with a rough crowd, he was fatherless and she was a destitute crack addict with only drugs and death in her future.

"My grandmother took me to church, put me back in school, got on my case about studying. She saved me," he repeated.

Eventually he won a college scholarship.

"That's why he loves what he does so much," Abby said, licking ice cream off her lips. "He sees himself in these kids, their potential. He can set them on the right road, because he's been there, on his way down the wrong one himself." They exchanged fond glances.

Yeah. Sure, I thought. I liked her. Under other circumstances I might have liked him too. But certain questions iced that possibility. Did he rape Sunny too? I wondered. Did he help beat Ricky? Did he jam the gun to the boy's head and pull the trigger?

"I always think, There but for the grace of God . . ." he mumbled. "I'm so lucky."

I smiled, my heart a stone in my chest. He *was* lucky. He had it all: a career, a nice wife, and a family he loved. The good things in life that Ricky Chance would never experience because he was doing the big dirt sleep.

"I regret my youthful mistakes," Charles Wells was saying, "deeply."

"I'm sure. Everybody makes mistakes," I said. "It's just that some are a helluva lot bigger than others."

He nodded, face somber. "I can't help but think that if Andre, Mad Dog, and his cousin, Stony, had the chance I had, their lives might have turned out different too."

"Stony?"

He shifted uneasily in his seat, aware he had misspoken. "You know," he muttered. "Parvin Stokes, Mad Dog's cousin."

"What happened to him?"

"Got into a scrape." He shrugged. "Some kinda fight over a stolen car. The judge said, 'Since you like fighting so much, join the army or go to jail.' So he enlisted."

How nice for the army, I thought.

"Won a medal in the Gulf War, a hero for a while. Then he got into another scrape, did some time, and got dishonorably discharged."

"Where is he now?" I asked.

"He was there tonight. Didn't you see him? Saw you talking to his little cousin, Shelby. He was wearing a black T-shirt with Andre's picture."

He was the glowering man who had whisked her away from me, I realized: suspect number four. Andre Coney, Ronald "Mad Dog" Stokes, Charles "Cubby" Wells, and Parvin "Stony" Stokes. Where was number five? A little shudder rippled down my spine, as though someone were tap dancing on my grave.

"Who was the fifth guy you all ran with, just before you moved to Grandma's?"

He stared across the table at me, then shrugged.

Abby interrupted with another confession. "Not only am I always hungry, I'm always going to the little girls' room." She excused herself.

"She's so nice," I said, as we watched her depart. "You must worry about your youthful mistakes catching up to you."

"Say what?"

"Say a crime with no statute of limitations, like murder. You remember that Christmas? The young couple?"

"Those were the darkest years of my life," he said quietly, guilt written all over his face. "I was just a kid." He swallowed. "I know that age is no excuse, that we all have to take responsibility for our actions. I'll regret some of the things that happened until my dying day. But I didn't kill anybody."

"If you were there, you're as guilty as the shooter, even if you didn't pull the trigger."

Agitated, he called for the check.

"Does your wife know?" I asked.

"Don't talk to her about this. Please. She's pregnant. I don't want her upset."

"Maybe you should consider that and talk to the police," I said. "They're investigating it again; this time they're putting it together. They know Andre was there, and Mad Dog. Maybe if you tell them what you know, you can make a deal."

I reached for the check as it arrived, but he tore it out of my hand, sprang to his feet, then fumbled to pay at the cash register, intercepting Abby as she left the rest room. She turned to give me a bewildered wave as he hustled her out the door.

He was there, I thought. He's somebody else now, but he was a monster then. One of them.

I thought of his wife, their baby, and the troubled teens he counseled. If only his self-destructive crack-head whore of a mother had sent him to safety sooner. Those cruelest of words: If only.

12

I called Burch about Cubby Wells and Parvin Stokes, street name Stony, first thing in the morning.

"Wells is the weakest link," I said. "Not a stone-cold con like Mad Dog or Coney, never was. He reformed, got an education, and tried to atone. Too late, unfortunately. Squeeze him. I bet he'll crack.

"Also, I think Mad Dog's sister might spill something. I'll try to talk to her at the funeral today. How did Nazario and Sunny hit it off?"

"So far so good. Says he has to talk to her again," Burch said. "Didn't wanna push it till he had both feet in the door. I think he'd like to get more than that in the door. You should hear 'im. 'She's so talented, so smart, so noble.' Like he never saw a broad before.

"Said he never woulda recognized 'er from your description. Guess it's all in the eye of the beholder. But so far, Pete said he's taking it slow."

One eye on the clock, I transcribed notes into my laptop while nibbling *tostada* and sipping coffee. Funeral services were at ten. I quit at nine-fifteen, donned a suitably subdued navy blazer, then scooped up my ringing phone as I fed Bitsy.

"Hey, sweets."

Fitzgerald's voice startled me.

"Heads up," he said cheerfully. "The depo was rescheduled. I'm at the Golden Glades Interchange, 'bout twenty minutes away."

Panic washed over me. Was this Tuesday? It was. Oh, no! I'd totally forgotten.

"You there?"

"Sure," I said weakly. "You made good time."

"Hit the road before daylight. Should be rolling up to your place shortly."

"Okay." I said. "Don't rush. Drive safely."

Stifling the urge to make a run for it, I scrambled around my apartment instead, straightening up, stashing files and stacks of newspapers under the bed, and trying to remember. Had I promised to cook the man a gourmet dinner? It all seemed so long ago. The few food items in my freezer were unrecognizable, wearing frost beards. My mind raced.

The *News* food editor insists that anyone can whip up a quick gourmet meal using only the basic staples found in any kitchen. My only staples were cat food, dog chow, and half a bottle of Jack Daniel's Black. I suddenly wanted a quick swig. It was nine twenty-five in the morning, for God's sake.

The doorbell rang as I brushed on blusher. The man must have driven like Dale Earnhardt.

There was Dennis Fitzgerald, on my doorstep. Light-haired and muscular, clear gray eyes, and an all-American smile. Warm, intelligent, a sexy man, a good man, but not the man I wanted.

We hugged, but I neatly evaded the big smooch.

He noticed my jacket. "What's on the agenda?" he asked. "A surprise?"

"Well," I said. "There *is* something I thought we could do together, unless you had other plans."

"I was hoping we'd lock the door, take the phone off the hook, and pull up the drawbridge. But," he said, strong arms encircling my waist, "I'm up for anything you've got in mind. God knows, Britt, you're never boring. I just like to be with you."

"Good," I said.

"I must admit, I've had more romantic dates," Fitzgerald confided, as we joined the slow-moving procession to the cemetery.

"Sorry," I said. "I tried to talk them into keeping him on ice, but the family was hellbent on burying this guy."

My last trip to that particular cemetery had been to cover the latest grave robbery. Miami members of the Santería cult use human skulls and leg bones in their rituals. Guess where some go to find them? Willie Sutton, the legendary Babe Ruth of bank robbers, reportedly said that he robbed banks "because that's where the money is." Same premise.

Santería's magic number is seven, for the seven African deities. The woman who lost her skull on that occasion had not a prayer of resting in peace. Her not-so-final resting place was the seventh gravesite in the cemetery's seventh row, beneath a headstone with an inscription stating she died at age seventy in 1977.

"Even the dead aren't safe in Miami!" her horrified granddaughter had wailed.

Cemetery security appeared to have been beefed up since then, however. There was not a decapitated chicken, disturbed grave, or dead goat in sight.

Ida Sweeting wept inconsolably as church choir members sang "I'll Fly Away" at the graveside. Cubby and Abby Wells were conspicuous by their absence. The Reverend Earl Wright and his black-shirted contingent were a presence but left their protest signs at the gate. As he detailed his outrage in front of the television cameras, I spotted Shelby Fountain along with her cousin Stony and a man I assumed was her husband. She and I exchanged glances but had no opportunity to speak.

"Who's your friend?" Fitzgerald murmured, nudging my arm.

Shelby's cousin Stony had focused an angry narrow-eyed glare on me during the minister's reading of the Twenty-third Psalm. He was tall and muscular with short wiry hair, a military bearing, and a gold earring dangling from one ear.

As he and Andre's family members scattered handfuls of dirt onto the casket being lowered into the ground, my thoughts were irreverent. One down, I thought. Four to go.

Lottie, shooting pictures from a distance, gave me a thumbs-up when she spotted Fitzgerald. She sidled over to me when he went for the car.

"You didn't tell me you had a date for this shindig," she said.

"I forgot. He showed up, and I don't know what to do with him."

"You need instructions? That man is hot."

"That's why I don't want to be alone with him," I said. "I just can't."

"Great guns and little fishes! Have you been smoking loco weed?"

"Thank you for your sisterly support," I said.

Fitzgerald drove while I used my laptop and put together a brief story on the funeral for the city desk.

Lunch was romantic, in an elevated flower-filled gazebo in an oceanside garden at a beachfront hotel. The sounds of the sea, the exotic shadows of palm fronds, and drifting clouds in an azure sky were the perfect backdrop for champagne, cold shrimp, and ripe pears poached in honey and showered with shaved almonds.

He nuzzled my neck while I filled him in about the case, the story, and Sunny herself. As I did, it occurred to me that, like her, I avoided reality by talking only about work. At least Sunny had valid reasons for being screwed up. But Fitzgerald was a good sport.

"What's next on the agenda?" he whispered seductively, as we strolled the beach hand in hand, the surf swelling at the edge of a silver and turquoise sea.

He looked expectant.

"Well," I said, champagne and honey still on my lips, "you know what a movie buff I am. My heart beats a little faster every time I walk into a theater lobby and smell the popcorn, but I rarely get to movies because of my hours."

He blinked.

I took him to the Gay and Lesbian Film Festival under way at the Alliance. He quit holding my hand about halfway through. He looked thoughtful as we left, brow furrowed. "You trying to tell me something, Britt?"

"No," I said innocently, and checked my watch. "I just heard it was a good flick. You know, they're showing *Rebecca,* an old Hitchcock flick, in Little Havana. We can make it if we leave right now."

After *Rebecca,* I enthused about the new enhanced uncut reissue of *Godfather II* at a nearby multiplex. It was dark by the time we staggered out of that theater.

"What now?" he said quietly. "There must be a midnight screening somewhere of a movie you've only seen three or four times."

"No," I said. "In fact, I think we've overdone it. I've got a splitting headache. I'd rather just go home."

He studied me for a long moment, then drove me back to my apartment. He parked outside and we sat for a moment in the dark.

"What's the deal with all the mixed signals, Britt? You've done everything you could all day to avoid being alone with me. Is this a game? I don't get it."

"Sorry," I said. "I really do have a headache."

"Who wouldn't after a triple feature? Hate to tell you this, but I really couldn't stand the one with the subtitles. And if I smell popcorn one more time, I'll puke." He paused. "You forgot about us, didn't you?"

The question hung, unanswered, between us. He gave up waiting for a reply. "You call me in the middle of the night and then forget our date. I don't think you're on drugs, you're not a drinker, and you never struck me as a tease. But why encourage me to drive hundreds of miles and then avoid me? What's the story?"

"It's me," I said, in a guilty whisper. "I just got really wrapped up in what I'm working on. . . ."

"Don't we all?" He sighed and gently ran his thumb along my jawline. "It's that other guy, isn't it?"

"I'm hopeless. Neurotic," I said.

"Woulda been nice to know that before I drove all the way down here. I better hit the road. It's a long haul back."

I was surprised he even bothered to walk me to the door. I opened it and he turned to leave, Bitsy bouncing around his feet.

"You should have a cup of coffee before you go," I said. "I'll make some."

He hesitated, eyes suspicious. "Sure."

He sat at my table watching me savagely grind the coffee beans at high speed.

"I didn't mean to jerk you around," I said miserably. "I've always been lousy at relationships." I dumped in the water, steam rising. "Everybody has emotional conflicts at times."

"That's the problem with women," he said, "especially you Catholic girls. You think too much. Make everything too complicated. With all that's happened lately, Britt, you must realize that so much of what used to be important really isn't. Life is too short. The world is a dangerous and complicated place. Sex should be simple. This is not about relationships or emotional decisions. It's about biology, two healthy hot-blooded people who are attracted to each other. You, me, raw sex."

"That's supposed to make me feel better?" I couldn't help laughing.

He shrugged and opened his arms, expression hopeful. Still laughing, I straddled his chair, sat on his thighs, and hugged him. Only a hug, I thought. Then a kiss. Only one, then another, and several more. Then he was unbuttoning my blouse, I was unbuckling his belt, and soon there was no room in the chair.

"Thanks," I murmured later as we drowsed in my bed, the hypnotic blades of the ceiling fan cooling our overheated bodies from above.

"For what?" He nuzzled the hollow of my throat.

"My headache's gone."

"Just call me Doc. I wonder if it was the oral medication or the physical therapy?"

"You know, Doc, I think I feel another twinge, right here." I pointed to the spot.

He worked warm lips against my skin. "Hmmmm," he murmured. "Looks like time for more therapy, but first I'll have to perform another physical examination. Hmmmm. What have we here?"

* * *

We sent out for food at 4 A.M. There is something to be said for a city that never sleeps. Our order arrived in twenty minutes, smelling heavenly, pasta drenched in tangy meat sauce and warm crispy garlic rolls oozing olive oil.

We ate in bed, fed each other, then got frisky with a cardboard shaker of fresh grated parmesan and romano cheeses.

My expectations were exceeded.

I tossed the bedclothes into the washer and drove off to see the parents of murder victim Ricky Chance. Fitzgerald was gone, back to Daytona for an afternoon court hearing in an old case. I hated seeing him go; I was relieved to see him go. I had so much to do.

The Chances' number, from an old phone message in Burch's files, was still good, listed at the same address in Heather Chance's name.

I could have called first, but people tend to resist revisiting old tragedies, reopening old wounds. Sometimes it's easier simply to show up. The address was a garden apartment in Aventura, a North Dade municipality of relatively new water-view high-rise condos and apartments.

Heather Chance answered the door. An attractive well-tailored brunette, she had a crisp polished veener. The set of her shoulders, the angle of her chin, her confident smile, all projected an image, someone who gets things done, a professional, a woman who has kicked her way through the glass ceiling. A teacher, as I recalled. A leather briefcase sat on a gilt-edged Louis

XIV table in the foyer. Perhaps I'd caught them both at home.

"I'd like to talk to you about your son, Richard," I said, introducing myself. "I'm writing a story about the Cold Case Squad, detectives who have taken on the investigation."

Her hands flew to her throat, eyes flooding. She had morphed instantly from polished professional into heartbroken mother.

"Ricky's case? You want to know about Ricky?"

"Do you have a moment?"

"Of course." She swung open the door. "Please, come in."

Something about the apartment's warm and inviting decor seemed oddly off-key, but I couldn't place what it was. Ricky's framed photo was prominent on the mantel, and one wall was adorned with an artist's montage of pastel drawings of him in sports scenes, apparently sketched from photos. No sign or sound of Sean Chance, who'd probably already left for his office.

Motioning me to a cushiony indigo sofa, Heather perched on the edge of a floral-patterned armchair, her pose almost girlish, eager and expectant. She had to be in her early fifties and, though immaculately groomed, she looked every day of it. "It's such good news to hear they're working on it again. Do you think they might actually make some headway this time? It's been so long."

"It's possible," I said cautiously. "They're following some new leads. Sergeant Burch is still in charge."

"I remember him." Her smile was rueful. "I'm sure he doesn't have fond recollections of me. I spoke to him, or left messages, almost every day to keep them from forgetting, to keep them working on it. I was desperate to see the case solved, so it wouldn't happen again to another mother's child. I even resented it when the detectives took a day off, or a vacation, or even went to lunch. My *child* was dead. How could they relax, eat, or enjoy life? How could anyone?" Embarrassed, she looked down at the hand-hooked floral rug in shades of rose and cream. "Not surprising that after a time they began to ignore my calls. Finally they made it clear that they would call me when they had news. In other words, Don't call us, we'll call you. I'm still waiting."

"They worked it with everything they had. They must have been as frustrated as you were," I said. "Do you still teach?"

"Oh, no." She looked startled. "I couldn't. After it happened, I couldn't see a child without seeing my son.

"I couldn't even deal with Sunny, the girl with Ricky that night. She survived, you know. Of course my heart ached for her, but at times I wanted to wring her neck. I wanted her to remember those faces, to help the police more. God forgive me, but at times I hated her and her parents. She was alive; Ricky wasn't. She had her life. They had her. They even had young Tyler, but we were left with nothing. Ricky was our only child."

Her eyes drifted to his framed photo.

"Of course," she said, refocusing on me, "I found other reasons to resent her. I wondered why Ricky was with Sunny, when there were so many girls in the world. He could have dated anyone. If he hadn't singled her out, he never would have been at that place, at that moment in time. I'd wonder whose idea it was to stop at that ice-cream shop. Hers? She was probably what attracted them. She stood out, with that blond hair. . . . If only Ricky had taken her straight home . . . I blamed myself as well. They were too young to date. Why did I permit it? If only I'd insisted that Ricky stay home with us that night."

"It's natural," I said. "What if? If only. When bad things happen we all think that way. It's understandable."

She nodded. "You're right. I learned later that a lot of survivors go through that sort of thinking. I guess it seems almost trivial now, with all the people in New York who didn't even find bodies to bury. At least we had that, a decent funeral, the chance to see him, touch him one last time.

"I wanted desperately to talk to Sunny but hardly ever saw her after she was released from the hospital. I'm sure she was avoiding me too, afraid to face me. Sean insisted we sell the house and move. I was sorry I agreed. I cried for weeks after. I never wanted to leave the place where Ricky took his first step, had his first Christmas, got his first puppy. All those happy times. His basketball hoop was still mounted on the front of the garage when we followed the moving van out of the driveway. Sean was sure the move would help, but it only made the loss worse. I used to drive back to our old house all the time. The new owners must have thought I was stalking them. I got hysterical when I saw they'd cut down the tree where Ricky had his tree house. He and his dad built it when he was eight."

"So you moved here?"

She shook her head. "We moved to a Brickell Avenue condominium. It was big and cold, like a mausoleum, the people there all tucked away like corpses. I thought that every time I walked down the hall. How do you compare that to a home with character, memories, and living reminders?

"I was devastated. You can imagine the sort of companion I was to Sean." Her smile was sad. "He finally announced one day that we were still young enough to have another child. 'You can't grieve forever,' he said. 'We have to go on with our lives.' He couldn't understand why I recoiled at the thought. He didn't carry our son for nine months, didn't give birth to him. After raising a wonderful boy and losing him after seventeen years, how could I do it again? How would I ever let another child out of my sight?

"That's when Sean stopped attending meetings."

"Meetings?"

"The Parents of Murdered Children. I couldn't give it up. I was president of our chapter for three years. I still attend regularly. They're the only other people who understand what it's like, the only people I feel really comfortable with. Everywhere else, people start to talk about their children, then they ask about yours. . . ." Her voice trailed off.

"When did you leave the place on Brickell?"

"We lived there for less than three years, though it seemed much longer."

"And then?"

"We divorced," she said simply.

That explained it; the chinoiserie wall covering, the

gilt wood stool, the floral fabrics. Exquisite but strictly feminine, the apartment had no trace of a masculine presence.

"I got my real estate license. I specialize in water-front property, mostly in Golden Beach. I've been doing really well, a member of the million-dollar club."

"Good for you," I said. "But I didn't know you two were divorced. I'm sorry."

Her right thumb and index finger massaged the naked left ring finger where she'd once worn a wedding band. "We were childhood sweethearts," she said. "Married for twenty years, happy, content with our lives—it all changed in one night."

"Do you and Sean stay in touch; do you still see each other?" I asked hopefully. "Maybe you'll eventually . . ."

"How romantic. It must be nice to still think like that," she said wistfully. "He remarried less than six months later. She's younger. I hear they have three small children, a big house in Pinecrest. I haven't seen Sean in years."

"And are you . . . seeing someone?" One of the perks of being a reporter is that you get to ask questions other people are too polite or too embarrassed to ask.

"I haven't even dated," she said, "except for a man in my parents group, and he was more screwed up than I am. I've learned that sudden death is easy; what's difficult is going on with life. Work helped me immensely. It still does. Real estate is demanding, extremely detail-oriented, and incredibly satisfying when you manage to match the right family to the right house, a home where they can be happy.

"I can't tell you how grateful I am that you came here. It would be my dream come true if Ricky's case could be resolved. I think about them out there somewhere, enjoying their lives, hurting other people. I would do anything to see them brought to justice. Please tell Detective Burch not to be afraid to call me. I promise not to make a pest of myself this time."

Smiling, she thanked me again for coming. I paused outside after she closed the door and listened to the silence in the rooms behind me.

She was right, I thought, driving back to the paper. Ricky, gone in an instant in a blinding burst of gunfire, was technically the victim. But it was his mother's life that had been left vastly diminished. It was she who experienced the loss and the sadness. The mother, not the boy, was left to dwell on his promise, his unfulfilled dreams, his lost future. The killers had left her impoverished and suffering, robbed forever of the son who had enhanced her life.

The newsroom was oddly quiet as I walked in. Reporters and editors had gathered in small knots, faces grave.

Another budget cutback? I wondered.

Lottie bustled down the hall from photo. "Britt," she said, out of breath. "Did you see the ambulance leave?"

"No," I said, heart sinking.

"Ryan," she said. "Said he felt like shit, stood up to go home, and just hit the floor, passed out cold."

The desk directly behind mine was empty, the chair pushed back, his SAVE THE WHALES coffee mug still half full.

"Ryan?" I frowned. This had to be a joke. "It can't

be. What happened? Is he in love again? Did Gretchen give him another cockamamie assignment?"

"Britt, he looked terrible." Her honest brown eyes were so concerned that I felt ashamed.

"He's probably all right," I assured her, trying to convince myself. "You know how he's been complaining lately. He's such a hypochondriac. Men are such babies. Don't worry. I'm sure it's nothing serious."

"They took him out on a gurney," she said gravely.

"Where?"

"The ER at County. Gretchen went in the ambulance with him."

"Jeez, that would be like waking up to see Satan at your bedside. Poor Ryan. Wish I'd been here," I said. "I could've gone with him or at least followed, to drive him home later."

Nobody had left the newsroom feet first since the garden editor's nervous breakdown. She had to be restrained; her screams echoed down the hall. She never came back. She sued, instead, for disability benefits, citing job-related stress due to deadline pressures—and won. Reporters would hoot in derision at mere mention of her name. The woman had never had to survive riot-torn streets, see gunshot victims up close, or be threatened with arrest. Unlike our multiple daily deadlines, hers was once a week, for chatty Sunday features on mulching, organic gardening, and topics no more controversial than how to repot a poinsettia.

What was this with Ryan?

Lottie and I headed for coffee in the cafeteria where I filled her in on what I'd been working on—and Fitzgerald's visit.

"The Gay and Lesbian Film Festival?" She winced. "The poor guy must have whiplash. At least it ended happily," she said, with a wink.

"But it shouldn't have."

"Why not? My inquiring mind wants to know. A romantic lunch, a romantic evening—"

"And the next thing you know, your socks are off," I said. "But he's the wrong one, Lottie."

"Men do that all the time. It don't matter to them if it's the right one, long as it's somebody warm and willing."

"Sure, but we're supposed to be better than they are."

"Well, I may have eyes for Prince William, but I don't aim to stay single and celibate till he comes to his senses and breaks down my door."

Back at my desk, I found a message to call Dr. Donald Hartley. His nurse put me right through. He thanked me for returning his call. "I heard the disturbing news," he said gravely.

"Which disturbing news?" I asked, my mind racing through the short list: K. C. Riley, Ryan, my unfortunate love life?

He paused. "Is that question a sign that you're not having a good week?"

I had to smile. "Just the usual. It seems I always have more than enough disturbing news to go around."

He chuckled, a warm charismatic sound. "I'm referring to the tire on your automobile. Maureen and I heard belatedly that you found it necessary to call a tow truck. I only wish I'd been there to help or that

Tyler had been of more assistance. Sometimes he can be quite thoughtless."

"No problem," I said. "He had his own car trouble." What could I say? The truth? That his seed had produced a perverse and deranged vandal? "It's okay, Dr. Hartley."

"No, it isn't," he said kindly. "And please call me Donald. I had my office manager contact the Goodyear store near your newspaper office and arrange for new tires to be put on your car. No charge to you. It's the least I can do after you drove all the way up to see us."

"That's so nice!" I said, adding that I could not possibly accept. He insisted.

So did I. "It's against newspaper policy," I finally explained. "Reporters are not permitted to accept anything that we can't eat or drink in one sitting. It's an ethical thing. Tires are definitely out, but I appreciate the gesture."

"Is there any other way I can help you?"

"No," I said. "I saw Heather Chance. She's in real estate now, doing very well. She and her husband are divorced."

"I'm sorry to hear that." He sounded genuinely saddened.

"Otherwise, things are moving along. I'll keep you posted," I promised.

Sunny must be crazy, I thought.

I called the hospital, but Ryan was still in the ER. Another call caught me about to leave the office.

The breathy voice, uncertain and hesitant, was almost a whisper.

"This is Britt. Who is this?"

"Somebody you wanted to talk to."

I nearly blurted her name, but she sounded so guarded, I bit my tongue. "Right," I said. "We met the other night at—"

"At Andre's viewing."

"I'm so glad you called," I said. "Can I come by your place to talk?"

"No way," she said quickly.

"How about here, at the paper?"

"No, I don't wanna come there."

"Well, where are you now? We can meet someplace."

"I was going over to the Kmart," she said softly, as though she was not alone, "to get some things for my kids."

"The one on the Boulevard?"

"Yeah, next door to Busy Bee Car Wash."

"Where? It's a big store."

"The garden department? In the back, at the opposite end to the registers. In half an hour?"

"See you there."

13

Shelby Fountain stood in the back of the screened-in garden center, nearly obscured beneath the hanging baskets of spider plants and butterfly orchids, surrounded by spindly young palms, staked hibiscus bushes, and bougainvillea overflowing huge pots.

We rendezvoused in a shaded, shadowy corner permeated by the wet earthy smells of potting soil, wood chips, and living things, out of sight of the cash register lane, obscured from customers browsing the flats of bright blooming flowers on sale up in front.

She had a box of disposable diapers in her shopping cart, along with two small pink periwinkles in four-inch pots.

She greeted me with "I shouldn't be doing this."

"Why not? My impression was that you might want to talk about it."

She shrugged uncomfortably, in obvious distress. "They may not be the best family, but they're *my* family. If they knew I spoke to you . . ." She paused. "They can't know I said anything."

"I understand."

"I care about them," she said. "but I also have Jesus Christ in my heart and what you said the other night, about the people who got hurt—well, I know that's true."

"On Christmas Eve, fourteen years ago," I said, "a teenage couple was abducted."

She nodded slowly as I spoke. "I remember. I remember that night." She spoke softly as the arching fronds of a multi-trunked areca palm created dappled shadows on her face. "I was eleven. My brother had just come home from juvenile detention two days before. They let him out for Christmas. They told him to stay away from those boys he always got in trouble with, but first thing he did was hook up with them again. They went out that night, Christmas Eve.

"They left big and bold, like they was up to no good. Came back late, agitated and worked up, whispering among themselves."

"Did they say where they had been?"

"Not to me. But Mad Dog had blood on his clothes. And they had a gun."

Her gently spoken words raised goose bumps on my arms.

"Mad Dog used to scare me. I didn't like being in the house alone with him or his friends. They'd tease me and . . . my brother was always trying to put his hands on me. I used to lock myself in my room with my little sisters. I took care of them."

"Where were your parents?"

"My daddy ran off after my baby sister was born. My mama worked and had a boyfriend. She wasn't home a lot."

"What happened that night?"

"Mama had Christmas presents on layaway up at Sears, and I was waiting for her to bring them home so we could wrap them and put them under the tree. But the lady she worked for was having a party that night, and Mama had to stay to help clean up. She still wasn't home when the boys came back. I was there by myself, baby-sitting my two little sisters. They were 'bout four and six then.

"Andre was real upset. They was all scared and excited. They didn't want me hearing what they was talking about. Mad Dog told me to get out of the room."

"Who were they, exactly?" I counted them on my fingers. "Your brother, his cousin Stony, Andre Coney, and Cubby Wells. There was one more, a fifth boy. Who was he?"

She stared, expression thoughtful, as though she didn't know whether to believe me. "You don't know who the other guy was?"

"No, should I?"

"I thought you did, I thought that was one of the reasons you were here," Shelby said, her face pinched with apprehension.

"No. Why? Who is he?"

"If you don't know," she said evasively, "I'm not going to be the one to say his name."

Fearing she would shut down completely, I changed the subject.

"What were they driving that night?"

"Had a white van. I never saw it before. Musta had a stolen tag. I remember Andre was out in the alley changing the license plate before they left. I knew they was up to no good. Later he said he had to take it back where he got it. I never saw that van again.

"Mad Dog changed clothes, then tol' me to wash his bloody shirt and pants. Warned me not to say anything to Mama about it. I did what he said." She winced, as though stabbed by a sudden pain. "I guess that makes me an accomplice to whatever they did."

"No way," I said. "You were eleven years old, for heaven's sake, intimidated, scared, taking care of your little sisters on Christmas Eve. You did nothing wrong."

She fingered the cross hanging from a silver chain around her neck. "But I lied," she whispered, "and I stole."

"What do you mean?"

She chewed her lower lip and didn't answer.

"When did you see the gun?"

"They was hiding something from me before they left. But I knew what it was. I heard them talking. Andre took it in a burglary. Took it from a house up in Miami Shores a few days before Mad Dog come home from Youth Hall."

"Did you ever get a good look at it? Could you describe it?"

She smiled, as though embarrassed. "Oh, I got a real good look at it. Real good. Was a revolver type, shiny, chrome. Not too big, but not real small neither."

The way she said it prompted me to ask, "How did you manage to get such a good look at it?"

" 'Cause I stole it."

"When? Why?"

She sighed. "When they went out again, to take the van back, they didn't take the gun with them. I don't know why, maybe in case they got stopped. I knew they'd done something bad. I didn't want to see Christmas get ruined for the little ones again," she said earnestly. "I was tired. I just didn't want any more trouble. My mama's boyfriend was coming over for Christmas Day. Mad Dog never got along with him. They'd got into fistfights before; once they broke the coffee table. Me and the kids was all screaming. I was afraid. . . . I didn't want any gun in the house. I was tired of trouble. After they left, I went into his room and found it, wrapped in a T-shirt, shoved under the mattress."

"What did you do with it?"

"Put it in my pocket. It felt heavy. I wanted it gone. It was late, I wasn't allowed out, or to leave the kids alone, but I wanted it gone. I ran down the street with it. It was raining hard. I was scared. I just wanted to get rid of it."

"What a stand-up little kid you were," I said, imagining a frightened eleven-year-old on a cold and wet Christmas Eve, out in the dark alone, on a mission to dispose of a murder weapon. "Too bad there wasn't a cop around, you could have given it to him."

"If I'da seen a cop, I'da run the other way." She frowned. "I was scareda cops."

"What did you do? Think it might still be wherever you left it?" How amazing it would be if, after fourteen years, we found the murder weapon—and the eyewitness who could put it in the killer's hand.

"I was half drowned and crying," she went on. "Scared my mama would come home while I was gone and I'd get a whupping. Used to be a bar down by Fourteenth Street, on the corner. Think they called it the Circus. It's not there anymore.

"I was looking for the Salvation Army box across the street, looked like a red brick chimney. A man used to ring the bell and people would drop in money. The gun was still wrapped up in the T-shirt. I was gonna drop it in there. Thought they'd know what to do with it. But the chimney box was gone.

"Nobody around except a car outside the bar, engine running, steam rising off the hood. A lady in the passenger seat was waiting on the driver to come out. She called me, like; 'Whatchu doing out here in the rain, child? Where's your mama?' I had to get home. I didn't know what else to do. I just handed it to her. 'Here,' I said. 'Merry Christmas.' She started to say something. But I ran, faster than I ever had in my life. Didn't stop until I got home. Thought I'd never catch my breath again."

"Do you know who she was? Did you ever see her again?"

She shook her head. "Pretty, probably in her thirties. Had on dangly earrings, all rhinestones. Seemed nice. She was a grown-up; I wouldn't know her again if I saw her. I smelt liquor on her breath when I walked up close to the car."

"What happened when Mad Dog realized the gun was gone?"

"He didn't come back till next morning. Searched his whole room, then the rest of the house, my room too. Acting wild, kept saying he was looking for something, throwing things around. Twisted my arm and asked me if I took anything out of his room. I said I didn't know what he was talking about. He probably believed me because I had never lied to him before. That was the first time. He asked me if any of the other boys had come back over when he wasn't home. I said I didn't see nobody. Sometimes," she said, eyes grave, "when it's important enough, I think Jesus forgives a lie."

"Absolutely," I said. "I'm sure."

"All of them acted crazy after that night. Andre came over, started crying and punching at the wall. Kept saying it wasn't right, wasn't fair."

"What do you think he meant?"

She shrugged. "Everybody heard 'bout those kids being shot. It was all over the TV. First time I ever saw Mad Dog and his friends watch the news. They stuck close to home for a while, kept to themselves. 'Cept Cubby; he disappeared. Moved away. Never saw him again till the other night. Man looks good. Has a nice wife."

"Right," I said. "I like her too. Did you ever ask your brother point-blank if they did it?"

"Once or twice. Denied it, slapped me for asking. Kept saying not to talk about it to nobody. But I used to think about it," she said, "specially around the holidays. Now that I'm a mother myself, it's been coming back to me more often. I got kids, two of them. Sometimes I just lie awake at night, thinking about the mothers. With what happened on nine-eleven, it seems like evil is overtaking the world, like the prophecies in the Bible."

"Would you discuss this with a detective?"

"No!" She stepped back, almost knocking over a leggy, wide-leafed philodendron in a plastic pot. "This is just between us, Shelby to Britt. You know that. I been wanting to tell somebody for a long time, just didn't know who. Sister or not, it's dangerous. I've got my own kids to think about. And my mother would never forgive me for making more trouble. If they knew I told somebody, I wouldn't have a family, maybe not even a life."

"I understand. But the gun is very important. If we could just track it down . . ."

"What happened to the girl? The one who lived?"

"Deaf in one ear from the bullet wound, she's an artist now. The dead boy's parents couldn't handle the loss and got divorced. He was their only child."

Her eyes misted as I slipped my notebook into my pocket.

"Thank you," I said. "You were a wonderful child, so brave. You still are." We hugged. She smelled like baby powder and Spearmint chewing gum.

"You be careful," she said. "They thought nobody remembered, that it was over. Now they're all hinky again, calling Cubby, fighting with each other, and talking 'bout you." There was genuine concern in her eyes. She checked her watch. "My husband is real close to my brother and my cousin. He wouldn't be happy if he knew I was here."

"Is there any good time for me to call you?"

She shook her head emphatically. "Between the answer machine, caller ID, and the kids who might pick up the phone. . . . No. Besides, there's nothing else I can say."

"But what if I need to touch base with you?"

"If it's urgent and you really need to reach me, I drive my oldest to school, first grade at Banyan Elementary, drop her off at seven-thirty every morning. I drive a beige Hyundai. I always get out and watch until she's inside the building."

I jotted that down.

I called the office on the way to police headquarters.

The news was not great. The hospital had admitted Ryan for tests. He sounded weak but chipper, when I got through to him. He was worried.

"Don't let anybody else use my desk, Britt. They'll mess it up and I won't be able to find anything. Or my chair; don't let them fool around with my chair. I finally got it adjusted perfectly. And would you check my mailbox for messages?"

I promised. "What do the doctors say?"

"Not much, just that my blood count is low. They're doing more tests tomorrow."

"You're anemic," I said. "That explains everything. You don't eat right, you don't get enough sleep. That's why you're anemic. Want me to call your folks?"

"Naw, I don't want to worry them. Remember how upset they were when I was lost at sea?"

An assignment from Gretchen had turned into near

disaster when she sent Ryan to do a first-person account of what it was like to be a Cuban refugee adrift on a tiny raft in the shark-infested Florida Straits. The plan went awry; he was lost and presumed dead after a huge air and sea search—and came home a hero. Lottie and I met him at the airport. You never realize how much you cherish your friends until you think they're gone.

We said goodbye as I parked outside police headquarters.

Craig Burch and Sam Stone looked startled. "How the hell did you get in here without an escort?" Burch asked.

"Everybody knows I'm on the story," I said. "They're so used to seeing me now, I'm like a piece of the furniture."

"Don't count on it," Burch said. "Thanks to you we're back on Riley's shit list. What the *hell* have you been doing?"

"Helping you," I said, put off by his attitude. "Wait till you hear the latest."

He rolled his eyes at Stone. "Do we need your help? Did Custer need more Indians?"

"What's wrong now?" I asked impatiently. His foul mood was bringing me down. "If you recall, you're the guys who asked me to do a little legwork."

"Heather Chance gave me a call." He glared at me sternly as though I were an errant child.

"So?" I shrugged, trying to keep the annoyance out of my voice. "She promised not to make a pest of herself this time."

He and Stone exchanged baleful looks. "Right. Unfortunately, I wasn't here, so she asked to talk to my supervisor, to thank her for reopening the case."

"Damn." I dropped into the chair beside his desk. "She didn't shoot the poor woman down, did she?"

"No way. Riley's too smart for that. She just said, 'You're welcome,' and then blindsided me when I walked in the door. Didn't know what hit me."

"Where is she?" I stole a guilty glance over my shoulder. Her office looked dark.

"Slammed out of here ten minutes ago. Think I'd be standing here talking to you if she was around?"

"Sorry," I said. "But I have something that will make you boys feel better fast."

"What, you pushing Prozac?" Stone said.

"Maybe she's getting outa town, way outa town," Burch said. "Becoming a foreign correspondent."

"Not funny, when I've got the cure for what ails you," I said. "A witness."

Their faces changed as I filled them in, without using Shelby's name.

"She's scared, afraid to talk to you. But she can confirm a lot of things."

"Did she say where they got the gun?" Stone asked eagerly.

"B and E of a house. Thought it went down in Miami Shores four days or so before that Christmas Eve."

"Excellent," he said. "Miami Shores has only about ten thousand population. Can't be many guns taken in burglaries there during that week. Let's just hope the gun was legal and the victim reported it. If we can locate the police report, get the serial number, we can see if it's surfaced anywhere since. Might still be out there, recoverable. If your witness can put it in their hands that night—we might have something to run with."

"She was only a little kid at the time," I said. "I'm not sure if she can ever be persuaded to testify, but she might. If not, it might give you enough to flip one of the others."

"How come this witness never spoke up before?" Burch asked.

"She's grown now, a mother herself. Her conscience has been bothering her."

"Funny how people suddenly discover their conscience," he said, "once they have kids."

"She's also depressed, apprehensive about nine-eleven and the war."

"Who isn't?" Stone said.

"How nice of our legal system back then to turn Mad Dog loose on the community for the holidays," Burch said. "Merry Christmas, Miami."

"Yup, sent him home angry, hopped up on teenage testosterone, and out of control," Stone said.

"Sounds like he's the shooter," I said. Now that Riley knew, I asked them, did we still need to withhold the information that Coney was a suspect? "I can use it in my next story," I said.

Burch shrugged. "Riley's gonna make us miserable anyway. Why the hell not?"

"Way to go," Stone said. "She'll take the bows when we close it."

Visiting hours were over by the time I found Ryan's hospital room. His roommate, an elderly man, was dozing, but Ryan was awake, halfheartedly watching talking heads dissect gloomy news on CNN. He looked tired but seemed happy to see me.

He flicked off the TV. "What a weird war," he said. "Bam! Boom! Bombs away, take that. Now, here's some lunch."

He felt better, he said, but still didn't know when he could go home. I kissed his cheek and delivered his mail, along with a stack of magazines I'd picked up at a newsstand on the way, *Esquire, Time,* and *Playboy.* "Thought you might want something to read," I said, "or pictures to look at."

"You should see some of the nurses here," he said, with a low whistle. "I love nurses: their white uniforms, all starchy and clean, and those little white squeaky shoes. This place is full of them."

"Not surprising," I said, "since this is a hospital."

Lottie, Villanueva, and Howie Janowitz had visited earlier. Lottie had brought cheerful sunflowers in a tall blue vase and a bakery box of chocolate chip cookies.

A big shiny-green plant from the paper had a card signed *From the Newsroom.* And there was a giant fruit basket filled with gourmet biscuits, sausages, and cheese—from the firefighters union, Ryan sheepishly admitted.

"I'm big with the fire department," he said. "Their PIO called to say they entered my story in a national contest."

I helped myself to an apple. "You mind?"

"Naw, guess you're entitled, since you actually wrote it. But hands off the chocolate-chip cookies."

He was wan but smiling when I left, enthusiastic

about a pretty young nurse who'd popped in to say I had to leave. She'd promised to look in on him again before her shift ended.

"She's so cute," he whispered, after she left. "Single, too. I think she likes me."

"Who wouldn't?" I said.

I drove home listening to the chatter on my police scanner and wondering why young Andre Coney had wept and punched walls in apparent rage and frustration after the crime. Did he actually have a conscience as a lad? His later record reflected no such hint. Perhaps it was fear. The possibility of a homicide rap will give even hard-core adult criminals bad cases of the heebie-jeebies. Maybe he was afraid the missing murder weapon would resurface, leading police to him. Or was it something else? Most of all I thought about the little girl Shelby Fountain had been, the woman she had become, and how life can be so damn hard for good people trying to do the right thing.

14

Lottie sashayed down the hall, a stack of photos in her hand, as I checked my mail next morning.

"What are you doing?" she demanded. "Nobody opens their mail anymore, not without gloves and a space suit."

"I do. I wouldn't miss my crank mail for the world," I said. "I just called the hospital. A stranger visiting the patient in the next bed answered and said Ryan had been wheeled away for more tests. Have you talked to him today?"

"Yup," she said. "He's in love. Hope nurse Nancy don't break his heart."

"Let's treat them to dinner at his favorite place when he gets out," I said. "Think she'll come?"

"Sure. I'm up for that," she said. "I just wish they'd

quit messing with him and let him go home before he catches something. Hospitals are full of sick people. You know doctors, they're like policemen; no bad situation they can't make worse."

"For sure," I said. "It sounds like they're running every test in the book. CYA, I guess. Scared of being sued if they miss something."

She pulled up a chair and began to spread out her photos. "Hell-all-Friday, Britt, why didn't you tell me Sunny had cheekbones to die for? Did you know her mother modeled? And guess who showed up during the shoot? Detective Pete Nazario, scampering around underfoot like a lovesick Chihuahua."

"Sunny Hartley?" I blinked. "You shot Sunny's picture?"

"Yup. Not for our piece, for the Lively Arts section on Sunday. She's hot. Thought you knew."

I didn't. She read me the art critic's lead:

"The Miami art scene, once a cultural wasteland, is now alive with hot young emerging artists."

She raised an eyebrow.

"He's featuring Ten to Watch, the top ten twenty- and thirty-something artists," she said. "Whole package is gonna run in color on the front of the Arts and Entertainment section. Sunny's near the top of the list. Her first big show is about to open at a South Beach gallery.

"Sorta camera-shy at first," she said, "but loosened right up once we started discussing her work."

"She never said a thing about it," I said, vaguely troubled. The pictures were stunning. Sunny, pensive and sophisticated, posing with her cold stone statues, her hair loose, strong body lithe and graceful.

"Ain't she a natural?" Lottie said, peering over my shoulder.

"You can make anybody look good," I murmured.

"Sure don't hurt to start with a face like that. Most young artists would kill to get this kind of exposure. This'll be a surefire career booster. Big-time."

"Did you talk about the case?"

"Nope. The assignment had nothing to do with it. Didn't want to bring it up unless she did. Don't even know if she knows I know."

Sunny, I thought, surprising as usual. "What was Nazario doing there?"

"Helping out with the lights, equipment, and all. But he's definitely got eyes for her. Sparks flying, hormones jumping. Ain't love grand?"

Later in the day, a judge refused again to reduce bond for Hector Gomez, the shopkeeper—in part, I was sure, because the Reverend Earl Wright led raucous demonstrators in a noisy protest outside, then filled every seat in the courtroom.

Andy Maguire was off, so I covered it. The defendant, in a rumpled oversized jail uniform, gave me a hopeful sad-eyed nod as he scanned the gallery for a friendly face. His wife, a small round woman, caught up with me in the corridor outside.

"Hector talked to you. You saw him," she pleaded. "Please tell them he never meant to hurt nobody. Tell them my husband is not a bad man."

"I'm sure he isn't," I said. "Have the public defender, your lawyer, check out the story in tomorrow's paper. There will be some details on the dead man's character."

Her eyes brightened. "Then, you think, they will let Hector come home?"

I sighed. "I don't know." Probably not, I thought. "But your lawyer might find it interesting." I told her not to worry, easy for me to say, then watched her walk the gauntlet alone, past the angry, shouting protestors outside.

I wrote the story identifying the dead burglar electrocuted in Gomez's shop as a suspect under investigation in the old Christmas Eve rape and murder.

I already had a quote from Heather Chance, so I called Sean Chance as well. His new wife answered. She insisted on knowing my business with her husband before letting me talk to him.

"It's in reference to a news story I'm working on," I said.

"What story?" she demanded, children playing noisily in the background.

Simply curious or jealous? I wondered. Unsure how much she knew about the old case, or how she might react, I said I preferred to tell him.

"What story?" she repeated.

"A follow-up on something from years ago," I said lightly.

A child shrieked, then began to howl.

"Sean! Sean!" the woman shouted. "Sean! Are you

deaf? Why in hell is Danny crying again? Pick him up! Now! Can't you see I'm on the phone? Would it kill you to lift a finger for a change?"

Maybe raising a young trophy wife along with a second family isn't such a barrel of fun after all, I thought.

"Now," she snapped irritably, "just what is it you want to talk to my husband about?"

I gave up. "His son's murder," I said crisply.

She put him on.

He took the news in stride, as though Ricky's murder were a remote if sad historic event from some distant lifetime. "It's a shock to have it come up again after all this time," he said softly. The noted architect added that he hoped justice would at long last be served.

I had heard the unmistakable click of an extension gently lifted as we spoke, so I mentioned that I'd already met the boy's mother.

"How is Heather?" he asked.

"Fine," I said maliciously. "Absolutely wonderful, and so happy to hear the news."

I called Cubby Wells next, but he didn't pick up his phone.

"Just wanted to let you know," I told his answering machine, "that you might be interested in a story running in tomorrow's paper." I left my number.

I also called the Reverend Earl Wright for comment on the judge's refusal to reduce Gomez's bond.

"I applaud his just decision," he boomed. "An eye for an eye. That man took a life."

"Would that apply to Mr. Coney too," I asked, "since he's now identified as a murder suspect?"

"I don't believe corrupt lies designed to deliberately

malign the dead, who are unable to defend themselves or their reputations."

At least the man was consistently inconsistent.

I turned in the story, then swung by the hospital to see Ryan. His face lit up when I walked in. He put down the black-and-white composition book he'd been scribbling in and happily reported that he had a Saturday-night date with nurse Nancy.

"So you know when you're going home?"

"Not yet"—he shrugged—"but I'll surely be released by then. I feel a lot better," he said, eyes alight. "I've been working on my poetry. You know how I always complain that I don't have time."

With his curly chestnut-colored hair and those big soft brown eyes with lashes any woman would kill for, Ryan did look like the young Lord Byron.

I called Sunny's number on the way home to tell her about the story in the morning paper. No answer. I detoured to North Beach, muttering under my breath. My knocking must have disturbed the musician upstairs. Barefoot and wearing baggy shorts, he padded halfway down, leaned over the banister to check me out, and then retreated without a word. What was that all about? I wondered.

Sunny eventually heard me, eyeballed me through the peephole, and opened the door. The process took longer and involved a lot more hardware than I remembered.

"Have you beefed up security?"

She nodded.

Did that explain the hammer in her hand, or was I

interrupting her work again? She scrutinized the lobby, then locked up behind me.

"There was a prowler," she said casually.

"What do you mean?" I said, alarmed. "What happened?"

She shrugged. "Someone tried to break in the other night."

"Are you sure?" I said.

She appeared calm, but she left the formidable hammer on a table near the door before leading me back through her high-ceilinged studio into the kitchen-living area of her suddenly shadowy and cavernous apartment.

"They picked the dead bolt," she said, "at two A.M. I had just finished work, happened to be in the room stretching, and saw the door inch open. The security chain caught it. It was weird. I called out, and when no one answered I rushed to slam it and then pushed a chair in front of it."

"Did you see who it was?"

She shook her head. "But next morning I found a half dozen burnt-out matches and cigarette butts in the lobby, as though someone had been waiting or watching. Maybe they thought nobody was home."

"Why didn't you call Sergeant Burch or me?"

"Why should I?" She looked puzzled.

"Did you tell Detective Nazario?"

"No. Why would I?"

"Did you call the Miami Beach police?"

This time she nodded. "I filed a report."

"Did you tell them about the old case?"

"No. This had nothing to do with that."

"But, Sunny, what if it did?"

"That wouldn't make sense. I've done nothing to provoke it. I'm not working with the police. Nobody from the past has any reason to stalk me."

She chose a Golden Delicious apple from a fruit bowl and offered it to me. Stomach churning, I declined.

She sat at her little dining table and took a bite.

"Stalk?" I took the stool across from her. "Has anything else been going on?"

She chewed, then swallowed. "I thought somebody was following me the other night."

"Oh, swell," I said. "Did the Beach cops take the matches and cigarette butts as evidence?"

She blinked. The idea never seemed to have occurred either to her, or to them.

"They didn't seem that interested," she said.

"Where are they?"

"I swept them up and threw them out."

"Not a good move, Sunny." I threw my hands up in exasperation.

She put the apple down and leaned across the table. "It was probably just some crackhead, or drunk, or homeless person looking for a place to crash." Was this to reassure me or herself? "This town is crawling with spaced-out weirdos, partygoers, and tourists on the make. Maybe one followed me home from the beach the other night. Sometimes after working long hours, I go for an ocean swim, just to stretch out in that warm salt water. It's wonderful for knotted muscles."

"At night? Sunny, don't tell me you do that at night with no lifeguards on duty."

"No chance of sun damage," she said lightheartedly. "My mother would be so proud."

I was not amused.

"Look," she acknowledged, "this did rattle me a bit. Had I been in the freezer, or asleep, I wouldn't have seen the door opening and they might have gotten in. But it's okay now." She smiled. "I kickbox, I stay alert. Jimmy, my upstairs neighbor, is keeping an eye on things. And now that the police know, I'm sure they're watching the building."

Like hell, I thought. I filled her in on the Gomez-Coney story in the morning paper.

"No more night swimming in the ocean, please," I said. "At least not until we know what's going on."

"This sort of thing, a burglar, a peeping Tom, happens to every woman," she said. "I'm lucky they didn't get in, and now they won't because I've taken extra precautions." Her eyes caught on mine. "I'm not paranoid, Britt. I was. After Ricky was killed I thought I'd never feel secure again. When your trust in human beings is destroyed, you're afraid of everything, even being in an elevator with a stranger or alone at a bus stop. You're afraid to pass an ordinary-looking guy on the street. I fought those fears. I took self-defense courses. I stay in shape. Fear will never rule my life again. I'm fine now. Although," she said, averting her eyes, "you never get completely over some things."

"Are you seeing Pete Nazario?"

She turned her deaf ear to me.

I touched her hand, forcing her to look at me.

"Look," I said, "I don't mean to invade your privacy, but—"

"I'm still trying to work through some things," she whispered. "I don't date a lot."

"Why?"

"Well, the first one certainly didn't end well, did it?"

"Look, Pete's a good person. I think he's interested in you, and I'm sure he'd want to know about this—"

"He *is* interested," she said flatly, "but is it a prurient interest because he knows I was a rape victim, or is it me he's attracted to?"

"In his line of work, victims are a dime a dozen. If he had a thing for them, he'd be a very busy boy. He strikes me as a pretty decent guy."

She sighed. "It would probably be best for me to tell every man I meet up front that I had a bad experience and can't deal with aggressive men. But I'm not comfortable doing that. My problem in a relationship is that the man has to be very, very gentle, you know what I mean?

"Physically," she said shyly. "I have to come on to them. It's awkward. So I usually find it easier not to start anything." She buried her face in her hands, clearly uncomfortable. "It would help if he knew that."

Oh, hell, I thought. Who am I now, Ann Landers?

"If you find him attractive, Sunny, see him. Have some fun. I thought you two might be hitting it off. With all the creepy stuff going on right now, it can't hurt to have a cop around. They're great deterrents. I used to date a cop," I said wistfully. "They really know how to make a woman feel secure."

"Because they're heavily armed?" she asked wryly.

We both laughed.

"You know," she said, gazing out toward the dining room and the headlights streaming past the big one-way picture windows, "one thing that always bothered me was that Ricky and I had Christmas gifts for each other, just little tokens. He wanted to open them before we went to the boat parade. I insisted we wait until later. I'll always regret that I never got to give him his present."

"What was it?"

She shrugged. "A book, *Leaves of Grass* by Walt Whitman. It had a bookmark, a note Ricky had sent me in sixth grade. I had it laminated. Silly, isn't it," she said, "how little things stay with you?"

"No, not silly at all. I guess the moral is *carpe diem,* seize the moment. Never let it get away. My friend Lottie, the photographer, always says that. I hear you two have met. The pictures are great, by the way. But now I wonder if you should reconsider having your name and picture in the newspaper."

"No," she said quickly. "I thought about it, Britt. The gallery owner says it's a rare and golden opportunity for my work to be recognized. The opening is this week. I've worked so hard for so long. She said it would be professional suicide not to cooperate with an art critic who's eager to praise my work."

Made sense to me.

Outside, as I unlocked the T-Bird, a car passed slowly. I turned to look. One taillight was out, but I couldn't see the tag number, make, or model. Did that same car drive by slowly as I was saying good night to Sunny a few minutes ago? It's surely not the only car with a burned-out taillight, I thought.

Still, I called the squad as I pulled into traffic.

Nazario answered.

"Just the guy I need to talk to."

"I've been thinking about you too, *chica.* I know you were being truthful when you first described Sunny to me. What I don't understand is how you could see her like that."

"Well, I've been wondering about you too, *amigo.* That manatee story? Was that rescue mission to Jamaica for real or did you make it up?"

"Every word, I swear, is true." He sounded offended. *"Te lo juro por mi madre."*

"You're impressive, Pete. Now please tell me you've been playing bodyguard, protecting Sunny by lurking in her lobby smoking cigarettes and leaving burned-out matches."

"*¿Qué?* What are you talking about?"

"I was afraid you'd say that."

His immediate reaction was to want to race right over there.

"Wait," I said. "She likes you. But you can't be macho, aggressive, and try to sweep her off her feet. No chest pounding. No Tarzan yells." I sighed. "There's something you should know. . . ."

15

I felt numb and powerless when I got home, as though shadowed by a sense of inevitable disaster. Was it Mad Dog's soulless stare? Sunny alone in that cavernous place with only a flaky upstairs neighbor for protection? Ryan in his hospital bed? Or was I simply overcome by the great depressed, stressed-out, and anxiety-ridden American malaise? Even the wind stirring in the Christmas palms breathed ominous murmurs. The hibiscus bushes, bright by day with their sweet and sunny open-faced blooms, swayed menacingly in the shadows, perfect cover for evildoers.

What if all this was not my imagination? My Aunt Odalys insists that I was born with a gift—or curse—*tengo un presentimiento,* the sixth sense that leads me into predestined paths. I believe her at times, when something or someone, spiritual or supernatural, perhaps my father, helps guide me through the minefields surrounding the truth. But my rational self knows that truth is a moving target found only through hard work, persistence, and rare strokes of luck.

Even Bitsy appeared overwrought and agitated, and Billy Boots had emptied a high shelf of books, now strewn across the carpet like the work of a mischievous poltergeist. He had also clawed Darryl's latest finger painting off the magnet mounts on my refrigerator door.

"Why were you fighting?" I demanded, picking up books. "What's been going on here?"

But dog and cat kept their secrets.

Lacking appetite, I sipped some soup and a glass of wine as I prepared for bed. A question nagged until I put down my toothbrush to call the squad, hoping to catch Nazario again.

Burch answered.

"What are you doing there so late?"

"You're starting to sound like my wife," he said glumly. "Stone had Miami Shores dig their old burglary reports out of the warehouse. Showed three guns stolen that week. One from a liquor store, two from private homes. One fits the description.

"Belonged to a judge. Bought it for his wife to use for home protection. They took visiting grandkids up to Disney World for a coupla days before Christmas. The house was ransacked while they were gone. Thief took the gun, cash, jewelry, and a VCR. No prints at the scene. The pawn-shop detail recovered a wristwatch. No sign of the gun. Stone's running the serial number to see if it ever resurfaced.

"I'm rereading the case files now. Trying to match up the cross-references of all the witnesses, suspects, people we interviewed, to see if any name we have now ever appeared then. I don't want to miss anything this time."

"I have a question," I said, curling up in my favorite chair. "Do the killers know Sunny's name? The *News* never published it, but did it appear anywhere else in the media, in any court proceedings or public venues? Did the kidnappers take her ID that night? Did she even have one? Sixteen years old, on a family outing, maybe she didn't even carry ID."

He cursed when I told him why I asked. "She shoulda called."

"She reported it to the Beach cops. She's okay. The prowler incident seems to spook me more than it does her."

"A tough kid, always was," he muttered. I heard him shuffling papers. "Her name was never reported anywhere, far as I know. But you know how news travels, same way you always find out things you're not supposed to know. People at the hospital knew who she was; so did her neighbors, her relatives. The nine hundred kids in their high school hadda know she was the girl with Ricky Lee Chance when he was killed. Her dad's a prominent doctor; I'm sure his patients, employees, and associates all knew the injured girl in the case was his daughter. Then there's the boy's family. People talk.

"Here," he finally said, "I've got it. Asked in my initial interview. She was fuzzy then, didn't remember if her wallet and student ID card were in the little purse she carried that night. Probably were, cuz we didn't find them when we checked the house, her room, or her school locker.

"Never found her purse or Ricky's wallet. He had it when he paid for the ice cream."

"Serial-killer types like souvenirs," I said, thinking aloud. "But these guys probably just took out the money and tossed them, like most two-bit thieves afraid of being caught with the goods."

He sighed. "We searched every inch of roadside, every garbage can, every Dumpster."

"If they threw them in the water somewhere, the rain that night must have swept them away. I'll try to reach the witness who saw them with the gun later. Maybe she also saw some of the victims' belongings. I just want some assurance that none of the suspects are looking her up now. God, that would be awful."

"Damn straight. But guys like them probably didn't care what her name was as long as they got what they wanted. It's not like she had checks or credit cards they could use."

"What about the car Ricky drove?" I said. "It belonged to her dad and probably had papers with the owner's name in the glove compartment. Were the suspects ever inside it?"

"Not that we know. We processed it, found nothing. 'Course the outside got rained on before we found it. The only interior prints we came up with belonged to Ricky, Sunny, and her family. Nothing missing from the car. No evidence of a struggle."

"Wonder why they didn't take it?" I said idly. "Never knew a teenage jitterbug who'd miss the chance to steal a car. What was it?"

"Five-year-old silver Volvo, nothing flashy. It was Maureen's ride, the mother's. Her husband took the *Sunshine Princess* up to the parade staging area earlier, then caught a ride back. They used the Volvo that night because it was roomy. Maybe the killers didn't see it. They saw what they wanted, and it wasn't a car."

Sunny, I thought, with a chill.

"To them she was probably just another victim," he said. "If they ever knew her name, they probably forgot it."

"But what if they always knew it and just never had a reason to look her up before now? Her picture, big and in color, will be in Sunday's paper." I told him about the story of the gallery opening and how important it was to her. "She can't hide," I said. "It wouldn't be fair to expect her to."

He agreed. "Those scumbags probably don't read the *News,* and if they do I'm betting it's not the section on art."

I hoped he was right.

The uneasiness invaded my sleep. This time the dark cloud billowing behind the woman in the blue sweater was populated by stone figures alive and menacing. Trying to warn her, I could not make her listen. She could not, would not, hear me.

Billy Boots hurtled off the bed when the phone

rang. It seemed to be part of my troubled dream. But by the third ring, I was awake and dazed.

"Britt." The voice sounded terrified. "Sorry to bother you this late, but I'm scared. I don't know what—"

"It's all right, Sunny," I mumbled, legs already off the side of the bed, bare feet hitting the floor. The glowing numbers on my bedside clock read 3:46 A.M.

"Britt, Britt, wake up! It's Onnie. Britt?"

"Oh, right. Onnie. I was dreaming. What's wrong?"

"Edgar. He's been calling and calling. He's threatening to take Darryl."

Edgar, her abusive ex-husband, was in state prison, serving a long term for assaulting a police officer.

"There's call waiting," she whispered, at a series of persistent clicks. "It's him again."

"They let him make threatening calls from prison in the middle of the night?"

"No, he's out! Here! In Miami! Why do you think I'm so upset?"

"Did he escape?" I pulled on a cotton robe and licked my dry lips.

"No. They released him."

"How could they? That's impossible."

"I saw him, Britt." Her voice rang with desperation. "He was here! I called the police. I was so grateful when they came. But they checked him out and let him go! They said he's legally free. There's nothing they can do."

A family court judge had terminated Edgar's parental rights. Onnie had divorced him, moved, left no forwarding address, and had a new unlisted telephone number. "How the heck did he find you?"

"Had to be his family." Choked up, she stumbled over the words. "His mother, his sister. They begged to see Darryl, said he shouldn't be deprived of the grandmother who loved him. She swore on the Bible she'd never tell Edgar where we were. It had to be her."

"Where is he now? Have you seen him since the police left?"

"No," she said, "but he's called three times. Even madder because I called the police. He was already furious about the divorce. He says we're still married, he wants his son—"

"Damn! Why do these things always happen at night when you can't call a judge and find out what the hell's going on?"

"I'm scared, Britt. He's going to do something terrible."

"Okay." I brushed my hair out of my face, beginning to think clearly. "Grab a few things, just toothbrushes and a change of clothes, and come here. You and Darryl can stay with me until we straighten this out. Bring your cell phone and if you even see him anywhere along the way, dial 911."

"Thanks, Britt, but I don't know. It's almost four already. Darryl's finally asleep. I hate to wake him up to run away like thieves in the night. I can't let Edgar drive us out of our home."

"Want me to come there?" I padded into the kitchen and began making coffee. "I can be there in twenty."

"Seeing you could make Edgar worse," she said uncertainly. "He blames you for helping me. You know what he's like."

"It'll be okay." I tried to sound confident. "If he's threatened you, we'll talk to his parole officer in the morning. They'll slam his bad ass back behind bars so fast his teeth will rattle."

"Think so?"

"Know so. Look, don't worry. If you feel secure in your apartment, maybe it *is* better just to batten down the hatches and sit tight instead of driving over here in the dark with him on the loose."

"I knew my life was too good to last." She groaned. "It's been so wonderful without him."

There was no going back to sleep.

At 7:30 A.M., Mommy-mobiles, school buses, and occasional dads were dropping the kiddies off at Banyan Elementary. Youngsters played and ran, shouted and laughed, lugged school books and lunches. Mothers were rushing after youngsters who'd forgotten their homework, snatching quick kisses on the run.

I watched morosely. Once you share a child with someone, I thought, you are irrevocably tied to that person forever, no matter what, for better or worse.

I spotted Shelby. Her little girl wore a tiny blue scarf and clung obediently to her mother's hand. She loosened up, tried to let go when she saw her friends. But Shelby walked her right to the door, then watched until the child disappeared into the building.

"Hi," I said, and smiled.

Startled to see me, she scanned the street to see if anyone was watching. "I can't talk to you anymore," she said quietly.

"All I wanted to ask was—"

She unlocked her car door and slid into the driver's seat.

"Wait a minute," I said.

Her window half down, she pretended to be giving me directions, pointing somewhere off down the street. She looked scared.

"That night," I said quickly. "Did you see a wallet or a girl's purse, anything they might have taken from someone?"

She looked terrified. "No."

She turned the key in the ignition and the car lurched away from the curb.

And I thought she'd begun to like me.

I picked up a sack of Krispy Kreme doughnuts and went to Onnie's. She had just returned from taking Darryl to kindergarten and was dressed for the office.

"Think it was safe to send him today?" I asked.

"Routine is important," she said stubbornly, pouring me a cup of coffee. "Especially to children from broken homes. I spoke to his teacher and the principal."

I arranged the jelly doughnuts on a plate. She'd also spoken to her lawyer.

He called back as we ate.

She asked questions, took notes, then rejoined me, face drawn.

"There is no parole officer," she said simply. "He finished his sentence and was simply released."

"But I thought he still had a minimum of two more years to do."

"So did I. I counted on it. The lawyer said it's some

sort of new early release program they implemented because of prison overcrowding."

"This could be a mistake. I'll look into it," I said. "Meanwhile, if he shows up and threatens you, call the police. He just got out of prison. I'm sure he doesn't want to go back."

"You know what he's like, Britt."

"Ask for a restraining order."

"A piece of paper won't stop a bullet," she said grimly.

We both knew she was right. I unclipped a small red leather-covered canister from inside my purse flap and handed it to her. "Here, take this for now. It's Sabre Red, the pepper spray the police use. Aim straight for the eyes," I told her, as she gingerly examined it. "It should drop him right there. Then don't wait around. Later this afternoon we can go out to the Tamiami Range and Gun Shop. Pick out a handgun and I'll teach you how to use it. I saw a nice airweight Smith and Wesson there last week. Then we'll start the paperwork for your concealed weapons permit. The process takes several weeks. You'll have to be fingerprinted—"

"But I'd hate having a gun in the house," she whispered. "With Darryl."

"I know, but the cavalry doesn't always arrive in time. In real life, it almost never does. You know that. You have to protect yourself. We all have to be responsible for our own safety. Especially now. It's the American way, Onnie."

I stopped at police headquarters and beat feet up to Homicide, hoping Riley wasn't in yet. Burch's expression as I stepped off the elevator told me I'd miscalculated.

He needed a shave and looked terrible, as though he hadn't slept. "We've got a problem," he said.

I didn't like the direction this day was taking.

"Riley?" I asked.

"Among others."

My heart sank.

"Start with the state attorney," he said. "Evidently Wayman Andrews from Channel Seven saw your story this morning and woke him up with an early call to ask when arrests were expected in the Chance case. The state attorney knew nothing. He hates it when that happens. Makes him look like the horse's ass he is. Then he read your story, spit up his coffee, and called the chief in a snit. Says his office should've been briefed and a prosecutor assigned. Which, of course, is SOP. He's hot to have his major-crimes chief take a statement from Sunny ASAP. He wanted to know who she's identified in a lineup. The chief, of course, knew nothing. And he hates it when that happens. So he called Riley in early to read *her* the riot act. Guess who Riley dumped on? Shit rolls downhill. And *I* hate it when that happens."

"Damn. It's all because the state attorney's running for re-election against real opposition this time."

"Yep. His office hasn't won a conviction in any real high-profile case lately. Emotions run high in this one: the Christmas season, innocent kids. We blow it and his opponent can throw it right back at him."

I caught the faint smell of liquor.

"Craig, are you okay? You make it home last night?"

He sighed. "Shit. I knew I forgot to do something."

"That's not funny," I muttered.

"Montero! Over here." K. C. Riley had opened her door.

She said nothing until we were inside her office. She sat, rigid, behind her desk, regarding me with contempt.

"I warned you," she said softly. "I offered my complete cooperation. But you fucked up, as usual."

She wore no makeup, eyes red-rimmed, as though she hadn't slept. Did anyone sleep well anymore?

"You must be thrilled," she said.

"What do you mean?"

"Don't pull that Miss Innocent shit with me. What you're doing to that girl is unconscionable." She pointed an accusatory finger at me. "And it's all because you have a beef with me."

"No, I've never had a beef with you, lieutenant. Ever. I think you're too tough on people at times, but I always thought we were on the same side. We care about the same things."

She reacted, eyes startled, and I realized what she was thinking.

"Justice is what I was talking about."

"Thanks for clarifying that point," she said sarcastically. "But it's not justice. What you care about is selling newspapers and your own personal interests. You don't give a shit about these detectives, this city, or the cases we might close. We're under the gun, facing severe budget cuts and commanders who couldn't care less about old cases that didn't go down on their watch. It's survival. As we speak, there's a move on to eliminate the squad and reassign these detectives.

"I'm working my ass off," she said, a tremor in her voice, "to save the squad, to convince the chief it's worth keeping in the budget. Numbers tell the story. I need stats. We need to close some cases. Fast. To spin our wheels on hopeless causes right now could be fatal. There is the human factor. We have people who beg us to take on a case, people who will do anything. And then there's the Richard Chance case. One possible perpetrator already dead, another in prison. No physical evidence, and a surviving victim who, even if she was not reluctant, probably can't remember anything of value anyway. That girl is lucky to be alive and walking and talking. She went through hell. The case would require her total cooperation. Old wounds reopened, old horrors relived. Her life would be interrupted again. All for nothing, if we fail. And should we succeed, Sunny's participation will be required not at one trial but perhaps three or four. How nice for her."

Her eyes glittered with anger.

"Look, I didn't mean to cause any grief to Sunny, the squad, or you."

Her expression was cynical. "Don't think for a moment that I don't know exactly why you did it. Your personal feelings are hurting innocent people. It's not fair."

"That isn't true."

She raised her hand to stop me. "You have to live with it."

"If you're inferring that we have a conflict in our private lives," I said indignantly, "you're wrong."

"Get out of my office. Don't let me see you in here again," she said, as though the sight of me was distasteful. "And stay away from my detectives. In the future, get your information through PIO."

"But I'm still working on the magazine piece—"

"I've had calls from members of both victims' families, some of whom are unhappy about your tactics, although not as unhappy as the state attorney, the chief, and my immediate superiors. You've been so very busy," she said sweetly. "I'm sure you have quite enough material for your story. Now get out."

She looked pale under her tan.

I rose to leave, knees shaky. Her cold rage was ominous. I would have preferred curses, shouts, and hurled objects. The chief would get over it the next time he liked a story I wrote. Ditto the state attorney—or, hopefully, his successor. But not K. C. Riley.

"By the way, Britt," she said. "the state attorney has called me twice this morning. He went ballistic when I told him that Sunny Hartley has declined to view a lineup. He said she doesn't have that option. He plans to issue a subpoena that will force her to cooperate."

"Would he really do that?"

She regarded me coldly. "And more. He swears that if she continues to refuse, he'll arrest her for obstruction."

16

I called Burch from a cubicle in the public information office. "The state attorney has got to be bluffing," I said. "He'd look so insensitive. Punishing the victim would be a public relations disaster."

"He'd know how to turn it around," the detective said. "You've heard the man's Mr. Sincerity shtick a hundred times. He'll call a press conference to look pained and say that sometimes those of us who serve justice have to do things we don't like, but it's our job."

The same line cops always use when doing unpleasant things to you, I thought.

"He'll say his job is not only to prosecute but to protect the innocent: your sister, your grandmother, you. That taking four murderers off the street any way he can serves the greater public good. Voters eat it up. That's how he keeps getting elected. You know the guy.

He knows how to tell people to go to hell in a way that makes them look forward to the trip."

Burch was right. I'd heard the speech before. Boyishly handsome, with Kennedy hair and a silver tongue, our state attorney was a truly devious political animal.

"I'm sorry," I said.

"My own fault," Burch muttered.

"Do you hate me?"

"Hell, no. I'm a big boy. I can take as much heat as anybody can dish out. Riley may be pissed off, but she's got no choice. She can't pull us off the Chance case now."

As I eased out of the police station parking lot, an unmarked car maneuvered alongside.

"Hey, news lady!" the driver yelled. "I didn't get my paper this morning. What the hell happened?" It was Nazario.

"Sorry, my bicycle broke down."

"Where you headed?" he asked.

I shrugged. "Back to the paper."

"Coffee?"

"Sure."

"I'm meeting Stone."

We settled at our back-room table at La Esquina de Tejas.

He seemed congenial, considering the situation. I asked about Sunny.

"The girl's got it happening," he said.

Stone groaned as he joined us. "Nothing worse than a *julio* in love," he complained. "They never stop talking about it. Babababababah." His fingers gestured like a constantly moving mouth. "What on God's green earth makes you think you've got a shot at her?" he asked the Cuban detective.

"So far she hasn't decked me, dialed 911 or pulled a gun," Nazario said.

"Sounds like you're making real progress," Stone said.

"The girl's talented. Her show is about to open at an art gallery. She's got guts," Nazario said. "And she didn't need affirmative action to make something of herself." He winked at me. "Unlike some people I work with."

They'd been out talking to old witnesses in the Meadows case, they said. They knew nothing about a new state prison early-release plan.

Stone's cell phone rang and he began taking notes during an involved conversation while Nazario and I revisited his favorite topic.

"Sunny really isn't that much of a loner," he assured me. "She just feels out of place."

"So do I," I said glumly.

"So do a lot of us. I can relate." He shrugged. "I always felt left out as a kid. Sunny's gun-shy about men, love, and sex, but the right person could overcome that. Her problem is that she's uncomfortable with average people who don't know what brutal and ugly things can happen. She thinks they'd look at her differently if they knew what happened to her. Yet she's not comfortable among victims either, traumatized or obsessed people. She's one of a kind. What she needs is somebody who's also one of a kind. Somebody else who's sorta out of place, you know, missing something. They could fill each other's needs and be happy."

He means himself, I thought. He's fallen.

Stone snapped his phone shut. ""'Good news. Progress on the gun."

My heart beat faster.

"Okay," he said, reading from his notes. "Serial number R-009206. Manufactured in Hamden, Connecticut, August 24, 1982. Sent from the factory warehouse to a Knoxville, Tennessee, hardware distributor. Shipped to a retail outlet in North Miami Beach two weeks later. The first owner, the judge in Miami Shores, bought it for his wife on Valentine's Day, 1983. He had it until Coney stole it just before the murder. Three years after Ricky and Sunny were shot, it surfaced again, seized from a Miami robbery suspect. A jury acquitted him, and his lawyer filed a motion to return the weapon to his client. The judge granted it and the gun was released to the attorney, who kept it as part of his fee.

"But not for long. Two months later it was stolen from his office, probably by another client. The gun was found six months later in a dead man's hand after a drug-related shooting in El Portal. Lucky us. Miami-Dade police departments dump their confiscated firearms into the ocean seven miles offshore once a year—except for little El Portal, just north of here. In an effort to raise funds, they keep the best weapons to sell. And"—he flipped the page of his small notebook—"they sold this one"—he looked up and smiled—"to a police officer."

The missing murder weapon sought for all those years was owned by a cop.

"Who is he?" I asked.

"He *was* a Broward County sheriff's deputy," Stone said, "now deceased. Killed in an on-duty crash during a high-speed chase six years ago. His widow sold it. The new owner registered it, according to computer records. Guess I'll pay him a call."

"Where?" I asked. "Here in Miami?"

He nodded.

"Amazing how guns resurface," Nazario said. "As far as we know it's been stolen three times."

"Today," Stone said, "ballistics can compare every confiscated gun to all our open shooting cases in a matter of minutes. But back then they'd only run ballistics at the request of a detective who thought a particular weapon might be linked to one of his cases."

"If we find the gun," Nazario said, "we need the witness to put it in their hands that night." His questioning eyes held mine.

I promised I'd talk to her.

Burch, they said, planned to brief the state attorney later in the day. This news put him in a stronger position to delay prosecutorial pursuit of Sunny.

Everything might work out, I thought. Back at the office, I called my friend Debbie, a Department of Corrections spokeswoman in Tallahassee.

"What do you know about a new early-release program?" I asked. "There's a former prisoner—"

"You too?" She sounded harried. "Everybody's been calling about that one. In fact, I just went over it in detail with another reporter from your paper. A guy named Janowitz."

Sure enough, the story was on the news desk's budget.

To allay prison overcrowding, a federal judge had ordered that for every new inmate sentenced to prison, one had to be released. One in, one out. After the state had lost its appeal, hundreds of inmates had been released, with more to come.

A hell of a story.

I called Onnie to explain and make plans for later.

"I don't like guns, Britt. Guns have no eyes, no friends. You never know if they'll protect your life or take it."

We bickered about the pros and cons of gun ownership, as newsroom staffers began to cluster around Gretchen's terminal at the city desk. The paper must have won an award, I thought. But no one was smiling. The faces were somber, shocked.

I told Onnie I'd call her back.

Lottie rushed to my desk as I hung up. Her face was flushed, tears in her eyes. "It's Ryan," she said. "He has leukemia."

17

It was the worst kind, according to our research in the library: hairy-cell leukemia.

Ryan was too young. Too special. Too good. We all echoed the same words.

We partied in his hospital room that night: Lottie, Janowitz, even Onnie. Others from the newsroom, the photo department, and the library brought books, cards, and copies of the paper. Ryan didn't look scared. He smiled a lot. He had taken voluminous notes while conferring with his doctors that afternoon. He had even seen the enemy, his own cells, under a microscope. He knew all his options and exhibited a reporter's keen curiosity about the illness, the possibilities, his prognosis, the treatments.

We put on a brave show. Reminded Ryan how he'd once been given up for lost at sea, yet survived. How he always landed on his feet. How he was tough, his doctors brilliant, the medications new and sophisticated; how he'd be swell. We even rolled the patient in the next bed over to join us. We told stories and jokes and laughed, as his phone rang, over and over. I'd brought a bottle of cognac. Nurse Nancy found us little paper cups, and we all drank. Even Ryan's doctor appeared and took a medicinal taste.

Ryan would start a course of treatment, injections of powerful medications, later in the week. We were cheerful, laughing and talking too loudly as we left.

We were all swell. Not until nearly halfway home, stopped at a traffic light, did I rest my forehead on the steering wheel and cry.

The light changed and horns blared. Gritting my teeth, I blew my nose, and at the next light I called the Cold Case Squad. Sniffing, I asked for Stone. "What happened? Did you get the gun?"

"You sound terrible, girl. You coming down with a cold?"

"No. I'm allergic—to bad news," I said. "That's why I called you. Give me some good news."

"Sorry to disappoint, but you better pop some antihistamine pills. The most recent owner says the gun was stolen out of his car three weeks ago."

"Oh, no! You're not serious. Did he report it?"

"Nope. Claims he didn't miss it at first. Forgot to take it out of the glove box when he left his car to be serviced. Didn't realize it was gone until a few days after he got the car back. Went back to his mechanic, who denied seeing it. He's a long-time customer of the guy and didn't want to make accusations until he was sure. Checked with his wife, searched his house, his garage. Said he kept hoping it would turn up."

I groaned.

"Sat down with the man and went back over his schedule, hour by hour, day by day. The car was never out of his control at any other time. His security system self-locks. Nobody else had his keys except the day it was serviced. The gun was there when he checked his service agreement the day before. I'm running checks on everybody employed at the garage. I'll rattle their cages in the morning."

"What are the chances . . . ?"

"We might still get lucky." He didn't sound optimistic.

I sighed as I parked, relieved to be home. I needed to sleep, to crash for a week, to wake up forgetting this day ever happened. A note hung on my door. What now? Had the building been condemned? I wondered bitterly.

"Please join us for tea or a glass of wine when you get home." I recognized my landlady's handwriting.

The Goldsteins are more than friends and always a comfort. Maybe they had somehow heard about Ryan.

I hesitated outside their door. Laughter and voices from inside signaled company. Happily married for sixty years, the woman is a dedicated matchmaker. What if the visitor was some man she wanted me to meet? Red-eyed, with cognac on my breath, I felt miserable and looked worse. I tiptoed away, as the curtains moved and someone peered out a front window.

"There she is now!" my landlady cried.

Too late.

"I thought I heard a car," she said. "So, you finally decided to come home."

I started to say I couldn't join them, but the words stalled in my throat as the door opened wide.

Major Kendall McDonald sat drinking coffee and eating her famous bundt cake.

I blinked as Mrs. Goldstein herded me inside.

"What are you doing here?"

"Visiting old friends." He smiled. "And waiting for you."

He had dropped by the night before as well, he said. Bitsy had barked, but I wasn't home. When I wasn't home tonight either, he intended to leave his card, but sharp-eyed Mrs. Goldstein had invited him in.

I drank a glass of Manischewitz and nibbled a piece of cake.

He looked wonderful, though a bit thinner in civilian clothes, his off-duty gun in his waistband. The only person on the planet I would have been happy to see that night.

Mrs. Goldstein was absolutely giddy and totally without subtlety. "It's wonderful to see you two together again," she said as we bade them good night.

"It is," he said. His hand lightly touched the small of my back.

"You should have called," I murmured, as she closed the door.

"There are some things I don't like to talk about on the telephone."

We kissed, soft and slow. Then I sighed, leaning against his chest, home at last, at least for the moment.

"I presume you're aware that Mrs. G is peering from behind the blinds," he said.

"I know," I murmured. "You're making her very happy. The woman lives for romance."

"Let's make her day," he said, and kissed me again.

I fumbled with my keys as I unlocked the door. Bitsy greeted McDonald with wild enthusiasm; Billy Boots stared from the sofa. "What brings you over to the Beach?" I asked.

"You." He took in the familiar room with pleasure, as though he felt at home.

"If it's about K. C. Riley," I said wearily, "she thinks—"

"I know. I told her it wasn't true. It's not like you."

"How awkward," I said.

"That's how it's always been with us," he said, "our jobs in the way, pushing us apart. We have to make it happen."

"Make what happen?"

"Us. I miss us." His silver-blue eyes were dead serious. "You and me. I did a lot of thinking, up in New York at Ground Zero and since I came back. It's time to decide what's really important and commit to it. If that's what you want."

I hugged him tighter. "You know how I feel."

"It's time, Britt, our time. Before either of us does something stupid. Life is uncertain. All I'm sure of is that I want to spend it with you. We can work out whatever happens."

He sat on my sofa, long legs stretched out in front of him. I curled up next to him.

"It's always been you, since the night we met," he said. "Remember?"

"Who could forget? Our eyes met across a blood-stained barroom floor the night the bartender at the Reno got shot."

"A great story for our grandchildren someday."

"But what about Riley? I thought you—"

"She knows. In fact, she told me that if it was right I should go for it."

"The woman hates me."

"No. I don't know why you two never hit it off. Kathy's a good friend, a stand-up woman in a tough high-stress job."

"I know," I said, feeling guilty.

We connected as though we had never been apart. I told him about Ryan. He told me what it had been like in New York.

"Working homicide for so long," he said, "I thought I'd seen everything, but to be there was unbelievable. Beams that were standing in the subway below the site were once part of the seventy-first floor of the World Trade Center. You would find a hand, a finger, or a foot and wonder if they belonged to a person whose picture you saw on a poster or somebody whose grieving family you met at a memorial. The anger, the helplessness, the devastation. So much in life seems insignificant now."

Later, as we clung to each other, he said, "Let's run away, Britt. Escape to one of the islands, maybe St. Thomas or Tortola. Just fly in for a few days. Get away from it all."

"When?" I stretched sleepily.

"I wish we could go now. But we're working on next year's budget."

"And I have this story," I said. "Let's do it as soon as your budget and my story are a wrap. We'll flee like fugitives. Travel light. No phones, no beepers, no deadlines."

"You and me, alone," he said.

"It sounds like heaven," I said wistfully.

We slept tangled in each other's arms.

He left at dawn to feed his own dog, a hound named Hooker, and prepare for another early budget meeting.

I luxuriated in bed, praying it wasn't all a dream. Eventually I stirred, showered, and dressed, loving the fact that life for me was about to change forever.

At the gallery in South Beach, a sturdy crew of workmen with heavy equipment was tackling the monumental task of installing Sunny's sculptures.

Sunny and the gallery owner, a middle-aged woman with platinum hair, black garments, and a tiny teacup of a dog that she wore like an accessory, were supervising placement of the pieces. Nazario was already there.

I felt giddy, my heart light. Everything looked and felt different. Love lifts you up. I even convinced myself that Ryan's diagnosis had to be a mistake. A snafu in the lab or a bad joke. Who could be sick on a day so full of Miami's glorious light?

Sunny looked serious. Stressed about the show, I assumed. I was wrong.

"Somebody vandalized the rental truck," she said

quietly, as soon as Nazario moved out of earshot. "We used it to move the smaller pieces yesterday. I parked it at the loading dock outside the dining room." She lowered her voice even more. "I sleep in there, Britt. I'm only half deaf and a light sleeper, but I didn't hear a thing."

"What happened?" I asked, thinking of her brother, Tyler. "Were the tires flattened?"

"Slashed to ribbons, all of them. Smashed all the windows with a pipe or something and cut into every surface with something sharp. I don't know why I didn't hear anything. I had to rent another truck this morning."

"You called the police?"

"I had no choice," she murmured. "The rental company required a police report for insurance purposes."

"Did they mention any similar cases last night? Teens on a rampage?"

She shook her head. "Not that they knew about."

"What did Nazario think?"

"He didn't. I handled it."

"You didn't tell him? Why not? He can help."

"Britt, I don't want that kind of relationship. I don't want him to see me as a woman in distress, somebody who needs to be rescued."

"Oh, swell," I said, exasperated. The woman was serious. "Sunny, we all need rescuing sometime."

She shook her head as Nazario reappeared with Cuban coffee for us and the crew.

When his cell phone rang a short time later, she was out on the sidewalk supervising the unloading of a large piece.

"Stone did it!" he told me, jubilant. "He found the gun! The mechanic's assistant gave it up. And it's the one! The serial numbers are right. We've got it! We've got it!"

"Cool," I said. "I'll try to talk to the witness. I wonder what Sunny will say?"

He shook his head. "I'm not telling her. Don't want to distract her now. This," he said, gesturing around the gallery, "is too important to her."

These two could be candidates for a daytime soap opera, I thought. Passion, dark secrets, and hangups from the past, with neither party confiding in the other.

The workmen lugged the huge piece inside, wrappings falling away as they positioned it in its designated spot. The sculpture was striking. Unlike most of Sunny's other work, which was graceful and romantic, these figures were fierce, almost threatening. Drawn to it, I watched the workmen clear the debris from around the base, then caught my breath.

My jaw must have dropped because the gallery owner materialized next to me, still cradling the tiny dog under her arm.

"Impressive, isn't it?" she said. "The moment I saw the slide, I knew we had to have it. It's an earlier work that Sunny wasn't particularly keen on exhibiting. Actually, it's reminiscent of the early Etruscans. Quite religious, but a pessimistic crowd. They believed that demon armies constantly menace the souls of the dead."

"And these would be the demons?" I asked, gazing at the chiseled figures forever captured and trapped in stone.

"Well, you wouldn't want to run into these fellows in a dark alley. Clearly this was influenced by the artist's studies in Italy," she said cheerfully, before flitting off to confer with the caterer.

I tugged at Sunny's sleeve. "The men in this piece. Who are they?"

She looked up at them, her blue eyes unflinching. "No one in particular. I rarely use models. I made them up." She shrugged and hurried off to examine the catalogs just delivered from the printer.

Had real-life nightmares haunting Sunny's subconscious emerged in her work? Chills rippled down my arms as I stepped closer. The leader in the tortured sculpture had raised, grape-like scars extending from his throat down to his private parts. The profile of another was a relatively good likeness of Mad Dog. Two were less recognizable, but the remaining figure, the largest, stood out in excellent detail. I knew that face. The fifth suspect? He had to be the one.

18

I found him at an inner-city church where clothes are collected for the poor and the homeless fed. Pleased to see me, he was ready, as always, to pontificate for print.

"You never mentioned that you grew up with Andre Coney," I said.

The Reverend Earl Wright removed the cigar from his mouth, licked his lips, and frowned. He wore a clerical collar and highly polished shoes with his well-cut suit.

"It wasn't relevant." His eyes darted to a trio of elderly volunteers sorting bags of donated clothing nearby. "I would speak out as strongly against the unjust death of any brother."

"You and Coney, Mad Dog, his cousin Stony, and Cubby Wells—you were running mates in those days."

"We were all young once. Hadn't seen Andre in years. Wish he'd come to me for help," he said piously. "I could have set him right with God Almighty and with himself."

"You remember the Christmas Eve rape and murder," I said quietly.

A dangerous light flickered in his eyes. He consulted his gold watch.

"If there's nothing else I can help you with, the Lord's work is always waiting to be done."

"Why not set things right for yourself with God by confessing the truth?"

He reacted, as though slapped. "You are wrong! I hope you are only misguided," he said softly, "but I warn you, you're treading on dangerous ground."

"Is that a threat?" I asked. "Here, of all places?"

"Take it for what it is and find something else to write about. I can point you to dozens of stories about poverty, prejudice, and people without hope. You're barking up the wrong tree with this one."

"The police are putting it all together," I said. "Wouldn't it be better for you to step forward and tell the truth at last? You're the one who could persuade the others to do the same."

He leaned close enough for me to inhale his stale cigar breath.

"Be very, very cautious," he whispered, malice in his voice.

He turned to the church ladies, his features instantly transformed like one of those kewpie dolls that change expression when you twist the knobs on the tops of their heads.

"Good day, sisters," he boomed, "and God bless! I want to see your beautiful smiles and hear your angel voices in church on Sunday."

They tittered, smiled, and waved fondly.

"And goodbye to you," he muttered in passing.

I drove to Banyan Elementary but couldn't spot Shelby's car among the traffic jam of SUVs, vans, and buses.

Perhaps her little girl was sick and out of school today, I thought. But then I was sure I saw her in a little red plaid shirt and navy skirt, waiting alone, eyes searching the street for her mother's car. I scanned oncoming traffic but didn't see her Hyundai.

Then a red Chevy pulled to the curb and a man behind the wheel waved. Startled for a moment, the child skipped to the car and climbed in. He helped her with her seat belt and they drove off. I couldn't see him clearly but assumed it was her father. Nonetheless, I jotted down the tag number and followed, keeping the car in sight as I called her home number.

She answered. "Shelby?"

"Who's this?"

"You know, we talked the other day. Did you just send someone to pick your daughter up at school?"

"Yes, my husband." She sounded as though she'd been asleep or crying.

"Are you all right?" I stopped following the Chevy and pulled to the curb.

"Remember," she whispered, "when you asked me to talk to a detective? I think I'd like to do that."

"Good for you."

"Is one of them named Sam Stone?"

"How'd you know?"

"They said he's been asking questions. I know the name. He helped my auntie once when her car was stolen, and he kept a man in Overtown from going out of business when kids kept stealing from his store. People say he's good."

"He is."

"When can I talk to him?"

"I'm sure he'll make himself available whenever it's convenient for you," I said.

"I can't go to the station house," she whispered. "Somebody might see me."

"Decide when and where you're comfortable. I'm sure he'll be there."

"You too?"

"Sure. I'll bring doughnuts."

"Gotta go," she said, as though startled. "Call you later."

With Riley guarding the gates at Homicide, I rendezvoused with Burch and Stone at the statue of the virgin in Little Havana. "Surprise," I said. "Guess who suspect number five is?"

They exchanged knowing glances.

"You already knew?" I accused.

"Nazario thought he saw the good reverend in one of Sunny's sculptures," Burch said.

"So did I," I said.

"Seems preacher boy grew up in the same projects, had himself quite a bad rep before he found Jesus," Stone said.

"Well, here's something you don't know. The witness's name is Shelby Fountain. She's Mad Dog's kid sister."

The detectives exchanged glances. "We figured as much," Burch said.

"Sam, you're the only one she'll trust. She says you have a good reputation in the community. She wants to talk to you."

"Obviously an intelligent woman." He gave me his beeper number. "Anytime, anywhere."

All we needed was her call.

But it didn't come. At one point that afternoon, I scooped up the phone, hoping it was Shelby, but it was Security in the lobby, instead. A visitor named Burch wanted to see me.

"Sure, fine." Odd, I thought, that he didn't call first.

I closed the file I was working on, profiles of the detectives for the magazine project, and went to meet him at the elevator bank. The doors slid open and people spilled out. Burch wasn't among them, or aboard the next one. Headed back to my desk to recheck with security, I overheard a middle-aged woman with short sleek brown hair and big dark sunglasses ask the receptionist where to find me.

"I'm Britt Montero," I said. "But I'm sort of busy right now. Is there something I can help you with?"

"I'm Connie Burch."

"Oh. Sorry. I thought you were someone else."

"You probably expected my husband." Her crisp words had an unfriendly edge.

"Sergeant Craig Burch's wife?"

"For twenty-one long years," she said. "Can we talk?"

"Sure." I showed her into the newsroom and rolled Ryan's chair over, next to my desk.

"My husband doesn't know I'm here," she began, lips tight. "But I'm not going to sit by this time."

I heeded the warning bells. "Is something wrong?" I am always up front with police wives when pursuing their husbands for information. Their lives are stressful enough without suspicious calls from a strange woman. Had she misunderstood, misread something? Did she spot my name in his address book, my card in his wallet, or hear messages I left on his cell phone or beeper? Was she jealous?

"Yes, there is," she said emphatically. "After three children and twenty-one years of marriage. I'm not about to kiss it all goodbye without a fight."

"Mrs. Burch, I cover the police beat for the paper," I explained carefully. "I'm working on a Sunday magazine piece about the Cold Case Squad. Your husband, his team, and their work will be featured. My relationship with him and the other detectives on the squad is strictly professional. I would never, ever—"

"You?" Her hand flew to her mouth, her expression one of startled amusement. "You thought—oh, that's rich! I've heard all about you, from my husband and from the other wives at SOLO meetings. You know, Spouses of Law Officers? *You're* no problem. It's her."

"Who?"

Connie Burch removed her sunglasses. Her eyes, dry and angry, burned with a resolve beyond tears; it was as though rage had taken over. She practically spit out the words. "Don't try to tell me you don't know. That Hartley bitch."

"Sunny?" I said, dumbstruck. "But she's—"

"No!" she burst out, furious. "Maureen. The mother!"

"Sunny's *mother?*" Way too bizarre, I thought, then recalled his comments, his wistful eyes when he spoke of her. Oh, shit. Sunny's mother.

"This time I'm not going to take it."

"She's the mother of a victim in a big case years ago," I said lamely.

"Tell me about it. The Chance case almost cost me my marriage. It would have, if she'd left her husband. My kids were little; it was the hardest time of my life. Now—when he's finally got decent hours so we can spend time together, with the kids just about grown, the house nearly paid off—now, he's started all over again. And I," she said, tapping her index finger on my desk to emphasize each word, "will not sit still this time."

"Are you positive?" I asked gently. "He worked so hard on that investigation, spent so many hours. I've seen the files, they're huge. It was a really high-profile high-pressure case."

"He's not coming home," she said, voice rising. A few heads turned our way. "He's drinking. It's the same pattern. He's back on the goddamn case and he's seeing her again. I can tell. I'm not stupid. Everything was fine between us, better than in years. And now it's all started up again."

"But he speaks so fondly of you, his family, even

your dog. A sheepdog, right?" I said. "I never thought—"

"Craig's no skirt chaser. He never ran around. The first and only time he ever cheated was with her. It was serious. He never got over it. She's always in his head, like some white noise that never stops. I knew it. I was stupid to stay. But we had the kids."

I shook my head in denial. "I've always thought of him as a good family man."

"That's the hell of it," she said, voice brittle. "He was! Then he meets her, a beautiful model who needs comforting, married to a rich, very busy doctor. Craig was never a drinker before her either. He obsessed so about that case because it was her child and he wanted to impress her."

"I don't know how I can help you," I said helplessly. "Why come here?"

Her face was dark, flushed. "It was you who got him involved in the case again. Since this somehow started with you, I assumed you knew. Well, this time I'm no naive, heartsick young wife with babies. I'm middle-aged, pissed off, and mad as hell. I'll be damned if he's going to toss me aside like a used-up tissue, not now. I don't care what happens. My life isn't worth shit anyway."

"You may be overreacting," I suggested. "His obsession was probably frustration at not solving the case."

"Or the frustration of waking up with me every morning and not her."

"I'm sorry. This must be difficult."

"Damn straight." She put her sunglasses back on

and stood up abruptly. "But I can and will make life a damn sight more difficult for a lot of people. Count on it. You can take it to the bank."

She strode out of the newsroom, her squared shoulders and rigid body language radiating her anger.

My immediate reaction was to delete from my story a reference to Burch as a family man. Would he still be married by the time it was published? Would he even be alive? The magazine had a two-week lead time. How awkward if she wasted him with his own weapon the week before the story landed on subscribers' lawns. I thought bleakly of Heather Chance and her lost marriage. How did this happen to people who love each other? Could it happen to McDonald and me?

Not yet anyway, I decided a short time later, when a dozen red roses were delivered to my desk. His card said *I love you. Run away with me*.

Burch eventually responded to my beep.

"Where are you?"

"At the crime lab," he said.

"Go home," I said. "Now. Take flowers—roses would be good, red ones. Talk nice and leave your gun in the car. Your wife is really pissed off."

"What makes you say that?"

"She just left here."

"Connie? Oh, shit. Goddammit. Sorry, Britt. What the hell is it with that woman?"

"Jealousy. Worst of all," I said, "it's not of me. Nearly laughed in my face when I assumed it was. Does this mean you don't find me attractive?"

"Jesus Christ."

"What's the story with you and Sunny's mother?"

He sighed. "Tell you about it one of these days, when we have enough time. Right now I got me enough grief without Connie losing it and running her mouth."

"What's wrong?"

"The gun," he said. "It's not a match. Ballistics says it's not the murder weapon."

"Impossible! Has it been altered? The barrel changed?"

"Not that they can see. We were so sure," he said, voice thin. "There hadda be another gun, or we're barking up the wrong tree."

Who else had used those words today? The Reverend Wright. I remembered his face in Sunny's nightmarish work of art.

"No way," I said. "Sunny might have seen the Reverend on TV, or his picture in the newspaper, but she sure as hell never moved in the same circles as Coney or saw his scars close up any other time but that night."

"We've got no proof," he said, "and a suspect who's a pillar of the community, with strong support on the street. That ain't gonna sit well with the brass. Wright worked with the mayor and the safe streets team during the last disturbance, cooled it down before the situation blew up into a full-blown riot."

Stone, he said, was reinvestigating other Miami Shores burglaries that week. A long shot at best.

He hung up. The news was a crushing blow after the triumph of successfully tracing the gun from hand to hand through Miami's byzantine underworld and criminal justice system.

As I sat, still holding the phone in shock and disbelief, a shadow fell across my desk. Morganstern, the *Hot Topics* editor, hair disheveled, his vest rumpled. "How's the story coming?" he asked casually.

"Fine." I lied through my teeth. "Couldn't be better."

"When do you think we'll get to see it?"

"Soon," I promised, digging myself in deeper.

"Got a complaint." He looked perplexed.

Uh-oh. Had Connie Burch visited him too?

"The woman," he said, confirming my fears.

Oh, shit, I thought, why me? "I'm taking out all references to him as a family man," I said quickly.

Morganstern regarded me quizzically, big dark eyes sad.

"C. J., K. C., something like that," he mumbled into his mustache. "The one with the initials, the lieutenant. Said you interfered with an investigation, got in the way, created a problem."

"Oh, her," I said.

"I promised to handle it."

"Oh?" I gazed up at him, heart sinking.

"You must be doing one hell of a job." He smiled. "Keep up the good work. I can't wait to see it." He started to meander away, then turned. "She'll still go along with the cover shot at the ice house, won't she?"

"No problem," I assured him. "You know how cops are."

He smiled again and nodded.

"I tell you, Lottie, Burch's wife was homicidal," I said later, at the hospital. "If I were him, I'd leave my gun at the office."

"Has to be hormones," she said, nodding, as we chatted across Ryan's bed. "Raging hormones. Poor thang. I've been there. I surge right outa PMS into cycle syndrome, then crash into postmenstrual syndrome. My hormones only operate on normal for about three hours a month.

"The power surges and the rage? You've seen me. Did I tell you what I did to that guy in traffic the other day? Didn't even try to cut me off, but I suspected he mighta been thinking about it. Sometimes I think I'm gonna explode, and I need chocolate, lots of chocolate, or I will die. Then I see a warm and fuzzy telephone company commercial about reaching out to touch someone, and it makes me cry—"

"I love listening to women talk," Ryan murmured weakly.

"We love to have you listen." I kissed his feverish cheek. His medication had made him queasy.

"We can break you outa here tonight," Lottie whispered conspiratorially, "smuggle you to Sunny's opening. We can stuff pillows under your blanket. Sneak you back in later. Betcha they'll never even miss you."

He shook his head, eyes serious. "Nurse Nancy keeps tabs. She's coming back with a pizza when her shift ends.

"It's great about you and McDonald, Britt," he said, as we left. "I'm happy for you."

"Me too," I said, blowing him a kiss. "It's the real deal this time."

McDonald, immersed in budget hell, had promised to meet me at the opening. The gallery was crowded. Elegantly dressed and well-heeled members of the cultural community mingled with South Beach's colorful and flamboyant creatures of the night, all drinking champagne and sampling hors d'oeuvres. Sunny looked beautiful. No one would ever suspect she'd had cold feet and considered not even showing up. She wore a gauzy long-sleeved white tunic over silk slacks, her blond hair swept up and back from her classic face. The gallery operator and another local art critic had her in tow, introducing her to the right people.

Nazario mingled as well, eyes rarely off her. Stone, dapper in a three-button suit and mock turtleneck, was chatting up the arts with guests who never suspected he was a cop. Burch stood alone in a corner, watching. I glimpsed what he was watching for when Sunny's parents arrived. The detective and Maureen focused on each other instantly, despite the crowd, their glances guarded. It's true, I thought. Surely her husband must know or suspect.

Perhaps that's why the doctor looked uncomfortable. He greeted me warmly, clasped my hand, and asked if I'd seen Tyler. I hadn't, and began to worry. Was Sunny's kid brother lurking out there somewhere in the vicinity of my car?

Maureen and Sunny embraced. Dr. Hartley pumped Nazario's hand as Tyler suddenly did appear, a flashy young girl on his arm. A photographer snapped the happy group together, freezing their images in time.

"How lovely," the gallery owner crowed, the ever-present little dog under her arm, as she, Lottie, and I watched. "You'd never know he was so against it."

"Who?" I said.

"Sunny's father, the doctor," she said. "After the invitations went out, he called to object. He was unhappy about the show and the publicity. Can you imagine?"

"I guess he's very protective," I said. "Worried about his daughter's privacy."

"He'd better get used to it," Lottie drawled. "Everybody seems to love her work."

As Sunny was spirited away to meet more VIPs, I encountered Tyler in the crowd. He looked flushed, as though he'd been drinking. "Last time I saw you," he said, "you were waiting for a tow truck."

"Thanks to you," I said.

He did a double take. "Me?"

"Yes. My tire was slashed."

"And you think that I . . . ?" He looked truly startled and offended. "Hey, I may be a prick, but I'm no son-of-a-bitch."

I was about to pursue the distinction when his date—who had pouty lips and a short cropped top that exposed her navel—found him, caught his hand, and dragged him off.

McDonald showed up and we gravitated across the crowded room to each other like heat-seeking missiles. If the other detectives were surprised to see us together in a social setting, they didn't show it. The enthusiastic crowd eventually dwindled, departing for dinner or local nightspots. Sunny's mother hugged her goodbye, their two blond heads close together.

"I'm sure you want to spend time with your friends tonight," I heard her say. "And Daddy has an early surgery."

I glanced around as they left, but Burch was gone.

The glowing gallery operator pronounced the evening "an absolute triumph, a huge success!" To celebrate, six of us—Nazario and Sunny, McDonald and me, and Lottie with a *Vanity Fair* magazine writer she met at the opening—repaired to the nearby South Beach club where Sunny's neighbor, Jimmy, played in the band.

Sunny actually got a drum roll on arrival. Excited and elated, she was more talkative than I'd seen before. "It was good to see Craig Burch again," she said, sipping more champagne. "He's aged. I almost didn't recognize him."

"I think he has a crush on your mother," I said. "Did you see how he looked at her tonight?"

"Old news," she murmured. "It's mutual. My parents used to fight about it. I even fantasized about her dumping my father and Craig Burch being my stepdad someday. I think she did, too. But she never had the guts."

"Wow. She actually considered divorce?"

She nodded. "She even left once, but dad got her back. He's a control freak, a manipulator. He controls her, controls Tyler; he'd control me if I let him. That's one reason I escaped to Italy and then never moved back home. He never liked any of my friends or any choice I made. He didn't even like poor Ricky, whom everybody really loved. He was such a neat kid."

Nazario took her to the dance floor. Her arms around his neck, slow dancing, they were oblivious when McDonald whispered something that made my pupils dilate and took my hand, and we left.

* * *

"Won't it be nice," he said, buttoning his shirt before dawn, "when I don't have to leave, because when we wake up together, we'll be home."

"Our home." I smiled and nodded back to sleep. The dream overtook my bliss like a horror movie scenario. Terrified people fleeing a deadly dark cloud of smoke and debris from a collapsing tower. Hellish blackness accelerating behind them as they ran for their lives. Then that face in the crowd. The young woman who walked as others ran. More and more slowly as screaming people streamed around her, until they were gone. And the blackness was no longer smoke, but a towering dark and angry sea. Alone, hair whipping in the fierce wind, she stopped to turn, about to embrace the evil gaining on her. Run! Run! I tried to scream. She haunted me still. But in this dream the woman who walked into the dark sea was Sunny.

19

Too much champagne, I thought, my visions of disaster now accompanied by a throbbing headache. I pulled on shorts and a T-shirt and jogged to the boardwalk. Running on the boards bounced my brain against my aching skull, so I ran beside the sea instead, on hard-packed sand at surf's edge. Laughing seagulls gliding overhead, the dramatic pink and gold morning sky, and a lilting breeze off the water all lifted my spirits as I bobbed and weaved to thwart the incoming waves in foamy pursuit of my running shoes. I stopped to snatch up a shiny shell tumbling in the surf. A perfect cowrie, speckled and exotic. My Aunt Odalys used them to divine the future. I thought of calling her but dismissed the idea. I knew my future. Sighing with happiness, I yearned to immerse myself in the warm salt water. Mornings like this recharged the batteries of my soul. I wished McDonald were there to share it.

I showered and then scanned the morning paper over coffee. In a follow-up to his story on the state's early-prison-release program, Janowitz had listed the names, crimes, and original sentences of released convicts from Miami.

I spotted Edgar's name, Onnie's husband, along with a few others I recognized, then gasped aloud. Ronald Stokes. Mad Dog. Free! He must have known when I was there. That accounted for his smug, arrogant attitude.

I lunged for the phone, hit star 67 to keep my name and number off her caller ID, and asked for Shelby when a man answered.

"She's not here," he said gruffly, children crying in the background.

"When do you expect her?"

"Who wants to know?"

"Alice Courtney. I'm a guidance counselor at Banyan Elementary," I lied.

"Don't know where she's at," he said, and hung up abruptly.

I dialed the squad. Stone answered.

"Did you hear?" I said.

"Yeah," he said grimly. "Got a copy of the report this morning."

"What report? You mean the story in the newspaper?"

"Let's start over," he said patiently. "You first. Tell

me what you're talking about, then I'll tell you what I'm talking about."

"Mad Dog got early release. He's out! Probably here in Miami, God knows where. The last thing he said to me was to tell Sunny he'd see her again, soon."

"Why do you think we were all there last night? The art world isn't exactly our milieu."

"You knew? Why didn't you tell me?"

"Excuse me. Who said we had to brief you on everything? We're actively looking for him, to have a chat. Keep missing him by minutes. Helluva thing, they're all scot free, with no supervision, no control, no nothing."

"Did Sunny know that's why you were all there?"

"No. She doesn't want protection, thinks she has nothing to fear because she's not working with us. Maybe she's right."

"Now," I said. "Your turn. What were you talking about?"

"Shelby Fountain, Mad Dog's sister. She's missing."

"Missing?"

"Walked to church for choir practice night before last. Hasn't been seen since, her husband says. When she didn't come home, he found out she never showed at the church. Filed the report last night. Missing Persons copies them to Homicide. I saw it this morning."

Dread curdled the coffee in my stomach. "That was only a few hours after I talked to her. She had to get off the phone in a hurry. She'd never leave her kids without a damn good reason," I said, truly alarmed. "You think her own brother would hurt her? Or Reverend Wright?"

"Not a clue. Let me know ASAP if you hear from her," he said.

While I'd been happily drinking champagne at Sunny's reception, Shelby was alone in the dark somewhere, like that scared little girl so many years ago.

I checked the office for messages. Two from Abby Wells.

"My husband's been very upset, because you keep leaving messages," she said.

"Has Cubby heard from Mad Dog?" I asked.

She hesitated. "I think Charles has been talking to him."

"And what about his sister, Shelby?"

"I think I met her at the funeral home," she said.

"That's her," I said. "She's missing. Disappeared the night before last, on her way to church. She has children."

"That's terrible, she seemed so nice. What could have happened to her?"

"Maybe Cubby has a clue."

"I doubt that. He's been upset. Two detectives came up here to talk to him. He hasn't gone to work since. What's going on?"

"Do you know what he told the detectives?"

"The same thing he told you. He didn't—they didn't—kill or rape anybody. He finally refused to speak with them anymore. My God, this is all so horrible! He drove down to Miami to talk to his old friends and came back even more upset."

"What about the Reverend Wright?"

"He's been calling as well. Was with them the other day. What's going on?" she pleaded.

"You love him, Abby. You're the only one with his best interests at heart. It's time to convince him to tell everything he knows."

"He was so young then, Ms. Montero. I'm sure that if anyone got hurt it wasn't intended; he wouldn't, he couldn't have—"

"Somebody did."

"I'll talk to him. I promise."

Lottie, Onnie, Janowitz, and I visited Ryan. The news was good: The doctors had balanced his medication and he felt better. Onnie had her restraining order and had pleaded with her former mother-in-law to intercede with Edgar. So far so good.

I left the hospital and drove toward home, listening to music, Kendall McDonald on my mind, telling myself that someday soon all would again be right with the world. A flock of night birds flew in a darkening sky, my spirit soaring with them.

Flashing red lights ahead, on the Boulevard, brought me back to Planet Earth with a thud. I killed the music and switched on my dashboard scanner. A minor accident, no serious injuries. Headed home, I locked in on the Beach frequency. The usual: a brawl spilling out of a South Beach club into the street, shoplifters on Lincoln Road, and a pedestrian hit on Collins Avenue. A hazardous-materials squad reported that it had identified the contents of a suspicious envelope reported by a jittery homeowner as a free soap-powder sample. The first officer at the scene of a 45, a dead body, came on the air excited, to change the signal to a 31, a homicide. The address, an old hotel in North Beach.

I took my foot off the gas reflexively and swerved north, my mind racing.

The twenty-minute drive took ten, while garbled radio transmissions confirmed my worst fears. Homicide was en route. One victim: an apparent tenant in the building. No next of kin was present.

Three patrol cars and a growing knot of curious neighbors and passersby out front. I abandoned the T-Bird in a loading zone and ran into the building.

The door to Sunny's apartment stood wide open. A young police officer stopped me.

"Hey, Britt, you can't go in there."

I turned to argue and saw the corpse on the stairs.

20

"Where's Sunny?" I gasped.

Jimmy, the sax player, lay sprawled on the stairs faceup. Blood leaked from a hole in his chest. It ran down his outflung arm, dripped off the edge of the open banister, and splashed in huge drops onto the faded lobby carpet.

Sunny sat hunched in a chair in her studio. A patrolman bent over her, barking questions into her bad ear. There was blood on her blouse.

"Is she all right?" I asked.

"Outside, you have to wait for PIO." The cop gestured impatiently toward the street.

"No, I want her here," Sunny said, raising her head.

The cop paused, then nodded.

I held her hand as she answered him, numb and dry-eyed, hesitating from time to time, eyes focused on nothing. Was she reliving that long-ago night, the young cop who took notes? She'd been working, she said. Heard the saxophone earlier. Didn't notice exactly when it stopped, but at some point thought she heard someone at her door. She called out, asked who was there. No answer. Moments later, she thought she heard a door slam. From her studio windows she saw a car accelerate and drive off at a high rate of speed. She couldn't see the make, model, or color through the picture window in the dark but did note that it was missing a taillight. She called upstairs to ask Jimmy if he'd heard anything. He didn't answer then, or a short time later when she tried again. She decided to check, stepped out into the lobby, key in hand, and saw him. She ran up the stairs. A bloody, frothy foam bubbled from his mouth. She couldn't find a pulse.

I stayed while she answered the same questions and more from the homicide detective.

Jimmy had mentioned a sister in Chicago. She knew of no other relatives or any enemies. He wasn't into drugs, though he might have smoked marijuana. He was not a heavy drinker or gambler. Did not appear to have many girlfriends, in fact was awkward with women. No, she didn't think he was gay. He did not flash money or jewelry. He was basically a quiet and mellow man who loved to play music.

"I'm so glad you were here," she told me later, head on my shoulder. "It's all . . . you remind me so much of Kathy. You're like her."

"Kathy?"

"The policewoman who stayed with me after Ricky was killed." She wiped her eyes. "Kathleen Riley."

"Oh. Right." I should have realized, I thought. "She's still trying to protect you, Sunny."

Nazario filled the doorway moments later, out of breath, hair disheveled, face stricken.

"*¡Dios mio!* Why did you not call me?"

He conferred privately with the Beach detective and then told Sunny to pack a bag.

He insisted on taking her to her parents, to a hotel, to his place, to my place, anywhere she wanted to go.

She refused. "My things, my work. I can't pack it up and take it with me. I can't let fear run my life."

Nazario worked the radio, issuing a BOLO—Be on the Lookout—for Mad Dog, his cousin Stony, Cubby Wells, and the Reverend Wright to be stopped and brought in for questioning only.

The streets would be unpleasant tonight for anybody with a busted taillight.

Sunny and I drank herbal tea as she cried for her good neighbor: his talent, his kindness, his friendship.

When I left, Nazario and the Miami Beach detective were taking an increasingly exasperated Sunny through a painstakingly precise minute-by-minute reconstruction of her movements during the past two weeks. I shared her exasperation. How, I wondered, would that help? Sunny wasn't a suspect. Why weren't they out on the street instead, beating the bushes, finding the bad guys?

The lobby crime scene was still roped off. Jimmy's body still sprawled on the stairs, now covered by a plastic sheet. One of his flip-flops had flown off when he fell back. I stood there for a moment, then made the sign of the cross for a man who awoke that day unaware he was about to become a case number.

It was already midnight. In the rush of my arrival, I'd left my cell phone in the car. I'd only driven a block before it rang.

"Britt!" She sounded nearly hysterical. "I've been trying to call you for hours!"

"Shelby! Is that you? Where are you?"

"A Denny's on Thirty-sixth Street." She sounded near tears. "I can't go home. I need to talk to that policeman. Right now!"

"Okay! Okay! Stay there."

"No. It's too bright. All lit up. Somebody will see me."

"Where?"

"I'll walk over to Miami Avenue. By those old apartment houses. Remember the one that burnt, across from the liquor store? I'll watch for your car. Is Stone coming?"

"I'll call him," I said. "Be careful. I'm on the way."

When Stone answered the beep and said he'd be there in ten minutes, I was already speeding west on the causeway.

As I crossed the Boulevard headed for the avenue, a police cruiser passed me doing at least seventy, sirens and lights flashing. Did Stone overreact and dispatch a patrol car? No, I thought. He was too cool for that. Two more speeding patrol cars raced after the first. A fire rescue unit in full emergency mode barreled along Northeast Second Avenue, air horn and sirens sounding. It lumbered through the red light and turned west, hogging the road. We were all headed in the same direction.

What was the big emergency? All the noise will surely spook Shelby, I thought, annoyed. The woman wanted to remain low-profile, have a secret meeting. The chorus of oncoming sirens around me could wake the dead. I prayed she wouldn't panic, run, and get lost again. I cursed impatiently under my breath, willing them to veer off, to go to their emergency.

They didn't.

My next reaction was a sick sinking feeling. My destination and theirs were the same.

The liquor store's shattered plate-glass window looked as though it had exploded. A middle-aged man moaned, rocking back and forth amid broken glass shards on the sidewalk, clutching his bloodied ankle with both hands.

A paramedic jumped off the rescue truck and ran to another form in the street nearby. He took her pulse, then got to his feet. His body language said there was none.

I ventured close enough to see the silver cross on a chain around her neck, then walked away, nauseated and trembling.

"Is that her?" Stone asked, from behind me.

He must have arrived before I did. He held his radio.

"Yes," I whispered. "That's Shelby." I clutched at his arm, my heart constricted. "Have them do something! They're not even working on her! They didn't even try! They can bring her back! They bring back people with no pulse all the time."

"The back of her skull is missing, Britt." His jaw tightened. "She's DRT: dead right there." Turning away, he spoke into his radio. "We've got a guy who took one in the ankle, and a kid around the corner who got one in the gut."

I stopped breathing. "A kid?"

"Teenager," he said. "Looks like a local gang-banger."

"Probably a drive-by," a young officer in uniform said. "We got us a little turf war in progress on the east side." He studied me, puzzled. "How'd the press get here so fast?"

Too late to file a story tonight. The paper had gone to bed. Not even TV had come out to this scene. Uniforms appeared convinced this was another drive-by shooting, the wounded teenager the intended target and the others innocent victims caught in the crossfire. The teen, en route to surgery, refused to talk to police.

The liquor store had just closed for the night, the manager said. As he locked up, his storefront exploded and he went down, hit in the ankle. He saw very little but thought all the gunfire came from one car. A second vehicle may have been involved, he wasn't sure. The man had worked a twelve-hour shift. He'd been tired and hungry. Now he was in pain. He didn't know Shelby, had never seen her before.

Stone followed me as I left.

"Bad night," he said, leaning in my car window.

I nodded numbly.

"Looks like somebody made a try at Sunny tonight," he said, "but her neighbor interfered and bought it instead. Now we've lost our witness. Both were threats to our suspects. You might be considered one as well. Be careful until we round up all the players."

"What do you do now?"

He sighed. "Inform next of kin, see if they can point

us to the others." His dark face glistened in the sweltering night, his voice dropped. "This is the part of the job I hate the most. Waking up strangers in the middle of the night, giving them the worst news they'll ever hear. Thought I wouldn't be doing it again, working cold cases."

He straightened up slowly, as though his body hurt, and studied the night sky for a long moment.

"Growing up, I always said I would leave this city. But it won't let you go. I think it's the sky here. It's so big and low and all around you, everywhere. It's on your skin; you can feel it. You inhale it, it's part of you and you are part of it and somehow you are one with this place."

He bent back down to my window, his eyes dark pools that reflected the night.

"Did you know that the department has informed us that it's against policy to use the word *dead* when informing next of kin? I *always* use dead or killed and I'm not going to stop. Sometimes, even then, they don't understand. Can't grasp it. You have to be straight with people at times like this. I'm sure as hell not going to say 'She expired,' which is what they told us to say. Some people right here, in the neighborhood where I grew up, don't even know what *expired* means. She wasn't a quart of milk, for Christ's sake."

"No," I said, voice hollow. "She wasn't."

"Go the hell home," he said wearily. "And lock your doors."

21

"Relax," Burch told me when I called his office at 4 A.M. "We're assembling our cast of characters. Even have the good reverend here. He's a real piece of work. Dragged him out of the sack with his choir director. How long we can hold any of them is another story. Nobody's talking; they're all getting lawyered up. Only one still missing. Stone got a tip on Mad Dog's location, missed him by minutes—"

"What about Cubby Wells?"

"He's here. His wife is calling every five minutes, driving us up the wall. Says he didn't kill anybody, rape anybody, or see anybody else do the deeds. Nobody else is even saying that much. The whole team's working, including the lieutenant."

"How come you never mentioned Riley worked the case too, protecting Sunny?"

"Didn't I? No big deal. K.C. was a kid, a rookie at the time. Didn't do any real investigating. We needed a female officer to baby-sit Sunny. She was a baby-sitter."

"Not important, but it explains a lot. I think they bonded."

"Super Glue wouldn't bond with that woman."

"I don't know. Maybe she's not so bad."

I tried to nap but couldn't. My mind raced at ninety miles an hour. Something tugged at my subconscious, something elusive. Flipping listlessly through the glossy pages of Sunny's show catalog, I stared again at the face I knew was the Reverend Wright's, and at Andre Coney's horrid scarring. The pictures had been reproduced from color slides.

I called Sunny on a hunch. "You awake?"

"You are kidding," she said wearily. "Who could sleep?"

"Is it all right if I come over?"

"You never asked before."

"My manners are improving," I said. "By the way, Sunny, do you have slides of all your work?"

"Sure, slides, photos, sketches."

"Right, you said you sketch the pieces first."

"At every step of the way, as well. It's an important part of the process."

Unable to face more herbal tea, I stopped at an all-night café on the way for some strong Cuban coffee and guava and cheese pastries to go.

The yellow crime-scene tape was gone, along with a section of carpet the technicians had removed from the stairs.

As I placed the small paper cups on her little table, I noticed a coffeemaker on the counter. “Something new?”

“A gift. From Pete.”

“How romantic.”

“He craves coffee.”

“I know. It’s a Cuban thing. I’ll teach you how to make it.”

“Okay,” she said, “but I doubt I could ever actually drink it.”

“I can teach you that too,” I said. “Here.” I handed her a tiny cup. “Drink this.”

She downed it like a shot of whiskey, eyes shut tight, then grimaced. “Oh, my God.” She gasped. “Will I ever sleep again?”

I sat on the floor beneath a halogen lamp in her studio examining slides, poring over pictures neatly encased in plastic, then looking through crammed sketchbooks. Her drawings depicted sculptures from all angles: works contemplated as well as those in progress or completed. Many included faces. It was similar to searching a book of police mug shots for a suspect. I flipped back several pages to reexamine one that jogged my memory. Where had I seen that face before?

“Who’s this, Sunny?”

She leaned over my shoulder. “Nobody. A face I came up with—you know, doodling and drawing.”

“You’re sure?”

“Yep, like most of them.”

“Here he is again,” I said, turning pages, “and again. Where’s the sculpture?”

“Never did it.” She shrugged. “He was too creepy to

spend the time with. When you work on a piece, you spend twenty-four hours a day with it. You have to like it. I learned my lesson about working on a project that makes me uncomfortable."

"Can I borrow this? I promise I'll bring it right back."

"Sure, but why?"

"It could be nothing. I'll explain later."

The lobby was dark, the newsroom empty. I checked the library and then called the squad. All the detectives were out. Nobody answered when I paged them. Maybe Mad Dog had been run to ground, I thought hopefully. Maybe they had him surrounded. I called the man whose face I saw in Sunny's drawings. No answer.

Puzzled, I called Sunny. No answer. Probably in the freezer. I wished Nazario had bought her a damn answering machine instead of a coffeemaker.

Moments after I hung up, the phone rang at my desk. Unusual at 5 A.M.

"I want to leave a message for Britt Montero," the voice quavered. "This is Abby Wells."

"Abby, it's me, not a recording," I said.

"I'm at police headquarters, in the lobby. They have Charles. They won't let me talk to him. Wait." There was silence. She must have put her hand over the phone.

She came back elated. "Oh, Britt, they told me he's going to be released, they're letting him come home! It'll just be a few minutes. I'm so relieved."

"I need to see you. I'm on the way," I said.

The lobby at headquarters was cold and quiet. Abby Wells shivered in a thin blouse, waiting on a wooden bench near the elevator. "They said it would only be a few minutes," she complained.

The elevator dinged at the fifth floor, and the light blinked at each floor on the way down. The door yawned open and Cubby Wells stepped out alone. He wore a rumpled T-shirt and blue jeans. He looked as though he had lost weight since the funeral. His eyes were red and bloodshot.

They embraced. She wept, he was teary-eyed.

The officer at the front desk glanced up, then resumed reading his newspaper.

Cubby didn't look surprised to see me.

"It's not over," I told him. "Let's get out of here."

He took a long deep breath as we stepped out into the moist warm air.

"I'm scared they'll charge him with a crime he didn't commit," his wife said.

"They probably will," I said. "Shelby's dead, so is an innocent man. Two people are wounded. This isn't an old cold case anymore. You have to tell the truth. You were there that night, weren't you?"

Abby began to cry.

"We can't talk here," he said.

We went back to the *News,* to the deserted, dimly lit, third-floor cafeteria. They sat next to each other across from me, holding hands, at a table overlooking the darkness of the bay and Miami Beach, a blaze of lights across the water.

"Tell me," I said.

He stared out the window. "We went after them," he said dully, "the boy and the girl."

"You saw them outside the ice-cream shop?"

He frowned and shook his head. "No. We waited for them to leave the marina. After they left the boat, we followed them down to that ice-cream place, trying to figure where to do it."

"You were just . . . waiting for anybody to leave the marina?"

"No, it was them. They were the ones we were after."

"You knew them?"

"No. See, it was a job. Andre's deal. He'd been busted for grand theft auto. Spent some time in jail. They had a program for youthful offenders then, doctors and dentists who donated their services to rehabilitate young inmates who had medical or dental problems that affected their self-image, their self-esteem, and contributed to them getting in trouble. They'd fix—you know—cleft palates, birthmarks, bad teeth. Even removed tattoos, pinned back big ears, and did nose jobs. Said they'd fix Andre's scars. This doctor, a plastic surgeon, he came to see Andre in jail, told him he could make him look normal, even make it easier for him to move his neck where it was too tight from the scar tissue. Andre was so excited. You'da thought it was Christmas morning. But the doctor wanted something first. See, he had this daughter."

I gasped, ice crystals forming in my blood.

"She wanted to date some kid, a teenage jock who lived in the neighborhood. He didn't like it. He wanted Andre to round up some guys to humiliate the kid in front of the girl. You know, so she wouldn't think the kid was such a big deal. Wouldn't want to date him.

"He didn't want his daughter hurt, only scared. Said it was okay if Ricky got smacked around a little. Andre was excited as hell, anxious to do a good job and get his scars fixed."

"So the trouble with the boat was faked?"

He shrugged. "Doctor told Andre they'd come out and get in the car. And they did. We followed them to the ice-cream store; we could've done it there but Mad Dog was afraid somebody might see us. We took them when they came out, went looking for a nice quiet place to work the kid over. He kept asking us to let the girl go. She was crying, asking where we were taking them. Every time we saw a spot and slowed down, somebody was there or it had too many lights or a police car would cruise by. Kept going south, turned on a dirt road, and wound up at that farm."

Tears welled in his eyes. Abby was already crying.

"We had 'em tied up so they couldn't get away. But when we took them out and were beating up on the kid—" He gulped, gasping for air to stifle a sob.

"Things got out of hand?" I said.

"A little. The kid pissed 'em off when he tried to fight back. Had a bloody nose, cut lip. Me and Earl were saying it was enough. But Mad Dog, his cousin, and Andre were whaling on the kid. Then we heard something. A big engine coming, high beams in the dark. We thought it was the cops, panicked, and took off."

"What happened to—"

"We hauled ass, left 'em there."

"Who shot them?"

Tears ran down his face. "I'm telling you, I don't know! They were alive and well when we left. She was intact, had all her clothes on. Didn't have a mark on her. Andre had a gun he stole somewhere, but he only used it to scare the kid. Nobody ever fired a shot."

"You sure he or Mad Dog didn't go back later to rape her?"

"Hell, no. I don't think any of us coulda found that place again if we wanted to. You know how dark it is down there, no signs, no lights, all those fields the same. We got lost getting the hell out. We panicked, thought the police were coming after us. Plus, she was never supposed to get hurt. If she did, Andre wouldn't get his scars fixed. He was scared the doctor would be pissed off because we left her way down there. But Earl said it would be okay. The job went right. When we heard later about the couple who was shot, we thought it couldn't be them. No way. But then they showed the kid's picture on television. It was him. When they said the girl with him got raped, shot, and she was gonna die, Andre went crazy. Out of his mind. Cried like a baby. Knew he'd lost the only chance he ever had to look normal. He called the doctor once. Man said to never call again and hung up."

"Why didn't you tell the truth?"

"Sure, we snatched 'em, took 'em to the murder scene, tied 'em up—but didn't shoot 'em? Who'd believe that? They were already looking for us. We had records. Even the doctor thought we did it. We'd go to the electric chair or prison for life.

"Andre never got his surgery. Now he's dead. And I might as well be." He covered his eyes, as his weeping wife comforted him.

A noise at the door startled me. A member of the night maintenance crew, an older man pushing a cart loaded with cleaning equipment, stared at us, turned, and left.

"So you're saying they were shot and she was raped by somebody else who left them for dead? Who?"

"The hell knows? Could be anybody. Coulda been cops for all I know."

I stared at him skeptically. "But how did Shelby get killed?"

"I don't know about that. She was a good girl. I know she was scared of Mad Dog, didn't like him around. When he came home from prison he insisted on staying with her and her husband. He was pissed off as hell about the case coming back to life, said nobody was gonna send him back to prison for something he didn't do. We were all talking about the girl, wondering how much she remembered, if maybe she could clear us. Everybody was pissed at those cops and you for stirring the pot with those stories. Earl Wright kept saying all along that we should stick together and just refuse to talk."

"Somebody else was murdered last night," I said. "In Miami Beach, a friend of the girl. What do you know about that?"

"Nothing, I swear. I was with my wife all evening, went to a show at her school. The kids put it on, a fund raiser for New York and Washington. Everybody there can confirm that. We were asleep when they came looking for me."

That, I thought, was probably why the cops had kicked him loose.

"Be straight with the detectives," I said. "If what you're saying is true, the statute of limitations ran out a long time ago on anything you did. Talk to Pete Nazario. Don't lie to him. He'll know if you do."

Cubby agreed. He would go home, shower and change, and then talk to the police. He promised. They left hand in hand.

Back in the newsroom, I tapped into the state database, ran a background check, and printed the results. Excited, I called the squad. Nobody there.

I drove back to North Beach in that cloudless darkness before dawn.

I saw a light behind the picture window of Sunny's studio, but she didn't answer her door. The dusty lobby was dark and shadowy. I tried not to look at the stairs. "Sunny?" Her name echoed through the creaky old building. The wind off the sea had picked up outside, and the hotel moaned and groaned in the dark, sounds you never hear in the light of day, as though the ghosts of all who had ever lived, loved, and laughed there were stirring.

I steeled myself and glanced up apprehensively at the staircase, half expecting to see Jimmy standing there, a bloody starburst staining his shirt. He wasn't. But somebody else was.

22

"Sunny? You scared me. What are you doing up there?"

Her hair was long and loose, her face white. She held a flashlight in her hand.

"The battery died," she said, and descended, joining me. "The power went out; it must be the wind. Then I thought I heard a noise upstairs. I was afraid somebody might be stealing from Jimmy's apartment. People do that sometimes, when they hear someone has died." She dug a key ring from her pocket. "Let me lock the front door. We usually don't bother. But with none of the other tenants in town . . ."

"Good idea," I said.

The front door bolted, we retreated to her apartment. Her studio, with its sheet-covered statuary, was illuminated by a battery-powered Coleman lantern.

"Part of my survival kit," she said. "It wasn't hard to put together after nine-eleven. I already had hurricane supplies—you know, water and canned food, candles and waterproof matches. I didn't spring for the gas mask, though." She looked scattered, face taut.

"There have been some developments," I said. "Things you need to know about."

A sudden knock at the door startled us both. Three sharp raps.

Sunny looked puzzled. "How did somebody get in? We just locked the front door."

"Who else has a key?"

"Only other tenants." She peered through the peephole, then began unlocking the door, throwing bolts open, unhooking the chain.

"Wait a minute," I said, alarmed. "Who is it?"

"A woman," she said. "It's okay."

"Sunny, don't!" Too late. She opened the door.

"Thank you, ma'am," the visitor said fervently. "I really need to call triple A, my car's stuck."

She brushed by Sunny and stepped inside.

"Well!" the tall raw-boned woman said, then looked Sunny up and down. "Look at you, now."

Sunny stared, expression odd. "Do we know each other?"

"You betcha, missy. You wouldn't be standing here now, without me." She glanced at me, still frozen in place.

"You *would* have to be here," she said pettishly. "I thought that was you when you came in."

"Sunny," I said, my voice a warning.

The woman reopened the door behind her. "Clyde. Get in here!"

The man wasn't wearing his baseball cap, but I recognized the same sharp features I'd seen in the old news photos and in Sunny's sketches. He was as tall as the woman but his shoulders were slightly hunched, as though he was reluctant to be there.

Sunny stepped back. I fought the instinct to do the same.

"Mrs. Pinder," I said. "And this must be Clyde, your husband. Do you recognize him, Sunny?"

Sunny frowned, bewildered.

"You sketched him. You think you never met, but you didn't dream up his face in those drawings. He's real."

Rebecca Pinder shot her husband a hard glance, then reached into her large shapeless purse and came up quickly with a small-caliber handgun.

She waved the gun at us, her finger on the trigger.

"Is that it? The murder weapon?" I asked.

I heard Sunny's deep breath.

"See?" The woman said sharply. "I told you they knew."

Almost apologetically, Clyde reached into his waistband and came up with a dark-colored revolver.

"Who are you?" Sunny turned to me, bewildered. "Pinder. Isn't she the woman who called the ambulance that night? I remember hearing that name later."

"Sunny," I said, staring at the guns, "the boys who abducted you and Ricky, they didn't assault you, and they didn't shoot you. He did."

Clyde hunched even more, eyes darting, his gun hand trembling.

"He has a record of sex offenses. Attempted rape, indecent exposure, lewd behavior. He did time in prison for it when he was in his twenties."

His wife regarded him with contempt.

"That was a long time ago," he protested, his voice a nasal whine.

Sunny shook her head. "I don't—"

"You had a head injury. You may not consciously remember the traumatic events. Your abductors were beating up Ricky but were frightened off by approaching headlights. They thought it was the police. It was probably Mr. Pinder in his truck. He found you."

"Saw a light, heard something out there. Thought somebody was stealing my equipment," Clyde protested. "When I got out of the pickup, there she was, all trussed up like a Christmas goose, young and pretty, blond-headed, just waiting for me. On my own goddamn property! What do you expect a man to do?" he said plaintively.

"You just couldn't resist," I said.

"That's enough, Clyde!" his wife snapped. "No point talking about it."

"When you finished with her, you panicked and shot them both."

"But . . ."—Sunny turned to the woman—"she helped me, she saved my life."

"Because when you showed up at the house, hours later, she didn't know what he had done. Am I right, Mrs. Pinder?"

"The damn fool," she said bitterly, gun in her hand, striding about the studio as though looking for something. "If I'da known, I never would've called the ambulance. We could've got ridda both of 'em. Nobody would've known. But the fool didn't tell me what he'd done until after they took her off to the hospital.

"We went through hell when you didn't die the way they said you would," she told Sunny, her words accusatory. "Thought Clyde would be arrested any minute. The farm was all we had. I couldn't have run it alone. But then the news said all she could describe was the boys who took her, and we started to breathe again.

"Now," she said angrily, "now, after all the hard years, we finally struck gold. All that cash money about to come in, like hitting the lottery. The Catholic church buying the whole damn shebang. And this has to come up to ruin everything.

"If all this was to come out now, it'd kill the deal. It's the *church,* for God's sake! Our pictures'd be on the news. The whole world would know what I've had to live with all these years."

From the scathing expression she fixed on Clyde, she wasn't referring to their guilty secret; she meant him.

"Clyde," she said sternly, "keep them here while I look around, figure something out. Either one-a them moves a hair, you shoot her dead. You hear me?"

He nodded grimly. His hand was steady now.

He waved the gun, herding us closer together.

"Hey, chickie," he murmured softly, eyes settling on Sunny. "You sure you don't remember me?"

He gave her a sick little smile.

"You wouldn't shoot us," I said reasonably, fighting to remain calm.

"I would," he said. "Just ask the little lady. Heard you're deef in one ear. Which one?"

Sunny turned, as though to indicate her left ear, and kicked the gun out of his hand. It flew about six feet, hit the floor with a clatter, and spun toward the picture window.

He and Sunny scuffled as I followed the gun.

I lunged for it, scrambling on all fours. As my fingers curled around the grip somebody stomped on my hand and I screamed in pain.

The rolled tops of her support hose were at my eye level as she kicked away Clyde's weapon and jammed her own gun to my head with such force that I thought for an instant I'd been shot. She twisted my hair in her hand and yanked me to my feet. We both saw Clyde pressing Sunny against the wall, his hands around her throat.

"Don't leave marks on her!" his wife screeched. "Can't you do anything right?"

He glanced at us and Sunny kneed him in the groin. He went down as she bolted for the door. Rebecca pulled the trigger and the world exploded. My last thought was that this was how it was for Ricky Chance. But I wasn't dead. Instead, I saw plaster fly off the wall above Sunny's head as she fumbled with the locks. She froze. Clyde, still on the floor, grabbed her ankles. Then she was down and he was on top of her.

I couldn't hear, my ears rang, my eyes flooded with tears.

As though from underwater, I heard Rebecca Pinder say, "I found the perfect place."

Shivers rippled up and down my spine as ice water oozed through my veins. I knew where we were going.

They marched us back to the freezer, as outside the picture windows the first hint of dawn crept relentlessly up the horizon.

"An accident, that's what it'll look like," the woman crowed, her words a distant underwater murmur. "Locked theirselves in by mistake. Happens to little children in old refrigerators all the time. Nobody can prove different."

The icy breath of the big freezer enveloped us as she opened the thick double doors. A six-foot block of ice towered atop the worktable, ready to be carved.

Rebecca Pinder puttered about, still holding the gun, collecting Sunny's tools with her free hand. "Don't leave nothing they could use to force the doors open," she told Clyde, who wore a grimace and was holding his testicles. "Make sure there's no phone in here, and take out those tools."

Sunny shivered, arms wrapped around herself.

"We'll freeze to death in here," she pleaded.

The woman's stare was sharp. "Don't look to me for sympathy, girly," she said. "You owe me. The last fourteen years were a gift you never would have had without me. A rich doctor's daughter, and what thanks did I get? A pretty little note on fancy stationery."

"Do you know how many lives are ruined because of what your husband did?" I said. "Even the teenagers he scared off have lived through hell because of him."

"They woulda done the same thing Clyde did. They

didn't take her"—she waved her gun at Sunny—"out there for a hayride. They had the same thing in mind but they got interrupted. And don't preach to me about grief and hard times. I know hard times. I'm only protecting what's rightfully mine."

"What's this," Clyde said, "a fire extinguisher?"

His arms loaded with Sunny's tools, he squinted at the nitrogen tank, standing against the freezer's back wall.

"Whatever it is, don't take no chances, get it outa there," his wife said.

Sunny and I exchanged glances. I had no clue how to operate the tank and no time to figure it out. Sunny had to do it. Fast.

I didn't know if she could or would.

She did.

When I saw her step back, toward the tank, I shrieked at the top of my lungs and tried to push the block of ice off the worktable. The ice didn't budge. A gunshot exploded. Shattered ice flew. His wife screamed a curse and Clyde took his eyes off Sunny for a moment. She snatched up the tank, turned a dial, and pointed the nozzle at his face. He refocused on her, no fear in his eyes. He must have expected a harmless foam.

I heard the hiss of nitrogen spray and a cry cut off, frozen in his throat. His eyes never changed. They remained open, still empty, his parted lips and tongue darkening shades of blue. His hair and eyelashes frosted.

Sunny continued to spray the man even after he fell. Ice crystals formed on the gun still in his hand.

His wife screamed his name. "What on earth?"

She rushed toward him. Shouting for Sunny, I scrambled around the far side of the worktable, out of the line of fire and out the door. Lungs aching from the cold, I held my breath waiting for gunshots. "Run! Run!" I cried.

Slowly, Sunny followed, then hesitated and turned back, like the girl in the blue sweater. I rushed inside, grabbed her waist, and dragged her out the door. "Run!"

"We don't have to," she said, as I slammed the freezer doors behind us. I thought she smiled for an instant, but I might have been mistaken.

"Should we call rescue?" I asked. "Is he alive?"

"I don't know," she said numbly.

"How cold is the gas in that tank?"

"About four hundred degrees below zero."

I ached all over as we huddled together. "It's all right," I whispered. "He tried to kill you."

"Twice," she said.

23

The telephone line was dead and Sunny had no cell phone.

I found mine in my handbag, kicked into a corner during the struggle. I dialed the number, hands shaking.

Seconds later, there were shouts and pounding at the front door and at the loading dock off the kitchen.

We stared at each other in panic.

"The Beach doesn't have that kind of response time," I warned. "Nobody does."

"Police!" The sturdy door seemed about to splinter under the heavy kicks and blows.

Sunny flung it open before they broke it down. Half a dozen detectives and uniforms spilled into the room off balance and stumbling over each other.

"How did you get here so fast?" I asked Sam Stone, who was breathing hard.

"Search the building!" he shouted to the uniforms.

"No, they're in here," I said.

"Where?"

"The freezer. She has a gun," I warned.

He and Nazario headed for the kitchen, weapons drawn.

They cracked open the freezer's double doors, then entered, first one, then the other, in shooters' stances.

"God almighty!" Stone said.

Rebecca Pinder was led out, huddled in a blanket, tears frozen on her cheeks.

When I asked about Clyde, Stone shook his head. "Talk about a brain freeze," he said.

Everybody was there or showed up eventually. Burch, K. C. Riley, the chief medical examiner.

"How did you get here so fast?" I kept asking. "How did you know?"

Stone finally explained. "We had warrants for Clyde and Rebecca Pinder's arrest," he said. "Went out to serve them but nobody was home."

"Warrants? What for?"

"Aggravated stalking. We knew Sunny was being stalked. So we retraced her movements for the last week, then pulled the tapes from all the security cameras on her routes.

"The average person is captured on videotape eight to twelve times a day," he said. "We played all the tapes hoping to see one of our suspects; instead, there was Rebecca Pinder, behind Sunny at the supermarket, in the bank, at the department store. When Sunny went to the post office, a security camera at the building next door picked up Rebecca and Clyde in the parking lot.

Burch recognized them. Can't beat those thirty frames a second," Stone said. "The camera never blinks. It's an unbiased witness. Which is more than you can say about people."

"You could have shown up sooner," I complained, trying to flex my swollen fingers.

Sunny gently examined my hand. "You want some ice to put on that?" she asked.

"No," I said emphatically.

I finished the Cold Case Squad piece that Morganstern was so hot to have, but it sat ignored on his desk for days before he read it, so typical of editors. Lottie came through, as always, with the cover art he wanted. K. C. Riley drew the line at actually sitting on a block of ice. Burch insisted privately that it was because any ice she sat on would never melt.

Instead, she posed sternly in the foreground, arms folded, as the solemn detectives sat or leaned on huge frozen blocks behind her. Great picture.

Edgar was threatening and harassing Onnie again, so I let her use my apartment while Kendall McDonald and I escaped to the British West Indies for a romantic week in Tortola. Darryl would love being near the beach and playing with Bitsy and Billy Boots.

Onnie and Lottie helped me pack.

"Hope you ain't aiming to elope, Britt," Lottie warned. "I hate weddings, unless it's mine, but I want to be there the day you get hitched."

"Me too." Onnie looked relaxed for a change. "You don't know how much Darryl and I look forward to staying here," she said. "It'll be like a vacation for us.

I've called the police so many times, but Edgar always splits before they show up."

"Only thing worse than a bad marriage," Lottie said, "is a divorce that don't work out."

"Tell me about it," I said, folding shorts and T-shirts into a zippered section of my garment bag. "Do you know that after Clyde told her what he did, Rebecca Pinder burned Sunny's bloody clothes and then pretended she'd hidden them somewhere, to hold over his head? She admitted to the detectives that whenever he crossed her, she'd threaten to turn him in. After DNA evidence began being used, she'd remind him that his own secretions could convict him.

"Hard to believe what families can do to each other. Look at Sunny's parents. Her father's evil little scheme to manipulate his teenage daughter took on an ugly life of its own that grew, spread out, and created more victims than he ever could have anticipated. To think, I even envied her for having her dad," I said.

"How is Sunny?" Onnie asked.

"Probably the healthiest member of her entire family. She's tight with Nazario," I said. "He's crazy about her."

"Damn," Onnie said in front of the mirror, holding my new bathing suit up in front of her. "I wish Edgar would fall in love. It would take the pressure off us. Sometimes things are quiet for a day or two and I think, Praise God, he's met a woman! But then he shows up, trying to kick down my door. My landlord's uptight, Darryl's having nightmares." She sighed. "I'd be relieved if he went back to jail. His mother is scared of him, thinks he's doing drugs. So why does she let him stay there? She enables the man. Is there any family that's not dysfunctional?"

"Never met one," I said.

"Dern tooting," Lottie said. "I can fight off my enemies, but God protect me from my kin. The sorry butts I'd like to kick the most all belong to relatives."

"Well, thanks, buds," I said, snapping my suitcase shut, "for the cheerful send-off. This is it. If the man doesn't propose, I don't know what I'll do."

"He will," Lottie said, with a sly wink.

When McDonald picked me up, Mrs. Goldstein was baking chocolate-chip cookies for Darryl, who, wild with excitement, was playing ball with Bitsy in the yard.

Our flight wasn't crowded and the hotel business was slow, with many people opting not to travel. It was as though the mountains and white sand beaches were ours alone. We ignored the news, forgetting Miami's trials and troubles and the world's, if only for a while. We slept late, sunned and swam, and explored other islands aboard a powerful cigarette boat piloted by a crusty Miami expatriate. We danced barefoot on warm sand, beneath a bright yellow moon and a million silver stars. When a troupe of musicians from the hotel played "I Can't Help Falling in Love with You," to a reggae beat, McDonald dropped to one knee and asked the question. I didn't know I was crying until he wiped away my tears. The answer was Yes—of course.

The musicians applauded.

"Some things are meant to be," he whispered. He even had the ring, momentarily lost in the sand.

Nothing ever felt so right. *We* never felt so right. We got back to the hotel late, but I called my mother and Lottie and Onnie and everyone else I could think of.

"First time you ever woke me up with good news," Lottie said, her voice sleepy.

"You go, girl," Onnie said, and put Darryl on the phone.

The wedding would be in the spring. My mother immediately spun into a frenzy of ideas, plans, and lists.

We tanned and talked and walked beside the sea for hours, discussing our future, our children, our home. I'd always been hesitant about bringing children into an uncertain world where so many are in need of nurturing. But my thinking had changed. We agreed that for each child we had, we would adopt one and then forget which was which.

We wore tropical shirts over T-shirts and shorts for the flight back. Fire and ice glittered from my ring finger.

We arrived home in the late afternoon. Onnie's car was parked outside so I knocked, then fumbled for my key. Mrs. Goldstein opened the door, clearly shaken, face drawn.

Relief in her eyes, she hugged me. "Thank God you're back, Britt, and that he's with you."

As she reached for McDonald, I saw Onnie inside. Her lower lip was cut and swollen, her face bruised, her eyes red and puffy from crying. My apartment was in an altered state of disarray, as though survivors had tried to clean up after a tornado.

"It's Edgar. He took Darryl." Onnie limped toward us, sobbing.

"Oh, no!" I said. "Where is he?"

McDonald put his hands gently on her shoulders. "When did this happen? Did you call the police?"

Mrs. Goldstein shook her head. "He threatened to hurt the boy."

"He'll kill him!" Onnie cried. "He means it, Britt. He'll kill him!"

"Tell us exactly what happened," McDonald said.

I helped her to a chair, sat her down, and held her hand.

"He was here, Britt. I'm so sorry. I'm so sorry."

Now I saw my hand-painted antique nesting tables, legs broken. The shattered shards of my grandmother's crystal vase had been collected and deposited on a shelf. A painting of a street scene in Santiago de Cuba, where my father was born, hung askew on the wall.

"It's not your fault." I touched her hair. "What matters is that you're okay and Darryl is safe. Edgar will go to jail for this, won't he?" I asked McDonald.

He nodded. "Don't worry," he told Onnie. "We'll get your boy back. But I'm going to have to call in the department's domestic violence unit."

"No! No! He's worse than I've ever seen him!" She clutched frantically at his arm. "He'll do it. He'll kill Darryl!"

McDonald sighed and looked up at me.

"How did he know you were here?" I asked her.

"I was so stupid! No one knew where we were staying. But I took Darryl back over to church this morning so he wouldn't miss Sunday school." She gasped for breath as Mrs. Goldstein handed her a tissue.

"I never saw him; he must have followed us." She wiped her eyes. "I was fixing lunch, a few minutes after we got back. Bitsy started to bark, then somebody knocked. I thought it was Mrs. Goldstein or that you'd arrived early. I felt so safe here. I opened it.

"He said he was taking Darryl. I tried to stop him and we struggled. He knocked me down, punched me. Darryl was screaming. I was so stupid."

Mrs. Goldstein saw Darryl kicking and screaming as his father carried him to his car. She found Onnie, half conscious on the floor.

"If only I'd been faster, if only I'd been quicker." My landlady wrung her hands. "I could have stopped him."

"I'm glad you didn't try. Where is Bitsy?" I asked, alarmed.

"Edgar kicked her," Onnie said. "She attacked him."

"Hy took her to the vet," Mrs. Goldstein said. "She has some broken ribs. They're keeping her overnight."

I retreated to the kitchen for a glass of water. Darryl's drawings of Bitsy and Billy Boots decorated the refrigerator. I burst into tears. Little boy lost. Brave little dog.

"Why didn't anybody call the police?" McDonald was demanding.

"The other tenants were all out at the beach, I guess. When I found Onnie, she begged me not to."

"The last thing he told me," Onnie said, eyes flooding, "was that if I called the police, I'd never see Darryl alive again."

"You think he'd take the boy out of the city?" McDonald asked.

"No. He's at his mother's." Onnie gulped. "I called about an hour ago. Edgar grabbed the phone, talking crazy. He made no sense. Darryl was crying."

"What does he want?" McDonald asked.

"I don't think he knows," Onnie said. "Wants me to undo the divorce, apologize, go back to him. In the next breath he says he's gonna make me wish I was dead, that I was never born, that he's going to make me pay."

"Let's go over there," McDonald said, "and try to size up the situation. How much influence does his mother have? Will he listen to her?"

"Used to," she said eagerly, wincing as she got to her feet.

"Would anybody like to see my engagement ring?" I said forlornly as we left.

"Oh, Britt," Onnie said, hugging me. "This is such a happy time for you and I'm ruining it."

"What else are friends for?" I shrugged, my arm around her.

Even McDonald smiled.

We promised to call Mrs. Goldstein as soon as Darryl was safe.

McDonald parked across the street from the duplex where Edgar's mother lived, then called the domestic violence unit with the address, asking them to stand by in case they were needed.

He asked me to wait in the car while he and Onnie went to the door. As they crossed the street, a woman came running around the side of the house. She looked disheveled and distraught. Something about her body language as she stumbled toward them propelled me from the car.

"He's crazy! He's crazy! He won't listen." She held one hand to her bloodied nose. "He's got gasoline! He's got his baby in there! Says he's gonna burn his-self up with my grandchild!"

She had told Edgar he couldn't stay. Ordered to leave, he did, enraged, and returned with a gasoline can.

Splashing gasoline around the living room, he was threatening to ignite it as she fled the house.

Onnie's knees gave way and I held on to her.

"Is he high?" McDonald said.

"Don't know." She whimpered, shaking her head. "I know he's been on drugs. I don't want him here. I'm scared of him."

"He's only six years old! Darryl, Darryl," Onnie said. "Please, please. Save my baby."

"Does he have a weapon?" McDonald asked Edgar's mother.

"Only kitchen knives, no guns that I saw."

Curious neighbors had begun to assemble.

"We need SWAT, a hostage negotiator, and a fire truck," McDonald said.

"No time for that!" the older woman cried. "Edgar was splashing gasoline all over the furniture."

Darryl's screams came from the house.

Onnie's eyes looked huge and terrified.

McDonald took off his shirt.

"What are you doing?" I asked.

"I want him to see I'm not armed. I'll try to talk to him and get Darryl out. Then we can leave it to SWAT to get Edgar."

"No," I said. "You don't even have a bulletproof vest. You're not armed."

"I know," he said, eyes on mine. "But the vapor could ignite at any time. A pilot light, the water heater, anything could touch it off. I'll just try to get the boy out." He turned to the woman.

"Where is Edgar?" he asked. "What room? Tell me exactly where the boy was when you last saw him."

Edgar was crouched in a corner of the gasoline-soaked living room when she fled, she said. He held Darryl's wrist in one hand, a cigarette lighter in the other.

"Stay back behind that fence," McDonald warned us, "no matter what you hear. If I don't come out, wait for the police.

"Call them now." He handed me his cell phone. "Start them rolling on a three signal, but tell them no lights, no sirens. I love you, Britt."

"Be careful," I pleaded, punching in the numbers.

I relayed the message as he walked up to the front door. He tried it, and it opened. He stepped cautiously inside as Onnie and I clutched each other.

"Edgar," I heard him say. "You all right in here? My name is . . ."

He disappeared into the house, leaving the door open behind him. For long heart-stopping moments, nothing at all happened. Then Darryl emerged, flying out the front door, stumbling, running, straight down the walk, away from the house. "Mommy! Mommy!" he screamed.

"Here I am, baby!" she cried, arms outstretched. He leaped into her embrace as the house erupted in a great roar. The roof lifted, windows shattered, and tongues of fire shot out each opening. A great ball of flame hurtled out the front door with a loud *whoosh,* then retreated as its intense heat forced us back into the street, away from the inferno.

Darryl was safe. No one else escaped.

24

They say you have begun to heal when it's not the first thing you think about when you wake up in the morning. Will I ever reach that place?

Other lives go on. Ryan is in remission and back at work. He won a national prize for the story on the rescue of the baby in the well. He was embarrassed, reluctant to attend the awards presentation.

Lottie and I insisted that he go. He returned lugging a huge and ornate plaque depicting heroic firefighters and a little child in bronze relief, then hid it under his desk.

Bitsy, my brave little dog, survived her injuries and is back at home.

The second-degree murder charges against Hector Gomez were reduced to manslaughter. He went to trial and a jury acquitted him in the death of Andre Coney.

The widow Pinder pleaded guilty to two counts of attempted murder and was sentenced to fifteen to twenty years.

Sam Stone pursued the Meadows case and found not the killer but nine identical cases in cities across the country. In Detroit, Chicago, St. Louis, and Portland, lonely elderly women who lived alone were murdered in their homes, then lovingly tucked into sleeping positions in their own beds. There are probably others. The most recent he has uncovered so far occurred three years ago. He is now temporarily assigned to an FBI task force in pursuit of the serial killer.

There was nothing Dr. Hartley could be charged with, due to the statute of limitations. There was talk that he might lose his license to practice, but no sanctions were taken against him. His wife Maureen left him but has not filed for divorce. However, with Craig and Connie Burch separated, anything may happen.

Though I still love them, it's difficult for me to see Onnie and Darryl. I still break down. Darryl said that Kendall McDonald threw him out the door, telling him to run as his father repeatedly flicked his lighter trying to make it work.

I still wear my engagement ring, and hang out with Lottie and Sunny. Their strength and optimism comforts me. Sunny broke Nazario's heart as I suspected she would. Sometimes the only way for a victim to heal is to never again see the people who remind you of the trauma.

Conversely, after hysterically railing at me for allowing Kendall McDonald to walk into that house alone on that terrible day, K.C. Riley and I clung together in shared grief. We talk often. It helps us both.

The detectives are convinced, though I remain doubtful, that Shelby Fountain was the innocent victim of a drive-by shooting unrelated to the crime that tormented her for more than half her life. Cubby and Abby Wells named their new baby girl Shelby.

In an unfair and troubled world, signs of hope begin to intrude on my despair. Driving home alone across the causeway, I see green spires, signs of growth, and new life reaching for the sky.

Acknowledgments

I am grateful for the friendship and expertise of Dr. Joseph H. Davis, Dr. Steve Nelson, and Dr. Howard Gordon, the genius of super-sculptor Amy Bryer, the brilliant and generous Coralee Leon, and artists Brooke Engle, Rosemarie Chiarlone, and Paula Harper. Special thanks to Bill Dobson; the Reverend Garth Thompson; Ann Hughes; Debbie Buchanan; Gay Nemeti Robson of the *Miami Herald;* Metro-Dade Police Intelligence Specialist Karen Austin; Angela and Frank Natoli; my agent, Michael Congdon; and the ice man Costas Metaxatos. My stalwart buddies Leonard Wolfson, Renee Turolla, Patricia Keen, Luisita Pacheco, and Molly Lonstein do their best to keep me on the straight and narrow and out of serious trouble. And when all else fails, the glamorous redhead Marilyn Lane swoops to the rescue like a superhero. What a sterling cast of characters! I am so blessed.